PRAISE FOR M

Tom Clancy fans open to a strong female lead will clamor for more.

(Miranda Chase is) one of the most compelling, addicting, fascinating characters in any genre since the Monk television series.

(*Drone* is) the best military thriller I've read in a very long time. Love the female characters.

Superb!

A fabulous soaring thriller.

Meticulously researched, hard-hitting, and suspenseful.

— PURE HEAT, PUBLISHERS WEEKLY, STARRED REVIEW

The first...of (a) stellar, long-running (military) romantic suspense series.

— THE NIGHT IS MINE, BOOKLIST, THE 20 BEST ROMANTIC SUSPENSE NOVELS: MODERN MASTERPIECES

Expert technical details abound, as do realistic military missions with superb imagery that will have readers feeling as if they are right there in the midst and on the edges of their seats.

— LIGHT UP THE NIGHT, RT REVIEWS, 4 1/2 STARS

Buchman has catapulted his way to the top tier of my favorite authors.

— FRESH FICTION

M L. Buchman's ability to keep the reader right in the middle of the action is amazing.

— LONG AND SHORT REVIEWS

The only thing you'll ask yourself is, "When does the next one come out?"

I knew the books would be good, but I didn't realize how good.

THUNDERBOLT

A MIRANDA CHASE THRILLER

M. L. BUCHMAN

Buchman Bookworks

SIGN UP FOR M. L. BUCHMAN'S NEWSLETTER TODAY

and receive:
Release News
Free Short Stories
a Free book

Get your free book today. Do it now.
free-book.mlbuchman.com

Other works by M. L. Buchman: *(* - also in audio)*

Other works by M. L. Buchman:

Contemporary Romance (cont)

Where Dreams
Where Dreams are Born
Where Dreams Reside
Where Dreams Are of Christmas
Where Dreams Unfold
Where Dreams Are Written

Science Fiction / Fantasy

Deities Anonymous
Cookbook from Hell: Reheated
Saviors 101

Single Titles
The Nara Reaction
Monk's Maze
the Me and Elsie Chronicles

Non-Fiction

Strategies for Success
Managing Your Inner Artist/Writer
Estate Planning for Authors*
Character Voice
*Narrate and Record Your Own
Audiobook**

Short Story Series by M. L. Buchman:

Romantic Suspense

Delta Force
Delta Force

Firehawks
The Firehawks Lookouts
The Firehawks Hotshots
The Firebirds

The Night Stalkers
The Night Stalkers
The Night Stalkers 5E
The Night Stalkers CSAR
The Night Stalkers Wedding Stories

US Coast Guard
US Coast Guard

White House Protection Force
White House Protection Force

Contemporary Romance

Eagle Cove
Eagle Cove

Henderson's Ranch
Henderson's Ranch*

Where Dreams
Where Dreams

Thrillers

Dead Chef
Dead Chef

Science Fiction / Fantasy

Deities Anonymous
Deities Anonymous

Other
The Future Night Stalkers
Single Titles

ABOUT THIS BOOK

The best ground-attack support fighter jets ever built—the A-10 Thunderbolt "Warthogs"—are falling out of the sky.

The Air Force brass repeatedly schemes to decommission this low-tech jet. They've been blocked by soldiers, pilots, and Congress...so far.

The "Hog" lies at the crux of a high-tech struggle for power. An interagency skirmish that now rapidly descends into a battle fought on a global scale.

Miranda Chase, air-crash savant for the National Transportation Safety Board, and her team dive in. The high-risk stakes mount in the battlespace—and a secret from their past could make them the next target. Miranda may become the spark that ignites a war.

PROLOGUE

Spieden Island, Washington, USA
Elevation: 137'

MIRANDA CHASE SHOOED A COUPLE OF SIKA DEER OFF THE
runway. It was a chill November morning only a few degrees
above freezing, so she didn't spend long about it.
A slow wave of sea fog was rolling in from Vancouver and
the Canadian Gulf Islands, adding a thick dampness to the
chill. The first of the US San Juan islands, Stuart and Johns,
were disappearing fast. If she didn't get aloft in the next
fifteen minutes, she'd be trapped here on Spieden Island
until the weak November sun burned it off.

The call from the National Transportation Safety Board
said that a new crash had been classified as urgent.

As if she would lag when there was a crash to investigate.

She opened the hangar door and began her pre-flight
checklist at the pilot's ladder, then circled the plane
counterclockwise. Tires inflated and clear of obstructions.

No leakage from the shock absorbers, brakes, or gear handling systems. No dings on the leading edge of the wings. All rote by now, but she never missed a step. She was her own ground crew, so it was up to her to make everything perfect.

Because of the frequent fog, she'd thought about installing an instrument landing system on her island. She liked that it would make Spieden one of the only grass strips in the world to have an ILS. The problem was that the outer and inner markers would have to be placed offshore in the deep waters of Puget Sound because, at two miles long and a half-mile wide, her island was too small to support the four-mile-long system.

Jones Island was in almost the right place, but it was a nature preserve that belonged to the state and they weren't interested in having an ILS beacon set up there.

Besides, her plane couldn't handle the Cat III equipment that would allow her to land in the exasperating near-zero visibility.

Her F-86 Sabrejet was neither pure North American F-86 Sabrejet nor the Canadair CL-13 Sabre Mk 5 variant anymore. One of the last ever produced before the line ended in 1958, she had tinkered with it over the years, including upgrading to the Mk 6's more powerful Orenda 14 engine. She'd also had to make a few modifications so that she could start the plane herself—normally a ground crew was required to handle the power connections for engine start.

But even with the upgrades it was still all authentically a Sabrejet, and old jet fighters didn't boast modern electronic suites. To shoehorn them in, she'd have to get a custom-designed cockpit—which was never going to happen. She loved the feel and familiarity of the old "steam" dial gauges mounted in the classic cockpit.

Her sole concession was a small tablet computer that attached to a Velcro strip on the right thigh of her flightsuit for GPS navigation and airport charts.

The preflight checks only took minutes. She rolled out onto the winter-dead grass as the first tendrils of fog began slipping across the field. Her time was shorter than she'd anticipated. She taxied ahead and punched the garage controller to close the hangar door. Normally, even though she lived alone on the island, she'd get down and padlock it from the outside. But this morning the fog was moving in fast.

Isolate.

Focus.

The island would be uninhabited by humans as soon as she was aloft.

Locking the door really didn't matter.

You're taxiing the airplane. Work the checklist.

Fuel tanks full.

Canopy Unsafe alarm dark.

Speed brakes retracted.

The sika deer were back, grazing along the runway as if antique fighter jets rolled by them all the time. They'd never yet run across the runway during a takeoff or landing, but she did hate disturbing their quiet island existence. They were startled every single time by the full-throttle roar of her turbojet engine.

She loved the deer. They were among the island's many survivors from when Spieden had been set up as a big-game-hunter resort decades ago. Thankfully the zebras, the far larger European fallow deer, and the like were long gone.

Some of the other remaining wildlife she was less pleased about. The incredibly territorial wild turkeys really needed to be cleared out.

There was one particular tom she'd named Dillinger. Especially fond of the acoustics of her front porch—he frequently launched his shrill call there at two in the morning. So far, he had eluded her efforts at capture or kill.

Perhaps she'd throw a hunting party. Which would include herself and...

"You really need some friends," Miranda could hear Tante Daniels teasing her. She had been doing that since she had been Miranda's governess, even more so since Miranda's parents had gone down on flight TWA 800 and she'd become the then thirteen-year-old Miranda's guardian.

Quite why Tante Daniels so enjoyed teasing, despite knowing better than anyone how much it confused Miranda, was beyond her. At least Miranda found teasing to be more easily identifiable than sarcasm. Why some people thought that double meaning was somehow a more efficient way to communicate was beyond her.

At the end of the runway, she turned her jet around and performed the final checks.

Flaps to takeoff.

Trim two percent nose-up attitude.

Altimeter to one hundred and thirty-seven feet to match the height of the northwest end of the runway.

The orange windsock drooped. Winds calm.

Miranda snapped in the oxygen mask, as she would be flying high, and tucked the tail of her helmet strap inside the chin strap so that it wouldn't tap against her cheek every time her jet hit an air pocket.

She called out her departure on the Unicom frequency in case anyone was in the area.

"Spieden Traffic. Sabrejet N19353 VFR departing to the southeast."

Miranda felt a satisfying sense of rightness with her custom tail number.

Airplane identifier N-Numbers painted on a plane's tail had only five characters—of which the first three had to be numeric. So, she'd started with the first five letters of the *Kryptos* sculpture in the CIA headquarters courtyard that she and her father had spent much of her childhood years trying to decrypt. She'd applied the Vigenère cipher (the same one used by the NSA and the CIA to decode the first two panels of the sculpture) using the word "Kryptos" itself just as the artist had when he'd initially encoded it.

KRYPT had become UIWEM once enciphered.

Rather than re-encoding that with a second word —"palimpsest" and "abscissa" respectively on the sculpture's first two panels—she'd applied the first alphanumeric encryption method her father had ever taught her. By using only the last number of each letter's position in the alphabet, 21-9-23-5-13, UIWEM had become 19353.

The custom N-Number was available from the FAA and she'd gladly paid the ten-dollar custom-number fee. The accompanying 20201 decryption key, for the tens place of 21-09-23-05-13, she'd ordered as a custom license plate for the island's tractor, which she mainly used for mowing the runway. Sometimes it worried her that someone would

M. L. BUCHMAN

decode the two together. Each time she reminded herself that it wouldn't cause any problems if they did.

Her radio announcement was only a little unusual, as no other traffic ever flew here—except the one time she'd invited her team to visit—but it was in the FAR, and even if she was the only person she'd ever met who regularly read the complete Federal Aviation Regulations, she did her best to follow them at all times.

Rules were comfortable.

She liked rules.

They gave a structure to the chaotic world.

Miranda paused for five seconds to listen for a response from some other flier stating that her departure might be a problem for them. There was no recommended waiting time, not even in the recent *Non-Towered Airport Flight Operation* advisory circular AC 90-66B. It was the first update since 1993 and she found it uncomfortable that it had no listening duration mentioned, just like its predecessor 66A.

Uncomfortable? Perhaps annoying was a better word. She reminded herself that she was getting better at identifying emotions, even when it didn't feel like it. At least the labels made them more tolerable.

She found it *annoying* that, as one of the lead NTSB accident investigators, she had reported on three separate accidents caused by a pilot who failed to allow sufficient time between an announcement and subsequent action. Three separate times she'd recommended that the FAA change their rules to include the five-second pause, but the National Transportation Safety Board only had the power to recommend, not to require.

Hearing nothing, she checked the skies once more

before pressing her toes hard on the footbrakes and sliding the throttle forward. As the Orenda 14 engine crossed twenty percent power, she released the footbrakes and the Sabrejet instantly began to roll.

The deer looked up in alarm and bolted for the Doug fir woods as always.

And there was Dillinger.

The male turkey scowled at her from a low hedgerow she'd recently planted near the hangar, but he didn't move. Maybe he had a stealth coating he used whenever she was out with a rifle or bow.

At a hundred and forty-five knots (a hundred and sixty miles an hour), she let the nose wheel lift. At one-fifty, she was wheels-up ahead of the first bank of fog prowling in through the conifers to the west. She tapped the brakes to stop the wheels from spinning, then retracted the landing gear.

Aloft, she was in clear blue skies.

Contacting Seattle Air Route Traffic Control Center, she initiated her filed flight plan and arranged for a fast climb to her best cruise height of thirty-one thousand feet. Now the only question was how fast could she get to Davis-Monthan Air Force Base outside Tucson, Arizona. It was illegal to fly over US soil at greater than Mach 1—an ability just within the performance envelope for her aircraft—but the law didn't say anything about flying at ninety-nine percent of the speed of sound.

She would cross from Washington to Arizona in under two hours. Once again, her team would unavoidably follow hours behind.

The wreck awaited and the NTSB team was on its way.

She waved goodbye to the island and punched south.

———

Achin, Nangarhar Province, Afghanistan
Flight Level 25: 25,000'
Nine hours earlier

"MC-SQUARED HEADING DOWN."

Major Carl Carmichael said it aloud in the cockpit just to see how it sounded. He still wasn't used to his new call sign —"MC-squared" had replaced his "Three-C" nickname almost overnight after his promotion from Captain Carl Carmichael to major two weeks ago. Most guys just got one nickname in a career, but his seemed to keep changing and needed some rethinking each time.

Riding the edge of the never-exceed speed, he dove his A-10C Thunderbolt II "Warthog" down from Flight Level 25.

The bitch-cold November sky over the Afghan mountains was a hard, crystalline blue that looked as if it would crack where the sharp glaciated peaks jammed against it. It had that dark purity of midmorning.

It was still dark down in the deep valleys. Real dark for some assholes once he showed up.

"Straight on down, boy. Straight on down."

Twenty-five thousand feet at four hundred and fifty knots (five hundred and eighteen miles an hour) meant thirty-five seconds to target. Actually thirty-one seconds as the ground elevation in the rugged front range of the Safēd Kōh Mountains was above three thousand feet.

A full dive in a Warthog was the best ride there ever was.

The design was fifty years old and his plane was forty. It was still the most kick-ass jet ever. The only plane in the US arsenal dedicated to close air support for ground troops.

Nothing touched it.

"Energy like light, we're kicking it with MC-squared according to old Einstein. Moving like the A-10 Thunderbolt we are, Nancy."

The action figure perched on the top of his flight console didn't reply; she just grinned as he worked on how best to use his new call sign.

The hop from Bagram Airfield a hundred kilometers away had taken only seven minutes and he was almost there. He'd crossed the desert flats and the rugged gray hills of the east.

As usual, command had ignored the unofficial Warthog motto: *Go ugly early.* The A-10 was a seriously homely plane, but it totally rocked. And the best way to help ground troops was to get a hog there *before* they were getting their asses kicked.

If they'd called him in before the squad of 75th Rangers had gotten pinned down and cornered in the brutal mountains outside the Afghani village of Achin, they wouldn't be in such desperate straits now.

Total airworthy F-35 Lightning II's at Bagram who could get there in a third the time he could? Zero. He'd be sure to rub that in at the DFAC tonight over steak and baked potatoes.

And the F-18 Hornets sucked for ground attack—at least compared to a Warthog—which is why he and his sweet old bird still had a job.

Medevac helos had launched at the same time he had but,

even slower than a Hog, were still twelve minutes-forty out. In twelve minutes there wouldn't be any need for the helos because there'd be no one left for the medical teams to rescue.

...If those rotorboys even dared fly into the valley filled with Taliban.

"No worries, boys and girls. Nancy and I are on the job."

His high-res thermal tracker let him catalog the situation quickly.

The Taliban were dug in on two different hilltops, pinning down the Rangers in the crossfire while their pals chased the good guys up a dead-end valley.

"Nasty little Talis. Let's get 'em, Nancy."

A cliff wall behind the Rangers and a platoon-size phalanx of Afghani ragheads coming at them fast had to suck.

"Ug-ly! That's the only word for it, Nancy. The only word. Ug-ly!"

A line of three broken US Army vehicles scattered in between the two ground forces said that the Rangers were probably now on foot, whereas the Taliban were still mostly mounted.

Technicals—pickups with heavy machine guns and even artillery mounted in the back—totally sucked. They had six of those, one for every two Rangers.

"Twelve minutes to get it all cleaned up, Nancy."

His sister was a bestselling romance novelist who worshipped Nancy Pearl—a major Seattle librarian who had encouraged Sis since early in her career.

When Carl had graduated from the Air Force Academy, Sis had given him the Nancy Pearl figurine. Ever since, he and Nancy had flown together. With short graying hair, big glasses, and a bigger smile, she was kinda sexy in her tight plastic top and red cape.

She'd begun her flying looking out the windshield, but when he'd found himself wondering about her ass hidden by the flowing cape, he figured it was better if she kept an eye on him.

At fifteen thousand feet up, he lased one hilltop gun emplacement and fired off a laser-guided AGM-65 Maverick air-to-surface missile. It would take care of that group in another fifteen seconds.

At ten thousand, he lased the other hilltop and kicked off his other Maverick.

Now he was getting some attention from the ground. The bad kind of attention, but he was ready for it.

"Time to do our dance, Nancy."

He jinked sideways and flipped through a hard wing-over-wing twist as he dove around the back side of the western ridge. From above he'd seen that the valley along the back of the ridge turned and led back up the valley the Rangers were pinned down in.

The two hilltops blew simultaneously.

"Ranger Ground to A-10. Nice shooting."

"Hold tight, boys, Nancy and I are comin' at you just like light."

Not bad. Still a little clunky. Had to be some better way to use his new call sign.

An A-10 Warthog's real strength wasn't its heavy armor—though Carl appreciated the well-fortified cockpit every time someone got a bead on him. Nor was it in the variety of bombs and missiles hanging from the eleven hardpoints on the hog's wings and fuselage.

The plane rocked the ground assault role because it had been built starting with a gun.

A damned big gun.

At its heart, the A-10 was two tons of 30 mm GAU-8/A Avenger rotary cannon that just happened to have a tough-as-hell twin-engine jet built around it. Each second it could deliver seventy inch-and-a-quarter by four-inch, high-explosive rounds at three times the speed of sound.

The Talis were about to have their line shredded.

"Ready, Nancy?"

He carved a hard turn at the valley junction over the crap town of Achin—half-a-hundred homes squatting among steeply terraced fields. Anybody who wasn't Taliban was probably al-Qaeda.

Sucky as shit place to be a farmer.

Nancy flashed her big smile as the sun shifted over her face through the cockpit canopy.

Most pilots sighted the Avenger cannon by eye.

Aim the nose.

Pull the trigger.

Ker-pow!

The heads-up display would show the gun's aiming point at different distances, but no real hog jockey needed it. Carl had made the cut to qualify in the A-10 Warthog straight out of flight school. Adding in a decade of tours in Iraq, Afghanistan, and Syria had made it automatic for him to aim and fire the jet's primary weapon.

Practice...and Nancy's head.

When her smile blocked the exact center of the A-10 canopy, the target was perfectly aligned in the gun's sights.

Flipping up the safety, he rested his thumb on the trigger.

Nancy's head was just lining up with the tail of the Taliban column. He could see that the soon-to-be total losers were still looking upward for his return from above after blasting the hilltop gun nests.

Instead, he had the throttle wide open and was cruising along at thirty feet above the ground from directly behind.

"Shoulda checked your six. Gonna ram it up your asses, dudes."

Steep valley walls to either side and an abrupt mountain wall at the head of the valley bounded his play area. He'd have a four-second, two-hundred-and-eighty-round pass, then he'd climb out and see what sort of mood they were in after that. Maybe drop a pair of Mark 80 iron bombs just to chew them up a bit as he went by.

"MC-squared. Fast as a Thunderbolt."

There it was. Damn straight!

He returned Nancy's smile and pulled the trigger.

———

Achin, Nangarhar Province, Afghanistan
Elevation: 3,943'

STAFF SERGEANT JASPER KENNING OF THE 3RD RANGER Battalion, Charlie Company dropped his radio but couldn't look down as it bounced off the rocks.

He could only watch through his rifle scope as the A-10 Warthog came apart in midair.

There'd been no incoming round.

One moment, their salvation had been racing up the valley toward them.

The nose cannon—ready to spit death from where it reached out between the Warthog's painted teeth and pissed-off scowl design—had started to spin.

Rather than a lethal stream of punishment for the Taliban column, the three missiles mounted directly to the underside of the main fuselage ignited.

Without releasing first.

They blew the shit out of the middle of the Warthog's belly.

Totally gutted, the plane twisted hard and dove smack into the ground.

The pilot never had a chance to eject.

The fireball climbed high in the sky and the narrow valley echoed with the explosion as its load of bombs and fifteen hundred 30 mm rounds cooked off from the center of the blaze.

For thirty seconds it was impossible to hear or even think anywhere in the vicinity until the explosives spent themselves.

Then the valley echoed with silence.

The Taliban troops remained hunkered in position. They hadn't even seen the Warthog coming up behind them, and there hadn't been time for them to do more than freeze where they were.

Stunned silence.

No victorious cheer came from the massed troops celebrating a successful takedown.

Just shock.

His own troops were just as frozen.

Happiness is a warm gun. His drill sergeant had a thing about quoting Beatles' lyrics like he was some fossil left over from the Stone Age.

Kenning's rifle wasn't warm, it was blazing hot from all the rounds he'd pumped out of it during their retreat, but the enemy had just kept on coming no matter how many they put down.

He was the very first to shake off the shock.

Looking aloft offered no solace. There hadn't been a spare Reaper drone to circle over their position for this operation, so no Hellfire missile was going to come down and shred the Taliban like God's mighty hand striking from above.

The A-10 unleashed another spate of explosions.

This time the cloud was black with the JP-8 jet fuel from the breached midline tanks.

"Rangers!" Kenning called out.

"Hooah!" The responses were few and weak, but they were there.

Three of his men were dead—including Lieutenant Bailey—their remains still back in the blown-up MRAP they'd had to abandon. A glance behind him showed that two more were never going to lift their rifles again.

The remains of his squad began forming up behind the scattered boulders that were going to shield their last stand.

The Talis shook off their surprise. They looked side to

side at each other. Then—they were close enough that Kenning could easily see—they smiled.

A unison war cry in Pashto declaring "God is great!" shook the valley. Like they needed to thank God for their bloodthirsty ways.

The Beatles' tune *When I'm Sixty-Four* took a swing through his head because Drill Sergeant McCluskey had said that's how old they'd be by the time he could make them into even marginally acceptable soldiers.

Sixty-four.

Yeah, that so wasn't going to happen.

———

US Air Force Agency for Modeling and Simulation (AFAMS)
Site C-3, Elgin Air Force Base, Florida
Elevation: Subbasement 2

A LOOP OF CODE TESTED THE GLOBAL R14A10ACH VARIABLE every three milliseconds as it had been since it was invoked seventeen minutes earlier by a higher-level process.

The test loop resided on a Cray XC50 supercomputer— one small section of which was running simulations for a group of fourteen pilots battling it out two stories above.

USAF Air Combat Command's Cray was four ranks of computing cabinets. Each cabinet stood six and a half feet tall, six feet deep, and a yard wide. Each cabinet was water-cooled by a blower cabinet the same height but half as wide. Three sets made a rank. Four ranks created a twelve petaflop computer—twelve quadrillion operations per second.

Fifty-seven thousand test cycles later—a hundred and

seventy-one seconds and a compute load so trivial as to be wholly inconsequential—the R14A10ACH variable tested true.

The subroutine proceeded through the next four hundred and nineteen lines of code in a cascading cycle lasting almost two full seconds.

In that time, the invoked process carried out just four steps:

Generate a one-word message.

Deliver the word to three separate secure cellphones.

After all three phones provided a delivery confirmation —over ninety-eight percent of the total elapsed processing time—drop the external connection.

Finally, the subroutine erased both itself and the program that had called it—a load of barely ten thousand operations requiring more than a billionth of a second compute time, but less than two.

1

Davis-Monthan Air Force Base outside Tucson, Arizona, lay at the far corner of her assigned West Pacific region for the National Transportation Safety Board.

It comprised the greatest concentration of military aircraft anywhere in the world. There were over three thousand of them parked in the storage area alone. Hundreds more were associated with the operational side of the busy Air Force base.

Miranda's approach circled her over acres of mothballed F-4, F-15, and F-16 fighter jets tucked tightly nose-to-tail. Ninety-six B-52 Stratofortress bombers snuggled up beside a hundred and twenty-three KC-135 aerial refueling tankers but no fuel hoses passed between them any longer. A hundred and nine Army Black Hawk helicopters sat beside seventy Navy Sea Stallions and another ninety-six Marine Corps Cobra attack helos—all sweltering in vast arrays.

The most important thing to her was that these were all aircraft that she didn't have to ever worry about. Parked in

Davis-Monthan's two-thousand-acre high-desert storage yard, they would all be unfueled and sealed tight. Many would have their engines and even their flight instruments removed.

There would be no crashes requiring an NTSB investigation among these aircraft. The dry desert air preserved them from all other types of harm until they were either remobilized or scrapped.

It was strange seeing the planes disassembled by man rather than by impact, fire, collision, or the many other causes that usually brought her to the site of an airplane's sudden removal from service.

Davis-Monthan was also a busy airfield with many aircraft in the pattern—some bound for missions, some for training.

It was the home of the 355th Wing. The resident operations units included most of the Air Force's A-10 Thunderbolt IIs as well as: Air Force Pararescue, an Electronic Combat Group that flew the EC-130 surveillance planes, and the Arizona Air National Guard's fighter jets.

It was a very busy place.

And apparently one plane that hadn't survived to add to the flurry or they wouldn't have called her in.

2

MIRANDA PUT HER F-86 SABREJET DOWN RIGHT ON THE numbers designating Runway 12, the very first safe position to land past the threshold. Flying mostly from the short field of Spieden, she wasn't in the practice of wasting runway length. At Davis-Monthan, she had to taxi well down the thirteen-thousand-foot runway to reach the first taxiway turnoff.

"Your team is awaiting you at Hanger 9," Ground Control informed her.

They were?

But that wasn't possible.

She'd given them the use of her Mooney M20V Ultra, which was the fastest single-engine light plane built, but it still traveled at less than half the speed of sound. It was very disorienting to discover that they'd already arrived from their base in Tacoma, Washington, less than a hundred miles from her own home.

She had anticipated a minimum of three hours lead time to organize herself and inspect the wreck.

Why doesn't anyone understand that a wreck needs to be approached slowly? So much pressure to go directly to the disaster itself.

Spheres.

That was the way to do it.

Weather, terrain, debris extent, the debris field itself... Each of these were best considered separately, working inward—rather than jumping to the remains of the downed aircraft and eventually the individual systems and failures.

It made perfect sense to her and she didn't understand why nobody else understood that.

Now she'd suddenly have people around her from the first moment. People who didn't think that the human factor was the last, innermost sphere.

So many investigators began with personnel. Pilot, controller, and mechanic errors were common accident causes, but there was no point investigating those until inspection of the accident had created a coherent contextual framework upon which to base interviews and other data-gathering strategies.

Even her own team didn't understand, except perhaps Holly Harper. But it was often hard to tell what she understood.

How had her crew arrived first?

There were no such things as time warps.

Yet her Mooney did indeed sit close by Hangar 9. She confirmed the manufacturer's tail number—definitely hers. Someone had once told her it was bad luck to rename a boat or ship, so she hadn't altered the Mooney's registration.

It was a ship of the air after all, and that was danger enough.

For her Sabrejet, she'd had to replace the military designator with a civilian number, so that had been okay. Not her willful choice, but a mandated rule of law.

And no bad luck yet, so maybe that wasn't a real problem.

She looked for some wood to knock on. It seemed to be protocol to knock on wood whenever luck was mentioned. Or was it only at the mention of *bad* luck? She hadn't observed sufficient demonstrations of the practice to draw a definite conclusion. The Sabrejet's interior was metal and a few pieces of plastic—no wood. She reminded herself to find some to knock on as soon as possible.

In the shadow of the hangar, she could see a military man in fatigues. An officer by the insignia on his sleeves. When she rolled close enough, she could see the birds on his collar points. Why was a bird colonel standing with her three team members? They were all watching her so intently that she almost taxied straight into the side of her parked Mooney.

Why did she always mess up when people were watching her? *Focus, girl. Focus.*

Cycling down, Miranda completed the shutdown checklist, opened the canopy (she was so short that she didn't have to duck as it rolled backward), and climbed onto the ladder an airman had hung on the side of her jet.

She was so rattled by their impossible arrival that she'd descended halfway down before she recognized it. It was an authentic Sabrejet ladder with the single hook at the cockpit and the two supports in exactly the right place. Usually she was lucky to have a painter's A-frame ladder placed unsteadily to the side. Of the nine thousand, eight hundred and sixty produced airframes, the remaining fifty were in museums or civilian hands and most of those no longer flew.

"They told me you'd be arriving in an F-86, so I had the boys dig out the right ladder," the colonel introduced himself with his explanation. "Arturo Campos at your service, ma'am. I'm the commander of the 355th Wing here at Davis-Monthan." He had sun-complected skin, dark curly hair cut military short, and just a hint of a Mexican accent.

Miranda had something else to figure out first and turned to her crew.

"How did you get here first?"

Jeremy looked down and Mike shuffled his feet.

Holly smiled. Or was it a smirk at the other two?

"Mike flew us down to Vegas," she answered in that thick Australian accent of hers.

It seemed thicker than normal for reasons Miranda couldn't understand. "Why?"

"Well, apparently Mike wanted to lose some money. Jeremy wanted to get thrown out of a casino for counting cards in Blackjack. Then—"

"But it's so easy," Jeremy jumped in with his normal enthusiasm. "I really don't understand the game. How complex can it be, even with a four-deck shoe? Counting cards just isn't all that hard. It seemed like easy money to me. Then I just—"

"Some of us," Holly cut him off. "We just stick with the poker table."

"Okay." Miranda assumed that had some significance. Oh. That's why Holly was probably smiling so much.

"You did well."

Holly started to speak, but Miranda had already shifted her attention to the colonel who was now glaring at her.

"Why am I being met by a full colonel?" She tried to suppress her alarm, but was sure that she did a poor job of it. Major General Harrington had been forcibly retired a month ago—for reasons that had nothing to do with anything so trivial as his greeting an NTSB investigator with a pistol aimed directly at her face.

"One of my planes just went down on the training range and I want to know why. I heard that you're the best there is, Ms. Chase. So I'm the one who sent for you."

Miranda decided that this was a much more comfortable greeting than being threatened with a handgun at a range of less than two meters.

Just to double-check, she glanced at the structural specialist of her team.

Holly nodded that everything was okay just enough to tip the brim of her yellow Waltzing Matildas hat—her favorite Australian women's soccer team. The hat Holly had given her was—

"I'm sorry. I left my cap on the mantle back home."

"What?" Colonel Campos seemed to think that he had some part in the conversation.

Holly pulled the one off her head, freeing her long blonde hair from its impromptu ponytail out the back, and handed it over.

Holly had insisted that it was important that the entire team wore them on each investigation and they had—five major investigations now in the last three months and many minor ones.

Miranda had learned that one didn't argue with Holly and expect to win. But with the rush to beat this morning's fog off the island—and Dillinger sounding sunrise with a shrill gobble at both two and four a.m.—she'd left her own behind.

"But what about you?" Holly's hair and fair complexion now shone brightly, uncovered in the hot sun.

Jeremy Trahn and Mike Munroe had remembered theirs and she felt worse for forgetting her own.

Mike offered his to Holly, which she pretended not to see.

"I've another in my kit, no worries," Holly offered a friendly shrug, her thick Australian accent now familiar enough to be soothing rather than jarring.

Miranda tugged the hat on and felt better about being in the proper uniform. She exchanged her flightsuit for her NTSB vest and hung her badge facing outward from the front pocket.

Once she was assured that all her tools were in place, she turned to the colonel who was watching her closely.

"What?"

He smiled easily. "You're not what I expected, Ms. Chase."

She was never what anyone expected, least of all herself. Unsure what else to say, she decided to keep it simple.

"I'm ready."

3

EXCEPT SHE WASN'T.

Colonel Campos himself flew them out into the immense US Air Force training area of the Barry M. Goldwater Range. Almost three million acres of Sonoran desert was reserved for bombing and dogfight practice. It was bigger than the state of Connecticut.

"We isolated the section with the area of the crash, so please try to ignore the other aircraft."

The significance of that statement didn't become clear until the Huey UH-1N helicopter's rotor had slowed to a stop.

Racing close to the sparse desert grasses of the softly rolling terrain, attack jets appeared to be very busy. Far above, a pair of F-35A Lightning IIs were engaged in an intense mock air battle of hard maneuvers—at least Miranda hoped it was mock. In the distance, she saw a trio of HH-60G Pave Hawk rescue helicopters flying low and fast.

Then she saw a slash of rounds firing from the helos'

side-mounted miniguns. An old vehicle parked in the desert convulsed as hundreds of rounds slammed into it.

She counted seconds.

Eight. Nine. Ten. Eleven...

And there was the heavy buzz saw sound. Even at a distance of two miles, the Minigun was so impressive that she felt decidedly unsafe.

She glanced at the other members of the team and tried to read their expressions.

Mike, the team's personnel specialist, was looking very alarmed as he always seemed to be around the military. But he was, as he claimed, the very best at interviewing people.

Holly barely glanced over to see what was happening. She'd probably become inured to such sounds from her years of service as an operator for the Australian SAS Special Operations Forces.

Jeremy was watching the dogfighting Lightnings far above with a rapt expression, leaning into the curve as the F-35 did a hard bank and climb. It was a surprise he didn't fall over with how far he leaned.

Thankfully there was at least one person other than herself focused on the task at hand.

Colonel Campos pointed back toward the base. "I've grounded all of the A-10s until you can tell me what happened here."

That was a significant statement. A third of all the Air Force's remaining A-10s were based here. That meant over eighty aircraft were presently grounded.

A high priority indeed.

Miranda didn't like to start with the crash itself as it

biased her view of what had happened, but it was such a curious sight that she couldn't help herself.

The A-10 sat on the desert as if it had been planted there.

Not parked, because its landing gear wasn't extended. Instead the plane looked planted so that it lay belly-flat on the ground...partly into the ground. Like a flowerpot left sitting in the garden too long and the garden had grown up around it.

Everything on the long Air Force gray-white fuselage appeared to be intact.

Perhaps if they waited long enough it would sprout.

This particular plane had an angry shark's mouth and eyes painted on the nose around the GAU-8/A Avenger rotary cannon. On an A-10 Warthog, the shark face was roughly as common as the warthog face for reasons no one had ever been able to explain to her.

"Is the pilot okay?" Mike asked a question she'd never have thought to.

"Yes, his ejection seat is over there," Colonel Campos pointed at an orange flag a few hundred meters to the west— directly beyond the plane's nose as he had ejected up and out. "We didn't touch it except to disarm and remove the seat's backup firing system. It's safe to approach now."

He'd been both thoughtful and meticulous. A very pleasant change from most of the overly self-assured pilots she'd met.

Jeremy jumped right in. "The pilot will be an inch shorter the rest of his life, but that happens from ejections."

"It *what?*" Mike looked aghast.

"The average ejection is between twelve and fourteen g of vertical force on the spine. Most of that spinal compression is non-recoverable. The older systems can fire even harder and they often broke the pilot's backs as well, though rarely catastrophically. Almost everyone in the modern era who had to eject has survived, even many at supersonic airspeeds."

Miranda thought about her Sabrejet, which had one of the oldest ejection seat designs still flying. A broken back didn't sound like something she'd enjoy.

Jeremy continued with the history of ejection seats from the first-ever, used by Luftwaffe test pilot Helmut Schenk in 1942. That was if one ignored Everard Calthrop's patented design, but never built, compressed-air ejection seat from 1916—and...

Miranda noticed the colonel rub his wrist.

No, he was brushing at the watch he wore. It was a simple man's watch—with a distinctive red barrel.

He noticed her attention, "I don't wear ties very often." Then he turned away with an odd look on his face.

She knew that the Martin-Baker Tie Club had been founded by the company for all pilots saved by an MB ejection seat—all received a tie, clip, patch, and certificate. The watch could be purchased separately, but only by club members. Even partly underwritten by Martin-Baker, they cost thousands of dollars apiece. They were designed to be tough enough to survive a second ejection.

There was something about his expression... But with his back to her, she couldn't look again to see what it might mean.

Instead, she turned back to the plane.

It was curious that it had landed flat despite the pilot's ejection. The seat had landed close by. Perhaps the pilot had guided it to a nearly safe landing and then ejected at the last moment as a precaution. Choosing what was called a zero-zero ejection—zero altitude-zero speed—was a very dangerous choice. A last-second tumble could disorient the ejection more than the seat's rockets could compensate for.

She waved Holly forward while Jeremy continued his discussion with Mike about record ejections: Mach 3 at over eighty thousand feet from an SR-71 Blackbird spy plane, underwater from an A-7 Corsair jet fighter after it had fallen into the ocean off the side of an aircraft carrier...

It made the space between her shoulders itch.

Maybe it was time to replace her F-86 Sabrejet's seat.

It might be original equipment, which she preferred, but it was getting very hard to find someone to service the old seat. And it was a first-generation design—not that far advanced from the German originals. Maybe it was time to call Martin-Baker for a retrofit of some fifth-generation protection.

The crash.

Focus on the crash.

Determining the extent of the debris field was a trivial task in this case. Several of the bombs from the A-10's hardpoints had been scrubbed off as the low wings had scraped across the desert. Flags, noting where each had landed, were scattered where the bombs had finally come to earth without exploding.

A long furrow marked the plane's smooth contact with the desert, like the trail left by a toboggan through fresh snow.

She and Holly set off to scout the edge of the debris field.

Except for the bombs—which had been removed—only a few bits and pieces had come off the plane.

Everything else was intact.

Miranda almost enjoyed the quiet and the gentle desert breeze. Together, they identified stray bits and pieces, but with only the occasional word between them until they were nearing the end of the circuit around the debris field.

"This should be easier than skinning a roasted tiger snake," Holly said once they'd completed their walk around the debris-field perimeter. "Though there is one thing this girl finds all sorts of puzzling."

Miranda liked that she didn't need to respond aloud to Holly. She could simply glance her way and wait.

Sure enough, Holly continued, "Why did they call the best NTSB investigator in the business for a simple crash? Not much like we need some aboriginal Elder wise in mysterious ways of the world to see what happened. Got too low or the engine died, and...splat!"

"Something took over the controls." The colonel had watched them walking the perimeter and, Miranda recognized, he had awaited them at exactly the point they would have completed their circuit of inspection.

"Some...thing?"

The colonel nodded.

"But..." Miranda pictured the A-10's systems. "The North American A-10 Thunderbolt II has a two-tier redundant hydraulic control system, and a mechanical control if both of those fail."

"You know your aircraft, Ms. Chase," Colonel Campos tipped his head politely, then winced and straightened slowly.

"Possible conflicts in the hydraulic systems?" Jeremy stepped in. "That might create the sensation that something else was controlling the aircraft. If there was an over- or under-pressure, it might easily be perceived as an unresponsive system..."

"Especially to a younger, less experienced pilot," Mike managed to get a word in edgewise, which was hard to do with Jeremy.

"...They might feel that the aircraft was behaving in a way that they would perceive as something else controlling the aircraft. Then—"

"Jeremy," Holly stopped him with a soft-spoken word. She was the only one who could. Mike's and her own attempts rarely succeeded.

When Jeremy had the bit of his systems specialty between his teeth, he was very hard to slow down. But this enthusiasm made him easy to forgive. Twenty-five and a genius, Viet-American with an accentless voice of the Pacific Northwest, and the excitement of she didn't know what.

"Let the colonel actually speak, buddy. You learn more that way," Holly chided him.

4

Jeremy knew he kept running off at the mouth whenever Miranda was around, but he couldn't help himself.

Three months.

He'd been part of Miranda Chase's NTSB team for three months and over a dozen investigations. He kept waiting for the glow to dim, but it hadn't. Each time he was called in, his luck kept being good.

He rapped his knuckles on his head.

"Why did you do that?" Miranda was the one who cut off Colonel Campos this time. But she wasn't watching the colonel, instead she'd looked at him.

He looked down at her. He was only five-seven. Only. He was the second tallest person ever in their family. His sister was like an alien from another planet, towering over them all at five-nine. Jeremy had teased her about that mercilessly, as someone at school had told him was his bound duty as a big brother—and he didn't want to fail at any "bound duty."

She'd finally made them all get DNA tests, *and* beat him up because she was way, way better at martial arts than he was.

He'd gotten back at her by refusing to fix her computer for over six months.

Still, he wasn't used to looking down at people other than his parents. Mike and Holly were both five-ten, but Miranda was just five-four.

Miranda was so slight that she looked as if her vest should be too heavy for her, yet she'd outlasted him on three major site investigations. He'd go to sleep thinking they were done and she would return to the site for another four hours in the middle of the night to check some facts.

It was amazing that the Number One IIC—Investigator-in-Charge—for the entire NTSB was a woman who made him feel tall.

"Why did I do what?"

"Knock your knuckles on your head."

Had he?

Miranda always flustered him, leaving him awkward and bumbling. He'd studied every single one of her NTSB reports dating all the way back to her very first in 2003. She had a clarity of thought that he could only aspire to and a methodology so meticulous that he often felt like he was in a sterile laboratory rather than the chaos of a crash site.

He didn't really believe in a higher power, but something had seen that he was assigned to *the* Miranda Chase's team.

Could it be something as simple as chance or luck?

Reaching up to tap his knuckles on his head, he froze. Yes, he had knocked on his head.

"Mom."

Miranda blinked at him in confusion.

Had he just called her Mom? Not unless she'd given birth to him when she was eleven.

He really needed to get his shit together around Miranda.

"*My* mom," and that sounded even more foolish, so he just plowed ahead. "Whenever there was a question about good luck, Mom would say knock on wood, then rap her knuckles on her head."

The others were just watching them. The colonel looked confused and Mike looked amused. It was Holly he kept an eye on—she was dangerous if he rambled too long. He rubbed his arm, still remembering the pain she was able to inflict with the merest touch when he got too carried away. Some weird military nerve pressure-point thing he never wanted to experience again.

"But your head isn't made of wood. It consists of brain, bone, and three outer layers of protective dermis," Miranda was quite insistent. "Around the brain there's—"

"Haven't you ever heard the phrase 'I'm a blockhead'?"

She nodded. "But blocks are stone, concrete, metal, or... Oh, wood."

"Right. So, if I'm blockhead?"

"It means...that your head is made of wood. But it isn't." Miranda frowned at him.

It was strange to discover that Miranda Chase was confused about anything—*ever*. But he'd seen it enough times now to know that sometimes she was anyway.

"It's just a saying," Jeremy tried to explain, wishing he was better at such things.

"And because of the metaphor that your head is made of

wood, it then becomes a readily available object to knock your knuckles against when you're speaking of luck. Especially useful if, as at the present, there isn't any wood close to hand."

Jeremy nodded.

Miranda tipped her head slightly to the side. "Good luck, bad luck, or both?"

Jeremy had to think about it. "Good luck. You knock on wood to not jinx good luck. Like my luck at being on your team. I can't begin to tell you how much I've loved working with you. I never imagined that—"

Holly drew his attention by tapping her own forearm with her fingertips. She did it precisely where she'd squeezed the pressure point on his own arm that first day and almost dropped him to his knees. His arm hadn't worked right for hours. He'd tried to do it to himself since, but hadn't been able to reproduce the mechanism. Online research about pressure-point and nerve-junction attacks had actually given him nightmares before he'd stopped looking.

Luck. Right.

"Uh...the luck that I'd be on your team."

Shut up. Right.

Miranda knocked her knuckles on the side of her head, then looked very relieved. "Thanks, that's been worrying me." Then, without pausing for breath, she turned back to the colonel. "How much experience have you had flying the A-10, Colonel Campos?"

He grunted and folded his arms across his chest. "Over ten thousand hours."

Since it was very rare for a fighter pilot to fly over five

hundred hours a year, that meant his numbers were amazingly high. Of course he was old—to make colonel meant he was at least forty-five.

"You say that the pilot said that something took over the controls."

He flexed his hands unconsciously, "I did."

That flexing must indicate something.

Miranda glanced at Mike Munroe. So Jeremy did as well.

He didn't know how Mike did it, but he could read people in ways Jeremy knew that he'd never master. Maybe Mike could read something in the colonel's gestures.

"So, colonel," Mike appeared calm. His NTSB vest was slung over one shoulder. He looked like he was just hanging out, maybe at a horse-racing track.

Jeremy had tried copying Mike's mannerisms in the mirror with absolutely no luck at all. Goofy nerd just wasn't a very cool look.

"Was this the first time you had to eject?"

The colonel flinched.

Oh! *He* was "the pilot" on this crash.

But he already wore a Bremont MBI watch. It stood out prominently on his left wrist. Jeremy had recognized it right away, though he'd never seen one in person. The back of every one was scribed with their Martin-Baker membership number and either their call sign or the date of their ejection. He was about to ask if he could see it. What font and font size had they chosen to—

"It's the second time. He has the watch," Miranda answered for him when the colonel didn't speak.

Mike looked at the watch but just frowned in

puzzlement. That was cool. He liked knowing something Mike didn't.

Would the colonel get a second Martin-Baker Tie Club membership? Maybe add another date to the back of his watch? But even more interesting...

"Did you lose more height the second time or did you already experience maximum compression from the first ejection? I mean, are you feeling additional loss of control issues from herniated disks? Or is it alignment variations that allowed the vertebrae to pack closer? I need to look that up. Perhaps—"

He didn't see Holly move up to him this time. Her quick squeeze on his shoulder completely stole his breath away. Even more startling than the forearm pinch. Suprascapular nerve, right near the Vulcan nerve pinch point. And it felt as if he'd be happier if it knocked him out.

Colonel Campos was scowling at him.

No one spoke for a long moment.

Maybe that hadn't been the best line of questioning.

Finally the colonel relented, yet spoke facing Miranda. "I *know* the handling characteristics of an A-10 Thunderbolt II. When I say that something took control of my aircraft, I mean that very literally. And it did it in such a way that if I'd been even a tenth of a second slower in my reactions, you'd be studying a wreck scattered across the entire landscape and speaking with my deputy commander."

"Oh." Miranda looked around like a confused owl caught out in the daylight.

Right, her spheres. He'd learned that Miranda hung onto what she called the "Music of the Spheres" for her investigations like it was some magic talisman.

"I already did the weather sphere, and there isn't really any terrain to record for the second one," he told her.

She nodded once, then looked around at the flatness of the desert terrain and nodded twice more.

"And you already did the perimeter walk." Jeremy wasn't sure why he whispered it so that the colonel wouldn't hear, but he did.

This time Miranda nodded three times as she acknowledged her third sphere.

"The hull, wings, and control surfaces all appeared to be intact," he prompted her again.

Then Miranda did one of those amazing things she did. From one moment to the next, she shifted from confused to commanding, having formulated an entire plan of attack faster than he could take a breath.

"Mike. Find out everything you can from the reticent colonel," as if he wasn't still standing there with them.

As she turned her back on the colonel, Campos looked down at the top of her head in some surprise.

Jeremy knew from experience that while Miranda never forgot *anything,* she would not be thinking at all about the colonel at this moment.

"Holly. I want you on mechanical factors. I doubt that you'll find any, but we need to look."

The only time Holly humbly took any suggestions was when they came from Miranda. She certainly never paid attention to him. And Mike, for some reason, always generated a negative response—typically in the form of derisive banter. Now, she simply turned and headed to the aircraft.

"Jeremy, you and I are going to go over the hydraulics

systems. It is the only force likely to exert sufficient control to overpower an experienced pilot."

One-on-one with Miranda Chase?

He knocked hard on the side of his head. *Twice.* This couldn't be real.

But when his eyes stopped watering, it still was.

5

"Lieutenant William Blake?"

"Here," Billy glanced up to see Lieutenant Colonel Kiley standing at the end of his cadre's table.

"Sir!" Billy jolted to his feet and banged the DFAC— dining facility—table hard. His mates cursed and muttered as glasses of iced tea and soda spilled over half-finished meals.

He'd look down later.

Lt. Colonel Kiley was the military commander of the AFAMS—Air Force Agency for Modeling and Simulation— installation at Eglin Air Force Base. Billy remained at attention.

"You have a sortie in ten minutes. If you're not in your seat, the flight leaves without you."

Billy knew it didn't matter that any sortie Kiley organized would be simulated. Scuttlebutt was that if a flier missed his start time, Kiley would dump him to the bottom of the rotation. And who knew how long it would take to climb back onto the active roster at all.

"Sir. Yes sir!" By the time he saluted it was to Kiley's back.

He looked down at the mess scattered across the table. "Sorry, guys."

"He apologized?" His buddy "Toucan" Jones looked down his big nose at him. "Next thing Lieutenant William Blake will start writing poetry for us. Get out of here, Poet. Don't ever keep an LC waiting." Of course, with buddies like that...

He'd hoped to leave "Poet" behind him in San Antonio, but it wasn't gonna happen.

He'd just met Kiley yesterday when he'd been haranguing the new arrivals during orientation—which included all ten of them at this table.

Billy started away.

"Hey, clear your own damn tray. We're not your maidservants, Poet."

He wished he could avoid the nickname. Mom was a hotshot English Lit professor at Fordham University back in the Bronx. So, because Eloisa Bly married a Blake, he was named for her favorite poet.

Tyger, Tyger, burning bright,
In the forests of the night...

And Mom wondered why he'd opted to fly the same jets his dad had before retiring to teach French linguistics. Jets were way cooler than being the butt of every senior high English class. The hottest girl in the class had made it clear that she liked him, but she refused to call him anything other than Tyger-Tyger.

Like an idiot, he'd been unable to get past that.

Give him math and science any day.

Now? It sucked that Tyger hadn't become his call sign. Too fancy for a bunch of air jocks; he'd gotten stuck with Poet.

He dumped the tray and broke into a trot.

Even though Kiley must have walked—senior officers never ran and the simulator building was too close to think of driving—he was already there and tapping his foot impatiently.

Billy checked his watch as he saluted. He still had four minutes to spare but maybe Kiley counted time differently. Or maybe he was pissed that Blake had arrived in time.

"Well, get your ass in the sling."

"Sir. Yes sir," he dropped the salute and trotted for the stairs. The simulators were one floor up.

In the ready room, five other pilots were milling about.

"You the one we waiting on?" someone snapped at him from the crowd.

He shrugged a response, like anyone ever told him anything.

"Shit! Whatdaya fly?"

"A-10C Thunderbolt II, sir."

"You dumb, flyboy?" A real insult to anyone inside the Air Force. The major confronted him from so close that he couldn't look down to see the man's last name.

"Sir. No sir."

"Well I say you are, so you are. What idiot opts for a forty-year-old piece of shit?"

He kept his mouth shut, but shouted in his head, *The kind of pilot whose dad flew A-10 Thunderbolt IIs in Operation Desert Storm and survived shit you couldn't handle, sir.*

He didn't recognize a single pilot. In fact—he scanned again—he was the only lieutenant in the room. Not a soul from his training cadre of first years. Everyone else was a captain or a major.

Was this one of those ante up or forever be the butt of every joke moments? Billy made a quick guess about what the Major flew.

"Ninety-four percent flight availability. Sir."

The guy did look pained at that.

Billy had nailed it.

The US military's most expensive weapon system ever, the F-35 Lightning II jet fighters, were lucky to hit twenty-five percent availability. It was about the worst introduction of a new aircraft in the Air Force's history.

"Fuck off, flyboy."

"Sir. Yes sir!" Billy saluted smartly and the major stalked off. Again, he missed a chance to see the guy's name. Major Ass-face would fit him just fine.

One of the other officers offered him a smirk, but it looked like a friendly smirk—sympathy rather than derision. "Bell" on the Captain's jacket, Billy noted for later.

The remaining three just flat-out ignored him.

Being the only junior officer in the flight was either a really good thing or a really, really bad one.

6

"I SHOULD HAVE PICKED UP THAT HE WAS THE PILOT," HOLLY rubbed her wrist.

Just like the colonel's gesture.

Miranda still didn't see the connection. Unless the big watch had hurt during the ejection. Or maybe...

Miranda tapped her knuckles on her head to test the idea. Yes, perhaps that was the colonel's symbol of luck—rubbing the watch he'd received for surviving the first ejection somehow helping him survive the second.

She'd never really believed in luck, having had so little of it in her life. The outsider to everyone except her parents. Them both dying in the plane explosion when she was thirteen and should have died with them.

All her years investigating crashes and no closer to understanding why?

She knew all about the *how* but that wasn't enough.

Miranda needed—

"I hate it when Mike gets something before I do," Holly was still grumbling.

"Why is that?" Jeremy asked.

The all too familiar darkness swirled murkily waist deep, dragging to pull her under.

"That's one bloke who's far too sure of himself. It's my duty as a woman to put men like Mike in his place." She faced Miranda. "Our duty as women."

As women.

Miranda caught a breath of clear air.

Miranda tried to make sense of her sudden inclusion in Holly's world. She made it sound like a noble calling. *Women.* As if they were something special for being that.

Holly sounded so certain.

Women.

She liked the idea of being part of something bigger than herself.

Lighter than herself.

But while she believed Holly on most other topics, perhaps Mike Munroe shouldn't be one of them.

"I like Mike."

"Well, sure you do." Holly looked to the heavens as if pleading for the sky to do something. "He doesn't see you as some hot Sheila just begging for a tumble in the tall weeds. I'd rather go a round or two with a saltie."

Miranda recalled that a saltie was the larger and more dangerous type of the two crocodile breeds that lived in Australia. She wasn't sure about the relevance of the metaphor.

After all, she didn't know of any salties currently in the

cool Arizona desert. Would they survive under the crystalline blue of the winter sky? Probably not. The arid desert here stretched from the usually dry river bed of the Santa Cruz River to the drier San Pedro River. Not exactly saltie country.

But if she had to choose between a saltie and Mike Munroe, the choice wouldn't be difficult. Mike was a very handsome man. But men like Mike didn't notice women like her.

In fact, most men ran the other way when they met her.

Of Miranda's seven attempts at relationships, five had made it past the first date. Three past a week. None past the second or third time in bed.

She would blurt something out. About how good or bad it had been. In public. At a restaurant or in the middle of a movie. Not knowing what to do with the emotion it always found an escape, and—by the time she figured out that it had been really inappropriate—she'd be alone again.

She watched a tumbleweed roll lazily by in the late morning breeze. She liked the juxtaposition. Mike would like to have sex with Holly in the tall weeds. Whereas Holly would probably rather lie down *with* the spiny tumbleweeds than with Mike.

Whereas she herself... What would she prefer?

To...solve the reason for this plane crash.

She moved forward to inspect the canopy.

"Stay in my tracks," she told the others. She didn't want the site contaminated.

"Oh, like we're the first to tramp about here. There's tracks everywhere, Sherlock," Holly scoffed, but she and Jeremy did stay in Miranda's tracks.

"Sherlock was a fictional man. You said I needed to

perform my duties as a woman. As I don't believe that I'm fictional, I fail to see the similarity." Miranda kept her eyes on the shifting desert soil.

"Benedict Cumberbatch," Holly sighed happily. "Not so fictional. Would definitely work for me."

"In the movies, Basil Rathbone came the closest for me," she had watched every single movie ever made about her hero detective. "Until I saw him being the French-slinging, villain-pirate in *Captain Blood*. Unable to reconcile the two, I never watched the old movies again. I have always preferred Doyle's original written Sherlock anyway."

Holly laughed. "Let's get to work."

"That's what I've been trying to do for some time now."

Holly laughed again and hugged her.

Unsure what to do, Miranda just stood there until she was done. Once Holly let her go, she asked, "Why did you do that?"

"Because you're so completely you, Miranda."

"Meaning what?"

"You'll figure it out someday," but Holly was smiling in a way that Miranda could only interpret as friendly. Then she turned aside to inspect the mechanical systems, logically starting from the aileron trim tabs.

Miranda moved to the shattered canopy and she and Jeremy looked down through it into the empty cockpit.

The ACES II ejection seat for the A-10 was not a subtle machine. At the top of the seat were a pair of canopy breakers—rabbit-ear steel protrusions. As designed, they'd shattered the thick, polycarbonate-acrylic-layered canopy when the seat had punched upward.

In her Sabre, an ejection would require six steps: hook

up to emergency oxygen bottle if over fifteen thousand feet, duck down to keep her head clear when she pulled the canopy eject lever on the right handgrip—firing it backward on its rails—sit up and lock the harness with the left handgrip, place her feet on the seat's footrests, push her head back against the headrest while tucking her chin, and finally pull on the right handgrip's trigger lever.

If she was under a thousand feet, her chances of survival would be negligible.

To use the A-10's ACES II seat, you sat back and yanked the big yellow handles at the end of the chair arms. It took care of everything else.

And you could do it from the ground, as the colonel had, with a reasonable hope of survival.

She mentally followed the arc up into the air. The colonel would have ejected because he was still unsure if his efforts to save the aircraft had been sufficient even at the last second.

After the canopy was shattered, rockets would propel him at three hundred miles an hour to approximately twenty stories into the air—auto-steering him to the correct angle.

At the apex of his arc, the seat would cut loose from the harness.

The seat would plummet to earth and a land...about where it still remained.

Now that he was separate from the seat, a charge would deploy the parachute still attached to the pilot by his harness—and he'd have a single swing before he returned to the earth...there.

But his parachute wasn't there.

Perhaps they had cleaned it up along with the explosives.

But...she walked away from the A-10.

"Hey! What are you..." Jeremy called after her.

The sound of feet trotting came up from behind. In her tracks, because Jeremy always listened.

She found what she was looking for well past the location of the seat—which would hold no unique information for her. It had done its job, saved the colonel's life, then fallen to land where ballistics had taken it.

But on landing, the Colonels' feet had made two deep punches in soft sand that would be where he first hit after a barely arrested twenty-story fall. Then the smoothly flattened area of a professional tuck-and-roll parachute landing. Beyond the end of the smoothed section was another deep furrow as the pilot was dragged by his chute twenty more feet before stopping against a large clump of desert grass.

"A strong tailwind," Jeremy observed correctly.

"Loss of lift in flight," Miranda noted. "A strong tailwind, especially a burst at the last moment, would drastically decrease the wing's lift that depends on forward motion relative to the air."

"Are you saying the colonel was incautious and too close to the ground when he lost too much lift due to some microburst?"

Miranda turned to look at him. "I was discussing facts. You're discussing conclusions."

"Right. Right. Right."

Miranda recognized the habit and understood that the closing of his eyes and nodding his head emphatically with each repetition was to focus his concentration.

Jeremy was driving the information into his mental

construct. Experience had taught her that it wasn't the most efficient method, but it worked.

"Don't think in a completed image, Jeremy. Think in a tree-shape of accumulating facts. Each piece has a place. We can now discern that there was a tailwind sufficient to drag a man into this clump of grass, but not through or over it. I have not tested this specific soil," she knelt down and scooped up a handful then allowed the sandy content to spill through her fingers, "but we can surmise that a wind speed under fifteen knots would be sufficient to drag the colonel."

"Especially if he was momentarily unresponsive or perhaps just happy to be alive and didn't think to cut away. We'd have to inspect the chute to be sure, but as it's not here, he probably carried it back to the base."

"Very good." Miranda knew that was more than she would have thought about the human factor. "And an emergency landing, without flaps..." She left the sentence open just as she'd learned to do when lecturing at the NTSB Training Center—the few times she'd let Terence talk her into doing so.

Jeremy was nodding rapidly. "Such a landing would be performed at a significantly higher-than-normal speed. Colonel Campos said that he had only moments to compensate and attempt to save his plane. Which means he would have still been at maneuvering speed, not landing speed. Therefore, the tailwind would have a minimal effect on the aircraft traveling at perhaps a couple hundred knots."

"But not *no* effect," she lifted a handful of the dry soil and shook it out between her fingers. It was light enough that even the light breeze carried it several steps away.

Again the rapid nodding. "Right. A possible factor,

though not a likely one. How do I learn to do what you do, Miranda?"

"Never stop learning." That was her father's voice. One of the last things he ever said to her before his death, though he'd said it so often she was still unsure if that counted as a special final instruction or not.

"I can do that."

"Good," Miranda dusted off her hands. "Back to the plane."

"Back to the plane," Jeremy agreed.

Miranda fished a hundred-foot tape out of her pack and handed the end to him. She positioned herself to measure the length of the pilot's skid and the distance to both the fallen ejection seat and the plane itself.

Again, facts.

7

No longer the center of attention, Billy took a moment to check out the Eglin Air Force base's simulator room.

It was still surprising that he was here.

He and the guys he'd left at the table in the DFAC had just graduated the Pilot Training Next program at AETC last week. The Air Education and Training Command at Joint Base San Antonio, Texas, had run his class through a six-month simulator course rather than the year-long course that included mostly classroom time and some trainer time.

He loved the simulators.

Pilot Next had given him unlimited hours. If he screwed up a flight maneuver, he wasn't taken into a classroom to discuss what had happened. Instead, they reset the flight to the moment he'd screwed up and he could keep reworking the moment until he nailed its ass.

He'd applied for the A-10 Warthog upon graduation, *and* gotten the assignment, which had transferred his training to Air Combat Command at Florida's Eglin Air Force Base. The

November temperatures were the same 50s as San Antonio, but it was still a balm to his New York blood expecting a bitter winter. Besides, his life was indoors. More simulators, and soon inside a fighter jet.

There was a little jostling for the stations, but there was no difference that he could see. It didn't affect him as they were all climbing into simulators labeled F-35 Lightning II—America's newest fighter jet.

He headed for one of the few labeled A-10 Thunderbolt II—America's oldest fighter jet. No one else headed for those.

The upper story of the training center was blacked out—no windows to look out, which was a good thing. He'd always loved watching the jets at his prior bases. Just sitting and watching the active runways for hours was one of his favorite pastimes.

Maybe someday he'd find a girl pilot who felt the same way. There was only one in his cadre, but she was engaged to some guy back in Wyoming. That's okay. He was patient and would find one like that someday. Until then, there were plenty of fine women available to an Air Force pilot.

He pulled on the headset goggles that were the only common element with the Pilot Next simulators—these rigs were very different than the ones he'd flown in San Antonio.

The headset would project all of the data, targeting, and threat information that would normally be projected on the inside of a helmet's visor. It would also track his eye movement and where his attention was focused.

Jittery equals bad, Billy reminded himself. *Steady, focused, scanning smoothly equals good.*

At San Antonio, he'd sat in a chair with flight controls

and four television screens—three for the view out of the cockpit and one for the instrument panel.

Here the seats faced into clamshells of four tall, curving panels. During yesterday's orientation, he'd been amazed at the clarity of the projections.

"These are 8K resolution," the head of simulations had happily announced. "Four times the pixel density of a 4k home television. All global terrains are accurate to a minimum of five meters, most within one meter." The instructor had added terrain-following radar overlays onto their views. "Now look left, right, and up."

Billy had been able to see the whole flight. Toucan's A-10, the four Lightnings, a pair of F-22 Raptors, even the two guys who'd been dumb enough to opt for the F-18s that *were* on their way out of service—the Air Force needed pilots until they retired those aircraft, but it was happening soon.

The A-10 would be around for a long while yet thanks to Congress forcing common sense down Command's throats. That, and the fact that nothing else could do the job half as well or at anywhere near the cost. An F-35 Lightning II, the proposed replacement, cost ten times as much as an A-10. And the hourly operational cost was stratospheric by comparison.

In yesterday's sim, he'd waggled his wings and Toucan had waggled his back. They were going to totally kick ass together.

But now it was just him and five superior officers—all in F-35 Lightning IIs.

"Today's simulated sortie," Kiley announced over their headsets, "will be over Syria. There is suspected Russian activity against anti-government rebels. You will *not* allow them to engage."

Billy took a deep breath to keep his hands and his gaze calm. He didn't want the eye sensors picking up on his nerves.

Incoming Russians. Perfect.

Lightnings against any fast movers. The Ruskies had about twenty fighter jets placed in Syria. Mostly the older aircraft, but the supersonic Sukhoi Su-34 "Fullbacks" were among them.

Not his worry. One of those came after him and his ass was toast.

But the Su-25 "Frogfoot"? That was his main game.

The Frogfoot was the fighter get you got if you started with an A-10 and then asked a bunch of drunk Russian engineers to redesign it from scratch. Take away the central cannon, because that was too tricky to design around. Next, make it smaller. Finally, mount the engines where you really wanted to put a couple racks of missiles instead.

Still dangerous as hell, but he couldn't wait to take one on.

And the best part was that the Syrians didn't have any Su-25s—they were all Russian. If he met a Frogfoot in battle, even simulated battle, it would have a Russian pilot and a Russian pilot's skill index setting.

The sim started.

They were launching out of Ramat David Airbase in northern Israel. With the deep chill going on in Turkey's psychotic government, the Incirlik Air Base must be falling out of favor.

The US had always been careful to not show that it was stationing aircraft in Israel.

If the sim was anything to judge by, that was going to change.

Cool to be in the know that command was even willing to test the idea.

He'd have to decide later whether or not to tell the other guys from his cadre about this. Of course, he'd lord over them that he was flying with a whole bunch of superior officers first, just to rub it in.

But the incredible detail and the visual surround let him almost believe he was in a plane. About the only thing missing was the motion of the large mechanical simulators. But as those cost over a hundred times this setup, he'd get a hundredth of the simulator hours.

The only other thing he wanted was his own bird.

A flight of six jet fighters was pretty spectacular. Real world they rarely flew in more than pairs. That meant the simulator training planners were beefing up a major scenario for them.

It was crazy that he was doing this during only his second day at Elgin. If this is the kind of thing they were going to keep doing, he'd bless Mom for naming him William Blake and driving him into the military.

For an hour they patrolled high along the border: north along the coast, then east just a few kilometers into Turkey. It was mostly high-level flight working on team coordination.

He tried not to think about what would happen if there was real trouble, as his was the only non-supersonic jet in the flight. In a battle, the Lightnings could all climb ten thousand feet higher and still be at a stroll as they left the area at twice his best speed.

It was as they were turning south along the Syrian-Iraq border that trouble first showed up on their radars.

8

Miranda and the rest of the team sat with their backs against the sunny side of the downed Thunderbolt's fuselage and conferred over club sandwiches. None of them had had breakfast, so they'd decided on brunch after they'd spent a couple hours at the site.

The colonel had made a point of taking their orders, then shuttling back to base in the Huey helicopter to fetch it himself.

"Feels good," Mike lay back against the A-10 with his hat brim pulled down far enough to hide his eyes.

"The desert down in Oz doesn't get this kind of cold," Holly's hat was tipped back and her eyes were closed as her face turned to follow the sun.

Colonel Campos kept his silence.

Miranda slipped the weather meter out of her vest pocket. Sixty-nine degrees Fahrenheit against an average midday high of sixty-five for November. She shifted the meter as far from the protection of the fuselage as she could without getting up. A seven-degree temperature drop. Was that a typical gradient from a protected environment or was the gradient unique to desert conditions? Perhaps...

"I've been thinking about—" Jeremy paused, and glanced at Holly, who looked as if she couldn't be bothered to move. Besides, her eyes were closed.

Miranda watched carefully, but couldn't see what he was waiting for.

A glance at the silent colonel startled him. He'd been watching her intently and was now suddenly interested in the A-10's starboard engine.

She inspected it carefully, but couldn't see anything of interest. It appeared wholly undamaged by the crash.

"What have you been thinking?" Holly prompted Jeremy without opening her eyes.

"Well... The condition of the aircraft's systems implies that while well maintained, the last major service wasn't recent."

"Fifty-seven flight hours ago," Campos confirmed.

"Exactly," Jeremy tried to lean forward, but was slightly mired by the sand. He planted his hands to push himself upright, forgetting that he still had half of a turkey sandwich in one hand. "Long enough since any major service that it's unlikely to be an error made in that process. But also, not long enough for it to be a parts failure."

"Sometimes parts just fail, Jeremy." Miranda wondered if Mike was asleep in the sun, but he wasn't if he was answering.

"What if they didn't?"

Miranda hated "What if?" questions.

What if her parents hadn't been aboard TWA 800 when an electrical fault blew it from the sky shortly after takeoff from New York?

What if she'd been on the plane with them instead of attending the final week of horse-riding summer camp—the last of her naive childhood tossed aside at thirteen as if launched away by an ejection seat?

What if this broke or that failed?

She far preferred the application of her *reverse* scientific method: what are the facts, what sole solution explains those facts, and no extraneous "what if" conjectures or wild hypotheses along the way.

However, as Jeremy enjoyed this exercise more than anyone else she'd ever observed, she'd become inclined not to stop the team whenever he began such conversations.

"You mean what if I'm right and haven't been making it up this whole time?" The colonel didn't look amused. Odd, she could read his emotions more easily than most even though they'd only spent the morning together.

"Exactly! What if some force did indeed take control of your aircraft?"

"Some force, Jeremy? What force? Aliens?" Mike kept up the conversation with Jeremy, as Holly now appeared to have fallen asleep in the sun.

"Well, that could certainly be one hypothesis, but I think it unlikely. If alien life was looking to make its presence known on Earth, I think landing a flying saucer in Central Park would be much more effective."

"Or blowing up the White House."

"Right. *Independence Day*. Though I'm more inclined to believe that any aliens would be benevolent and are simply waiting to see if we survive our self-destructive tendencies like climate change, runaway population, and technological advances in warfighting. Any which way, I can't see them tinkering with the flight controls of a forty-year old fighter jet."

"If not aliens, then maybe some tractor beam."

Miranda tried to decide if Mike was kidding around or not, but possessed insufficient evidence to reach a conclusion one way or the other.

Jeremy, on the other hand, didn't even blink. "It would be a repulser beam. Something pushing it toward the ground from above. It would be far more likely."

"Likely?" That actually got Mike's attention. He shoved his hat up enough to look at Jeremy across Holly.

"Sure," Jeremy bit into his sand-coated sandwich for emphasis, then went through a whole episode of coughing it back out and trying to wipe sand off his tongue—first with gritty fingers, then with a napkin.

Miranda checked to make sure the remains of her own sandwich were safely nestled in the exact center of her unfolded napkin, placed carefully in her lap. The sun had moved to align precisely with the diagonal slice, producing no shadow along the cut surface. She liked the connection of caloric consumption aligning with the solar maximum on a winter's day.

Except they weren't eating at 12:07, so it wasn't solar maximum. Still, she liked the alignment.

Jeremy rinsed his mouth with a swallow of soda. "Yes. I saw no signs of any vast equipment array in the desert, though I did walk well astern of where the aircraft impacted."

"You went looking for a tractor beam."

"No. I went looking for any stray parts or spills of hydraulic fluid. But while doing so, I didn't find any unexpected large arrays of equipment. So, if it was a mythical beam weapon, a repulser from above is far more likely than a tractor from below."

"He's got you there, Mike," Holly scoffed, proving that she was still awake.

"As much as is possible in the field, you've checked for mechanical actuators, unidentified cams on the ailerons control wires, and the like, right?"

Holly nodded and then opened one eye to watch Jeremy as he continued.

"The A-10 Thunderbolt II isn't fly-by-wire. You know, manipulate the control in the cockpit," he pointed forward, "and a signal travels down a wire to engage a motor to wiggle the aileron here." He grabbed the trailing edge of the wing and wiggled it. "It's all mechanical connections, by hydraulics and a backup of actual wires. Which makes much more sense for fly-by-wire—the mechanical rather than the electronic meaning, I mean."

"Yes, Jeremy, we all know what fly-by-wire is," Holly's glare had Jeremy stuttering for a long moment.

"Because the colonel experienced an apparent remote control of his aircraft—"

"Remote control?" Miranda sat up at that. It shifted the sun onto the face of her sandwich. With the breaking of the incidental solar alignment to the cut edge, she picked up the second half and continued eating.

"We've been proceeding on the concept that there is some system fault. What if there wasn't? What if the problem is that someone—"

"Or something," Mike pointed up toward the sky.

"Or something," Jeremy conceded, "did indeed take control?"

9

BILLY WAS LOOKING THE WRONG WAY WHEN THE FLIGHT LEADER called in the report over the radio that connected the simulators.

"I have a pair of unidentified bogies inbound from Tiyas Military Airbase." Tiyas lay almost exactly in the center of Syria—excellent strategically, a hideous posting in a burned-out desert hell.

But he found them fast enough. They were coming in high and fast on the radar, though he could only see one of them. Maybe his older radar couldn't isolate them as two separate aircraft.

The flight leader, Major Ass-face, began calling out tactics—none of which included him.

To hell with them! He knew his role and kept scanning the desert.

Even after six months in San Antonio—which just wasn't sensible to a New York boy—he didn't get how people lived in places like the Syrian landscape simulated around him.

He supposed even San Antone was better than this, which was a really extreme statement. Except for thirty kilometers along the Mediterranean and the narrow valley of the Tigris River, Syria was just a vast expanses of brown rock and lifeless dirt.

How could people be fighting over this for a nine-year civil war? Or the ten thousand years since the first settlements and agriculture had begun here?

The pair of fast movers were still arrowing in on their five Lightnings who had split into a pair and a trio.

Two on five and they were still coming hard.

That didn't make sense. They'd be badly outnumbered.

That's when he finally caught a clue.

The F-35 Lightning IIs were fifth-generation stealth fighters. There were only four fifth-gen fighter jet types in the world. The American F-22 Raptor and the F-35 Lightning II had been first. The Chinese were still having issues with their Shenyang J-31 Gyrfalcon.

But intelligence had reported two of Russia's brand-new Su-57 Felons were in Syria for testing in a live combat zone.

Fifth-generation stealth.

Just like the rest of his flight—except for him. An A-10 Thunderbolt II was old tech and would have the radar signature of a brick—a very large, very reflective brick.

He drifted his A-10 back from the pack by just a few kilometers. No more than fifteen seconds away.

Sure enough, the incoming blips shifted to remain vectored on his lone jet.

He hustled to catch back up as he radioed Major Assface.

"Flight lead, this is Alpha-one," he was the only A-10 in

the flight after all. "*I'm* the one on their radar. Also recall, a pair of Su-57s are known to be in-country."

No response.

He tried again.

Some kind of damn game. The bastards had jumped frequencies without telling him.

Complain to Lt. Colonel Kiley?

No points for whining.

He'd just fly his damn flight better than anyone else.

———

10

Colonel Arturo Campos couldn't make sense of this Miranda Chase.

If the source of her recommendation hadn't been the unimpeachable Chairman of the Joint Chiefs of Staff General Drake Nason, he'd have already booted her off the site.

Her people were leaning back against his crashed A-10 Thunderbolt, talking of aliens and repulser beams, and ignoring him as if he didn't know shit about his own aircraft.

The guy who talked the most—a slender Vietnamese kid, though with no accent—looked like he was about twelve.

The lovely blonde didn't say much, but when she did, it ruined everything.

His ex had been a New Zealander. Their accents were just similar enough to really piss him off—he so didn't need the reminder.

Shara had Dear Arturo'd him during his fourth tour in

Iraq and then tried to take his entire pension into her orthodontist-boss' bed. Thank Jesus, Mary, and Joseph that the courts had seen her infidelity the same way he had. Or thank his insanely expensive lawyer: brutal, but worth every damn dime. It had also helped his case that her new fiancé made five times the money he did. Hence the Dear Arturo.

For two hours Mike Munroe had questioned him in detail about the stupidest trivia. Every time Arturo was on the verge of dismissing him, Mike would somehow turn it around and keep him talking. He wasn't used to people who could manipulate him.

In fact, it was high time he got rid of these people. Too bad, as he found himself liking Miranda Chase despite her peculiarities. Or perhaps because of them. But her people were intolera—

"The colonel said—"

Mike's voice snapped his attention back to the rambling conversation.

"—that he saw no surge in the hydraulic pressure on either gauge. He tried popping the breakers on both, but he didn't regain control. Jeremy?"

"Yes, I can confirm that both hydraulic system breakers were pulled. I inspected the lines and reservoirs. The proper amount of fluids were in the lines and, as far as I can tell in the field, the right grade of oil—though I've taken samples to run back to the lab. If there's a mechanism, such as a hidden auxiliary pump or valving system, I was unable to locate it. The directional flow valves, in case of a system rupture, were intact and properly oriented."

Arturo could only shake his head in surprise. Civilians were able to leap so effortlessly from the ridiculous to the relevant. Before all his years of training in regimented military thinking, had he been able to think that way?

"Holly?" Miranda asked softly.

"Control lines look clean. There are a couple of crucial panels that we can't see behind until we get her up out of the dirt, but otherwise clean. I'm ready to unplant this bird and get it back to a hangar."

"What are we missing?" Again, such a simple seeming question from Miranda.

She was five-four, weighed about the same as an M134 minigun without the mount or ammo, and appeared otherwise non-descript with mouse-brown hair.

Yet her mind was sharper than a honed blade. And she also had absolute control of her team, just not in any way that he could identify.

"No microburst weather systems," Jeremy stated.

"No obvious broken control surfaces," Holly spoke up.

"The only pilot I've met less likely to be flustered by a mishap is probably you," Mike aimed a smile at Miranda. "I tried to mess him up and couldn't."

That assessment had Arturo turning to study Mike again. Clearly he'd found out things that Arturo had never intended to say, including how Shara had tried to take him for all he was worth.

But perhaps Mike had been testing and learning about him in ways Arturo hadn't anticipated? If so, what did it say about Miranda that Mike Munroe had said Miranda was even harder to fluster than he was?

Twenty years in the A-10s, he knew them cold and had always prided himself on flying them that way. In his opinion, those were the best type of pilots. Not Maverick, but

Iceman was the proper *Top Gun.* Ice cold and never screw up; just wear 'em down.

He now understood that was how Miranda dealt with crashes.

Not just with control, but with a chill brilliance.

He liked that.

A lot.

11

Keep chill, dude. Keep chill.

Billy chanted the mantra to himself.

He wanted to rip off the simulation's heavy goggles that were tracking his eye movement—and probably the tightness of his shoes and whether he was wishing he'd had a club sandwich instead of a double serving of lasagna for lunch, which was sitting pretty heavy.

But that wouldn't be chill.

Focus on the moment.

So, he was on his own.

Billy knew that the eye scanner wasn't the only thing monitoring his actions and transmissions. He wasn't sitting in an A-10 Thunderbolt II. He, at least, remembered that Lt. Colonel Kiley would be listening and assessing as well.

Well, if the flight leader wasn't worried about fifth-gen stealth fighters sneaking up on him, Billy still was.

If there really were Su-57s in the area, what would be the

best way to spot them? If they were as stealthy as intelligence briefings claimed, he wasn't going to pick them up on radar until he'd already stood out like a sore thumb on theirs.

Think, man. Think.

Su-57s were painted to blend in if viewed from above. If the Su-57s were even five thousand feet below the flight of Lightning IIs, they'd be tough to spot against the desert background.

The only realistic way to spot them was visually. Against the rough earth, much less likely. They'd be far easier to see as motion against the perfect blue backdrop of the simulated Syrian sky.

To see them sooner?

Get down.

He nosed over into a steep dive.

Billy kept glancing up, but all he could see was his own flight of five.

Not a word from Major Ass-face. Who probably wished Billy would "Go fuck yourself, Rook."

Billy kept his thoughts about offering a basic anatomy lesson to himself.

He'd drop ten thousand feet. Two miles down and still six above the Syrian countryside.

Still nothing above except the original two blips.

He'd descend down another three miles, then—

Something snagged his attention.

What?

What had changed?

His instrument display revealed nothing. Both engines running clean. Hydraulics at full pressure.

Nothing from the threat detector.

The background roar of the simulated A-10 remained unchanged over his headphones.

No, something outside the aircraft.

Again, nothing high. Not even a sun-glint off a canopy.

Down below. A pair of gray-white specs slashing across the black background of the Es Safa basaltic flows.

Su-57s? If so, he'd need help from above and he'd need it fast.

He tapped the zoom control on the flat LED of his targeting screen.

Not Su-57s. The wing configuration was wrong. But he knew what these were.

Su-25 Frogfoots. Frogfeet?

Ground assault aircraft. Appropriately enough—near the ground.

Rules of engagement said no firing before he was fired upon.

But it didn't say a word about scaring the shit out of some Ruskies. Time to show just what his plane could do.

A final glance aloft.

"Flight lead. This is Alpha-one pursuing two bogies at two o'clock."

No response, but at least he was doing his damned job.

He nosed his A-10 Thunderbolt II the rest of the way over until he was plummeting straight down.

A vertical mile later, and not a goddamn word from on high.

"By the way, flight lead, you have a pair of Su-57s coming up fast on your six." He'd spotted them on his last glance aloft—their distinctive wing configuration and white edging on the paint job made them easily identifiable once spotted.

Not even a squeak from above.

Well, fuck them all.

He enjoyed the rest of the ride down toward the two ground-attack aircraft just swinging clear of the Es Safa.

12

COLONEL ARTURO CAMPOS *STILL* DIDN'T KNOW WHAT TO MAKE of Miranda Chase, except that the woman was a total lunatic.

The CH-47F Chinook he'd called for from the base had lowered a cargo cable with a four-point lifting harness already hung. They'd picked his A-10 less than ten feet above the desert when Miranda called out for them to hover in place. Near the massive twin-rotor helicopter's load limits, that was a hard thing to do. A hover took much more power than maintaining altitude with forward motion.

While the pilots struggled to hover stably, Chase walked directly underneath the dangling A-10 before he could grab her.

His shout to warn her of the danger was drowned out by the sound of the pounding rotor blades.

The Jeremy kid looked up as he hesitated for a long moment—then rushed to join her despite the obvious danger.

She wasn't looking up.

Instead, she moved quickly, looking down—quartering back and forth across the slight depression his aircraft had punched into the soil.

Near where the tail section had rested, Jeremy pointed. She nodded sharply, shed her vest, and tossed it down on the ground.

Jeremy knelt on it, pinning it in place. Or like they were getting ready for final prayers.

She looked up for a long moment at the aircraft dangling a bare meter above her head.

Then, with an abrupt wave, she signaled him to dismiss the helicopter.

He radioed for them to return to base and place guards around the aircraft once they had it on the ground.

As soon as the helo cleared the area, he raced over to her. "Are you crazy? Standing underneath a thirteen-ton sling load and a fourteen-ton helicopter?"

She waved a hand around her as if that explained anything, but didn't deign to speak with him. He had no idea what the woman was thinking but she was clearly insane.

Squatting, she eased up the edge of her vest.

The young Jeremy shook loose a clear plastic sample bag.

"What the hell?" But they weren't paying any attention to him.

"You see it, right, mate?" The blonde Australian had arrived by his elbow.

"All I see is a woman with a death wish. And a young punk so into hero worship that he'd follow her right off a cliff."

"No, I don't think that's quite on. Though you may be right about Jeremy. What you see is a woman who has faced death and decided that it is of no interest to her one way or the other."

He turned to Holly. "What do you mean by that?"

It was one of the hardest lessons there was to teach a soldier. Only the very best Special Operations people learned that fearing death made death more rather than less likely when the margins got narrow. He'd learned it by ejecting from his aircraft—twice—and he still wasn't comfortable with the thought.

Fear caused hesitation. And out at the edge, hesitation meant death. That much he'd learned.

This Holly understood that—which said even more about the quality of Miranda's NTSB team. It made him wonder at both of their backgrounds.

"What you should be seeing is the ground," Holly made the same gesture that Miranda had made.

He inspected the sand at his feet, but didn't understand whatever these women seemed to think he was supposed to be seeing. Pancaking his jet to the ground hadn't even particularly packed the loose soil—just plowed it up into a neat furrow.

Except the furrow wasn't so neat.

The down-blast from the heavily laden departing Chinook helicopter had blown the light sands wildly the moment the wind shadow of the hanging A-10 had been moved aside. The deep furrow was still evident, but it had lost most of its definition.

"She walked under a potentially lethal weight load because..." He couldn't quite wrap his head around it.

"Because," Holly thumped him on the shoulder hard enough to hurt, "she cares that much about what causes a crash."

Just what had these women been through?

He turned to watch his A-10 being carried back toward base. The Chinook had climbed to a thousand feet as it headed back toward Davis-Monthan.

Yet even as he watched—the two aircraft separated.

It was such a small, lazy motion.

One moment they were connected by a long lifting wire with a cargo hook attached to a four-point sling carrying his A-10.

The next, there was a gap and the winch cable was dancing about with the sudden load release.

In slow motion, the two aircraft just...separated.

Then lighter by half, the helicopter had climbed abruptly.

And his jet, still wrapped in the lifting harness, fell from the sky.

Two crashes in one day was apparently too much for it. His A-10 Thunderbolt II hit tail first—hard.

Then exploded in a massive fireball that had them all ducking even though it was a mile distant.

"The same aircraft crashing twice," Holly commented close by his elbow, "that's not something you see every day."

Cargo hook failures didn't happen, not on helos in his command.

At least not until now.

13

THE CRAY XC50 AT THE EGLIN AIR FORCE BASE WAS RUNNING a training flight for five F-35s and a special A-10 flight.

Deep inside a different section of the code, it had been testing the variable R14A10DAVIS for eight hours.

The code finally tested true.

The subroutine proceeded through the next four steps:

Generate a one-word message.

Deliver the word to three separate secure cellphones.

After all three phones provided a delivery confirmation, drop the external connection.

Finally, the subroutine erased itself and the program that had called it.

14

FIVE THOUSAND FEET AND EIGHT SECONDS ABOVE THE PAIR OF
Su-25 Frogfeets, Lieutenant William "Poet" Blake flipped on
his missile targeting computer.

Billy could easily imagine the high squeal that would
sound in the Russians' cockpits.

"Hi, boys. You wanna just head your sorry asses back
home or do you wanna play?"

The lead bird rolled in a sharp twist and tried to bring its
guns to bear.

It fired too soon.

Billy was able to peel aside without a hit. As he did, he
launched a pair of 70mm Hydra missiles at each aircraft.

Number Two was too slow and lost a wing.

The pilot ejected even as his aircraft went into a
tumbling fall.

But the lead bird had kicked a load of chaff to fool the
missiles and was still after him.

Billy banked over ninety degrees, cutting a hard turn to the right.

Without hesitating, he slammed just as abruptly to the left.

He'd worked this out one long night on the simulator back during Pilot Next training.

As the S-shape crossed him ahead of the remaining Frogfoot, he released a round of flares right in front of the guy's nose. Then, rather than continuing the turn or making an expected climb for altitude, he took advantage of his speed and twisted into a dive.

He kept the joystick full forward, riding the edge of the Warthog negative-three g load limit. Billy imagined he could feel the blood rush to his head as his Hog swept through the downward loop that aimed him successively at the ground, upside down at the far horizon, then had him climbing straight up underneath the remaining Russian Frogfooter as it broke through his chaff wall.

"When in doubt, overkill is the best kind of kill," his dad used to tell him about his time flying in Desert Storm. Dad and his own A-10 Thunderbolt II had been on the team that killed over two thousand vehicles, including twenty-eight Russian-built Iraqi tanks, along the "Highway of Death" over two days in that miserable February—miserable for Saddam and his people at least.

Billy fired off an AIM-9M air-to-air Sidewinder missile, and then lit the big cannon.

Less than two seconds in range, but it was enough. Of the hundred rounds he fired, over fifty ripped into the belly of the Su-25 Frogfoot.

Then the missile struck.

Nine-point-four kilos of high-explosive dead-centered into the right-wing fuel tank.

The plane didn't explode.

It shattered.

Once he was clear, he looked back—and lost the view off the edge of the simulator screen.

Crap! The system was so good, he'd forgotten he wasn't flying.

This was incredibly awesome.

And he'd never get to fire off a six hundred-thousand-dollar missile in a real practice flight.

Doubly awesome!

He turned his A-10 enough to get a clear view on the simulator screen of the Su-25 moments before it crashed into one of the smaller peaks of Es Safa. No pilot ejection.

He'd totally rocked it!

"Splash two," he called out on the radio. The call meant that he'd killed off two aggressors, even if they were a long way from any water in this barren land.

No one answered, of course.

15

THE CODE ON THE CRAY XC50 SUPERCOMPUTER IN Subbasement 2 of the AFAMS building at Eglin kept testing the variable RI4AI0SYR.

It remained false.

A new instruction was loaded into the system. The load demand had surged in other parts of the system. Several milliseconds passed before the new code was executed.

16

Billy looked aloft and wondered how the F-35s were doing up above.

Certainly no one was helping him.

All jabbering on some other frequency.

Bastards.

He hoped the simulation was kicking their asses—hard.

He could climb six thousand feet per minute, which placed him seven full minutes below his flight. His own aerial battle had lasted under thirty seconds—theirs would probably be just as brief if they had to engage. He checked fuel, then began the long climb.

Once back at altitude, he'd have less than fifteen minutes on station before he either needed a refueling tanker or to turn for home.

No sign of any falling aircraft or battle flashes on high.

Maybe they'd all bugged out, in which case he'd kill the Ass-face as soon as he was out of the sim.

Best to climb up and see if he could help, but he'd keep an eye out below.

Less than a thousand feet into his climb, he heard a high squeal on his threat detector.

The tone was wrong for a Russian missile.

But it was right for an American one.

"Break off! Break off! This is Alpha-one that you're targeting!" They should see that clearly on their screen.

The tone didn't cut out until several seconds later.

If they hadn't heard him before, they probably didn't now.

He had the feeling that the targeting tone had stopped because they'd fired—not because they'd stopped tracking him. Once the missile was fired, it would lock onto his jet passively, either visually or by heat signature, and would no longer need external targeting guidance.

Speed and distance were now his friends.

He twisted into a hard dive and redlined the twin TF34 turbofans.

Heating-seeking.

If they'd fired at him, it was probably a heat-seeking missile.

And here he was, diving with his ass in the air and twin-engine exhausts making fifteen-hundred-degree bullseyes.

Head-on, the slender missile had the radar profile of a fat seagull, so he had no way to see how close it was.

Hopefully far enough.

17

THE A-10PCAS PROGRAM HAD BEEN CANCELLED BEFORE IT was truly begun.

DARPA—the Defense Advanced Research Projects Agency—had technically abandoned using an unmanned A-10 Thunderbolt II in 2012 as part of its Persistent Close Air Support program.

The PCAS program had successfully moved on to other aspects of the electronic battlefield.

But the unmanned A-10PCAS Thunderbolt II Warthog wasn't forgotten by the Air Force.

The flight of four F-35 Lightning IIs were currently in a fight for their lives in a dogfight high over the vast emptiness of the Syrian desert with two outmoded MiG-29 Fulcrum jets—and a pair of Su-57 Felons they'd never seen coming.

Independently, the remote-piloted A-10PCAS—driven by a pilot thinking he was in a simulation—dove straight for the ground with an American AIM-9 Sidewinder missile chasing after it at Mach 2.5.

The lead F-35 Lightning pilot hadn't fired it—though his plane had.

He didn't know about the simulation being run ten thousand kilometers away at Eglin Air Force Base. He didn't know about four F-35 Lightning IIs that were flying a completely different simulated scenario and wondering where the hell their A-10 pilot had gotten to.

All the flight leader knew was that he'd started the flight with an A-10PCAS but had lost radio contact with its pilot shortly after take-off. It had tagged along, but he'd been unable to contact it.

When his F-35 Lightning II fired the AIM-9 Sidewinder without his arming or releasing the weapon, he knew something was wrong. There were a lot of electronic systems in place to make sure that didn't happen.

His momentary distraction would shortly cause the first-ever loss of an F-35 Lightning II in combat—an event the Russians would bask in the glory of long after it had lost all meaning. It lost its meaning less than five minutes later with the downing of both of their brand-new Su-57 Felons deep in the heart of Syria.

The A-10PCAS, diving at its top speed of Mach 0.56, stood little chance.

The AIM-9's operational limit of twenty-two miles and the thirty-four second travel time from the high-flying Lightning II to the racing A-10PCAS would place the Thunderbolt at the outer limits of its range—if the A-10 had headed directly away at maximum speed.

Instead, it was diving toward the ground.

The exhaust of its dual jet turbines created an easy and

verifiable target for the Sidewinder's autonomous targeting systems.

The A-10PCAS reached the ground mere seconds ahead of the Sidewinder missile.

The Warthog released a cloud of chaff to confuse the Sidewinder missile—but the Sidewinder had been specifically designed to ignore such distractions.

As soon as it cleared the hot flares and chaff, it reacquired a hot target less than four hundred meters ahead.

Behind the momentary chaff screen, the A-10PCAS had been carving a seven-point-three-g upward loop, right at its control limits.

The Sidewinder punched through the chaff and into the clear—now facing the cold front view of the hard-turning A-10PCAS.

But the inferno created by one of the downed Su-25 Frogfeet—reignited by the A-10PCAS dropping an AGM-65 Maverick air-to-surface missile on the rubbish pile—captured the Sidewinder's full attention.

It plowed into the wreckage at three thousand kilometers per hour and fired its warhead.

Nothing survived bigger than a dinner plate except for a lone tire that rolled over a football field's length away before flopping down to rest in the baking desert heat.

The remote pilot of the A-10PCAS turned back for base and to hell with the simulated F-35 Lightning II's scrap metal tumbling down from where it had died fifty thousand feet above.

Hopefully it was Major Ass-face.

Lieutenant William "Poet" Blake couldn't have been more wrong.

18

THE CODE ON THE CRAY XC50 SUPERCOMPUTER IN Subbasement 2 of the AFAMS building kept testing the variable R14A10SYR.

It remained false.

But the positional reading of the A-10PCAS in Syria was flying out of the designated kill zone. This set a true value to a different branch of the subroutine.

The new routine proceeded through the next four steps:

Generate a two-word message.

Deliver the phrase to three separate secure cellphones.

After all three phones provided a delivery confirmation, drop the external connection.

Finally, the subroutine erased itself and the program that had called it.

19

SENATOR HUNTER RAMSON'S PHONE BUZZED AT THE SAME moment as his guest's, rattling hard on his desk's cherrywood where he'd set it facedown.

The Chairman of the Senate Armed Services Subcommittee on Airland flipped over his phone and glanced at the message.

Syria negative.

He slapped the phone back down. He'd been promised an A-10 Thunderbolt II mission failure in Syria.

"Goddamn it! Can't you people do anything right?"

Before his guest could answer, his phone rang.

No question who it was. He couldn't afford to ignore it. But he didn't want to deal with it either.

Hunter snatched up his phone, accepted the call, and spoke before the caller had a chance to.

"I'm late for a floor vote. We'll discuss this later."

He hung up the call and slammed the phone facedown again.

Then he steepled his fingers and considered the woman seated opposite him.

"I—"

He waved her to silence. She was definitely selling it, even if she wasn't actually. Word was she didn't trade sex, only exuded it.

Five-ten of stacked-and-fit white-blonde in a pitch-black power suit and one of those filmy scarves in hooker red tied about her throat. Sharing more cleavage than his wife had revealed as Miss Utah in her alarmingly risqué French bikini thirty years ago. At least it had been risqué for him as a 24-year-old, newly minted, Salt Lake City lawyer who'd never been outside of Utah and was co-opted into being a judge when his boss had fallen ill.

This was the goddamn nation's Capitol Building. Didn't she have any respect?

"Senator—"

"No goddamn excuses!" He flipped his phone over and back, over and back.

He knew that his nervous habit probably spoke volumes to a trained spook like the CIA's Director of Special Projects and he didn't give a shit.

"Did you fuck your way to the top?' Word on the floor was that she was screwing the Director. He was widowed, but she was twenty years his junior—right on the border of damning, but not *quite* over it.

"No," she refused to be flustered like any other woman was when he used the tactic. "But we could start discussing how your father-in-law bought you your seat in the 23rd District as a wedding gift."

And the spooks wondered why everyone hated working with them.

No one was supposed to know that except him and Marv —and his father-in-law had been gone a decade, since literally stroking out while screwing his latest nineteen-year-old fiancé. At least he'd kicked off before he'd married this one. It had saved a lot of money and hassle.

Rose knew her father's proclivities and had warned him on their wedding day, *"Don't screw around on me. Not even once. I can make you a powerful man or I can have your body dumped in an Arkansas prison where they'll fuck your pretty little ass to death."* She hadn't made Miss Utah by being naive or timid.

He hadn't doubted her threat for a second. He'd kept his wedding-day pledge and she'd delivered as promised.

His voice was the one in control of acquisitions and force plans for all five branches of the military and the National Guard. Chairman of the Senate Armed Service Committee was only a few terms away. Clint was a good man, but he was in his seventies—time for fresh blood.

Hunter wondered if this young CIA bitch, for all her looks, could even come close to matching Rose. Thirty years on, Rose still had the awesome body that had made her final ten in Miss USA—or as close as the trainers and surgeons could come. She also made a point of so thoroughly fucking his brains out every Friday night that he'd never think to stray. No complaints from him.

But young people these days...

Of course, Pop had said the same thing. Being a small-time Vietnam War hero and married to three wives gave him a perspective Hunter had never understood either. He'd gotten out of Pop's fundamentalist version of the church as fast as he could. The Mormons had excommunicated their family for its adherence to polygamy. And, with all the anger of a betrayed church elder, Pop had excommunicated his only son when Hunter disavowed them. Which was fine with him.

He'd thought CIA Director Clark Winston was smart enough to keep his dick in his pants. He certainly wouldn't have dipped it here himself—this woman was ninety-nine percent shark and maybe one percent female.

"A training crash in Arizona and a miss in Syria? That's all you people have given me so far. What the fuck use is that?"

"Don't forget the—"

"Everyone assumes that the A-10 in Pakistan was a shoot-down no matter what your damned software reported."

Hunter leaned forward to force his hands to stop fooling with his phone. Instead, he started playing with his letter opener—a Viet Cong knife Pop had given him when he was still a kid.

The nondescript blade showed its history. Battered with the forger's hammer and years of hard service. The leather-wrapped handle had been sweat stained by a Victor-Charlie whom Pop had taken down during his time as a tunnel rat—going down into those dark holes as a hunter, not hunted. That's where Hunter had gotten his name and he did his best to live up to it.

"We need results, young lady. No more of your spook gibberish. Or should I have a chat with my old pal over at the Senate Select Committee on Intelligence about the outdated methods and waste of funds that is the CIA?"

Actually, John hated his guts and it was completely mutual —but he could still make threats.

She opened her mouth and he cut her off, tapping the switch under his desk.

"Now, get out of my office. And before you go fucking your boss some more—or anyone else—get me some goddamn results." On cue, his secretary called and he picked up the landline, swiveling his chair enough to dismiss the woman, but keeping his eye on her.

He started talking to his secretary about paragraph four subsection B of he didn't care what bill.

Clarissa Reese rose smoothly to her feet.

Usually when he intentionally pissed someone off he could tell. Not so much as smoothing of her form-fitting power suit.

"Senator," she took her leave.

He waved a dismissive hand somewhere in her direction.

As she stalked out the door in her spiky red heels, he had to admire her long blonde ponytail and her very fine ass. He tried to think if Rose's ass had been better back in her heyday. Close call, even for a beauty show judge—the one indulgence he'd kept up in all of the years since. Though he was careful to never dally with a contestant again, despite the temptations and offers, he could damn well look.

After she was gone, he hung up the phone knowing that Sharlene would keep up a conversation about something innocuous on her end until after the guest was gone.

He inspected the blade in his hands. How much blood had it seen? Pointless American blood wasted in the jungle of Southeast Asia?

Well, not anymore.

This woman with her hot body, her designer clothes, and her ruthless demeanor was the tool he needed for this job, but she had no appreciation of history.

There was more than the present task at stake.

Decades of lessons learned the hard way from military history were at risk.

That and a hell of a lot of money.

20

CIA Director of Special Projects Clarissa Reese let nothing show as she strode out of the Capitol Building. Revealed nothing that the waiting driver would see during the long ride back to Langley.

They rolled past the White House—her driver had long since learned that was her preferred route.

She allowed herself one long look at the noble facade amidst the most secure compound in any city.

CIA Director Clark Winston would be in there, meeting with the President.

At her advice, Clark had recently offered a one-on-one weekly in-depth briefing to President Roy Cole.

She wanted to be there as well, but it wasn't her time yet. First she had to get Clark to think about the upcoming election and his role as *the* vice-presidential candidate.

Her initial plan had included waiting for President Roy Cole to complete his second term—there was little doubt he'd have one.

But one night, after Clark had predictably fallen asleep and she was showering, she'd realized there was no reason to wait the extra four years. If Clark became Cole's second-term VP, then he'd be only one term from a real shot at the presidency. It would also give her the run of the CIA four years sooner.

That thought had given her a far more satisfying orgasm than the one Clark had provided. He was learning but he had *such* a long way to go.

Step One was getting President Cole to depend on Clark. She'd hear tonight how that was progressing.

Step Two would be discrediting VP Mulroney, *but* not so badly that it reflected on Cole. Just enough to have the President seeking a new running mate.

That would take some thinking.

Clarissa would also make sure that she was Clark's plus-one at the next White House dinner.

The timing of when to become Mrs. Clark Winston was still going to be tricky. Clark would have to be confirmed as the candidate for VP and herself as Director of the CIA before that could be announced.

So much to do.

And sooner than any of that, Senator Hunter Ramson was going to receive an education in just how small a man he was. So dickless that he'd barely stared at her cleavage.

The reports said he wasn't gay—a pity as there were other methods she used to convince those people to cooperate. Nothing against them, they just had very predictable buttons. Lesbians she could treat just like she did the men and it always worked.

It didn't matter, sex was only the simplest of weapons.

Though usually it was more than sufficient. Well, he was going to learn just how nasty it could be to attack her.

The only question was which tactic to use on him next.

There were very few men she truly didn't understand, and Ramson was one of them. He communicated one way yet acted another.

Time to be very, very careful, Senator.

Actually, that time had passed him by.

She pulled out her burner phone, keeping it out of sight of the driver as she did so. Clarissa texted a message to a disconnected number.

Less than a block later, not even past the Lincoln Memorial, an answer pinged back.

Only five more hours until the next event.

Good.

21

"This is Colonel Arturo Campos. Report to base. Do *not* attempt to leave your helo."

He didn't know if he'd ever been so mad in his life. It was all he could do to hold his radio without crushing it in his fist—even if it was military grade.

"A Security Forces team will arrive to keep you confined. If you make any adjustments or changes to your aircraft other than shutting it down before I arrive, I'll have you all in Leavenworth so fast that your heads will spin."

He let go of the transmit key on his radio before he said what he was *really* thinking.

Arturo had risked his life to save that plane. He'd ridden her right down to the dirt before kicking free. Ejecting, his first time, at five thousand feet as a SAM missile had taken out his plane had given him a bad case of the shakes.

Ejecting again at zero-zero with ground impact less than a second away...he hadn't had a spare moment since to let the shakes set in.

Yet.

He changed frequencies to the Davis-Monthan security frequency. He needed his best mechanical team to inspect the cargo hook and release system and find out just who had not done their job.

Before he could transmit, he realized that someone was standing very close in front of him.

"Is that anger?" Miranda Chase was standing just two feet away and looking up to inspect his face as if he was a curious puzzle. Her dark eyes were wide as she studied him.

Before he could answer, she continued.

"Or is it fear? I can never tell."

Like he'd know.

"According to my studies, both are quite normal reactions to near-death experiences."

"I..." He what?

"We need the helo to land *here*. Have them turn back."

"I want them at the base and in isolation until they say why they destroyed my plane." Because cargo hooks *didn't* just fail, which meant someone had dumped his A-10 from a thousand feet and he was damned well going to find out why.

"They need to come here because my team will be able to inspect their systems before any evidence is corrupted."

"My teams at Davis-Monthan are—"

"Better than mine?" No facial expression. No raised eyebrow of challenge. No smug or competitive tone. Just a simple question.

He remembered what the Chairman of the Joint Chiefs had said, *"A strange woman, but the very best there is at what she does."*

Before he could think of what to answer, she walked away.

Once again her team was converging on whatever had been under the tail of his crashed airplane.

Miranda Chase was one of the only three IICs—Investigators-in-Charge—with top secret clearance in the entire NTSB. And if General Drake Nason said she was the best, maybe she *was* his best option.

He ordered the helo to return and land a hundred meters to the north. "And get a damned fire suppression team out here to extinguish my plane." It still burned strongly in the distance.

A small explosion scattered more pieces. Thankfully, all of the wing-mounted armament had been scraped off during his landing and already retrieved by the ordnance team. That only left the ammunition of the Avenger cannon mounted in the nose.

Another round of exploding shells.

Campos followed her over to the churned, then compacted, soil beneath where his plane had initially come to rest. He was going to goddamn strangle that flight crew.

Jeremy was down on his knees with a paintbrush, sweeping aside the fine grit as if he was unearthing a dinosaur fossil.

"What did you find?"

Jeremy stopped and squinted up at him. He realized that the sun was coming from directly behind him, a technique he sometimes used when questioning an out-of-line subordinate. This time he moved aside and Jeremy stopped squinting.

"Well, we're not sure yet. A mechanical device that would

have been positioned along the third joint of the right elevator. Dragging through the desert wasn't kind to it, but I'm thinking it might have been—"

Jeremy didn't appear to notice as the blonde Holly huffed out an exasperated sigh and began digging the device clear with her hands, tossing aside great swaths of dirt.

"—an auxiliary elevator tab trim motor. I'm hoping to find an indicator of how it was controlled. A line of hydraulic fluid in the sand might give me a clue to—" He looked down and screamed.

Holly was holding what was indeed an elevator trim motor.

"What have you done?"

Holly just shrugged as she inspected the motor.

It would normally be used to tune the plane so that no control pressure was required for level flight—and trimmed differently for a sustained climb or descent. A plane's neutral point shifted constantly as fuel was burned or armaments fired. The little trim tab could be set to neutralize these shifts.

"As they lifted the plane away," Miranda had moved up to stand beside him, again without his noticing.

That was changing from troubling to a little spooky.

"I looked at the underside of the tail. I could see a black mark along the joint between the tail and the rear elevator."

"But that makes no sense," Jeremy had once again turned away from Holly as if he couldn't help himself. "An elevator trim control motor should be internal to the tail structure, not stuck on from the outside. What kind of black mark?"

"This kind," Holly held up the small motor and pointed

to a line of black glue. "Bondo. High-strength epoxy. And hydraulic fluid."

"But that makes no sense," Jeremy repeated. "The trim tab motor is electrically controlled."

"This one wasn't, Jeremy."

"But that makes no sense."

Holly rolled her eyes at him as he continued.

Arturo started to laugh, but noticed no change in Miranda's expression as if it wasn't funny, or rude, or anything. It sort of killed the joke.

"I checked all of the hydraulic systems. They were filled precisely to capacity."

"Then there was some additional system installed."

"But that doesn't—"

Holly pushed Jeremy over so that he collapsed backward onto the sand. Then, perhaps thinking he had a point, she dug deeper into the sand.

She held up a small device. "A one-way hydraulic valve. The more you used the system, the more pressure was pushed into this device and held there. Probably until you couldn't counteract the forces."

"Right," Jeremy was nodding. "And on your plane, I'll bet there was a leak stopper valve so that once this was ripped off, you didn't lose any system pressure. That fits."

"Colonel," Mike moved up from his other side. "I'd suggest contacting your base security regarding who was the last person to inspect your plane prior to flight. I would wager that whoever entered the last preflight record is either suspect—"

"That would be me," Arturo turned to face him toe-to-toe.

Mike didn't even blanch. "Or perhaps a distraction occurred allowing someone else to access your aircraft for a moment prior to your flight."

This wasn't happening.

His job meant that he was constantly in demand and that the only peace he ever found was in flight. That's why he'd been aloft at four in the morning before his day began.

Despite the early hour, he'd been halfway up the cockpit ladder when there'd been a call for him. Landline. In the hangar. Some trivial detail that he shouldn't have been bothered with, but it had placed his plane out of sight for perhaps ninety seconds.

"Shit!" He had a saboteur on base at Davis-Monthan.

He radioed the base and ordered his assistant to pull up his plane's records.

"Flight control monitor device installation is the final entry, sir. The signature is Moynihan's."

"Pull him in for questioning." Moynihan had been on the flight line at Davis-Monthan for two decades. An ace mechanic.

"I'd like to, sir. But he was just sent to the hospital with a massive coronary. Not expected to... Please hold, sir."

Arturo could feel the blood draining out of his head and sinking into the sandy soil along with the spilled hydraulic fluid.

His assistant came back on the air. "Didn't even survive the ambulance ride, sir. Sorry, sir."

"Trace everyone who had contact with him in the last forty-eight hours. If you find no anomalies, go back another forty-eight. Then another. Bank accounts. Medical records. Gambling debts. Mistresses. All of it."

"Order a full autopsy," Mike had rested a hand on Arturo's shoulder that, goddamn it, *was* comforting.

He made the call because Mike was right.

Miranda looked at them as if they were speaking in a foreign language.

"To determine if he was poisoned," he explained to her.

"Why would he be poisoned?"

He opened his mouth to explain, then closed it again. It was too obvious.

Mike again proved his mettle. "In case he was deliberately killed to cut the back trail of possible reasons for his perpetrating an air crash of the base commander's plane."

For five long beats as the approaching helicopter grew louder, Miranda stared at Mike. Then she turned very slowly in a circle to inspect the desert: his ejection seat, the ditch his jet had dug into the sand, the scattering of flags that had marked where the munitions had been scraped off the wings, Holly still holding the control motor, and finally the settling helicopter.

Then she nodded to herself and walked straight toward the helicopter, ducking under Mike's arm as he hadn't yet removed his hand from Arturo's shoulder as if they weren't even there.

Whatever she used for a brain inside that head of hers had apparently assimilated the concept—and finished with it.

Mike shook his shoulder in a friendly fashion, then let go and turned to follow his boss.

22

Miranda paced the distance across the fine sand of the Sonoran desert to the Chinook CH-47F. At ninety-seven meters she reached the cargo bay door. Told to land a hundred meters from the A-10's initial crash site, the pilot had been very precise, placing the helicopter's center at exactly a hundred.

She was tempted to run a tape measure to see just how accurate that assessment was.

Unlikely for such a pilot to commit an error in releasing the cargo hook.

The cargo hook lay beside the aircraft—the pilot had left the cable dangling long rather than reeling it in, and set the hook down in plain view before shifting to one side to land so precisely.

Or had the pilot intended to place the hook at a hundred meters and was therefore three meters out of place?

Either way: careful.

The manual release lever on the cargo hook had not been turned.

The Chinook stood high enough on its four wheels for her to duck down and look up into the hatch at the center of the cargo bay. The I-beam supporting the hook had been placed in the hatch opening at the center of the cargo deck and the hook assembly attached to it. She could just make out the emergency manual release lever at the side of the opening.

If it had been used, it had been returned to the closed position.

"We didn't touch anything," a female voice spoke from close beside her. "Val Munson, Captain, US Air Force," the Chinook's pilot held out a hand. She must be the pilot as she'd descended from the right-hand door.

Assuming that the Captain was not mistaking Miranda for a Val Munson, she shook the offered hand and offered the same terse introduction. "Miranda Chase, NTSB."

Val nodded and pulled off her helmet. "And no, neither I nor my copilot pressed the cargo release at our stations."

Miranda knew that it would be very difficult to do by accident. The release button on the pilots' joystick cyclic was intentionally low from the rest of the controls and had a raised perimeter shield to specifically avoid accidental bumps.

"Jeremy, check the recorders."

"Who's Jeremy?" Val asked.

Miranda looked around to see him jogging over from the crash site with his full site pack, still too far away to have heard her. He always carried twice the gear everyone else did. That included an interface for the recorder. While it was technically illegal—all black box flight recorders were supposed to be returned to NTSB's labs for downloading— she knew the military was not likely to release this recorder to a civilian agency.

He trotted up to her, glanced once at the hook on the ground, bent forward and down to look in the cargo hatch just as she had.

Without the pack's waistband hooked, it slid up to hit him on the back of the head and send him sprawling into the sand.

23

Billy "Poet" Blake landed and parked the A-10. He didn't see the point as it was just a simulation, but over the comm circuit Lt. Colonel Kiley had insisted he take it all the way back to base. Maybe part of the new training here at Eglin.

When he dumped his helmet and harness, Kiley was standing next to his simulator.

And right behind him...

"You fucking bastard!" He shoved out of his seat and dove for Major Ass-face.

Kiley wrapped an arm around his chest and Billy couldn't do anything but squirm. Man was a crossbreed between a boulder and a serious layer of titanium armor.

"Why did you try to shoot me down?" Billy shouted at the bastard's face—impotent to do more at the moment.

Ashton. Billy could see his name on his shirt. He'd been close. Major Ass-face Ashton.

"What the fuck are you yabberin' 'bout, Rook?"

"You fired an AIM-9M Sidewinder at me after I fought off a pair of Su-25 Frogfoots." Okay, he shouldn't have said that last bit. "Frogfeet!" Worse.

"We lost your ass at the Lebanon border. Figured you chickened. Never heard a goddamn squawk out of you."

Billy rocked back on his heels. After making sure he'd eased up, Kiley released him.

He took a deep breath but didn't feel even a little bit calmer.

"I don't chicken. You don't survive the Bronx if you chicken."

"The Bronx?" Major Ass-face's accent placed him solidly there. "Shit man, where's your talk?"

"Mom's an English Lit professor at Fordham. Nothing but the Queen's English."

"The what?"

"Never mind. Where you from?" Because Major Ass-face's accent was as thick as his head.

"Allerton."

"My family live on the other side of the Bronx Zoo in Fordham Heights."

"Close enough. Rest of these guys are from those weird southern states."

"Like Jersey," said a Captain Bell, the guy who offered the friendly smirk before the flight.

"Shut your face, Tinker. That's south of the Bronx, ain't it?"

The rest of the guys relaxed as they bantered back and forth. But Billy glanced over his shoulder at the simulator.

"Well, if you didn't try to shoot me down, who the hell did? Who was I even talking to?"

They all turned to Lt. Colonel Kiley, who raised his hands palms out in clear denial.

24

"I HAVE A THEORY." JEREMY SAT ON THE COOL METAL DECK OF the CH-47F helicopter's ramp as he scrolled through the data on his laptop. Wide and long enough to drive aboard a pair of Humvees, everyone else had gathered here out of the sun.

He always felt a little like the Asian James Bond when he was reviewing Cockpit Voice and Data Recorder records outside the lab. Only a little, because while Bond had cool toys, Q was the ultra-cool geek. Jeremy just liked the idea of being Mr. Ultra-cool Bond who got the girls better than being the geek, even if that what he was. Because the geek *never* got—

"Which is?" Holly could pack an entire C-5 Galaxy's cargo hold of sarcasm into two words. It had hurt for a long time, but now he was starting to realize that she couldn't help herself. Everyone except Miranda caught the edge of her tongue, not just him.

"That you're a major pain in the behind." Jeremy couldn't

believe he'd just said that and could feel the heat rushing to his face.

Holly smiled hugely, "As sure as a shark has teeth."

Mike thumped him on the shoulder. "Just ignore her. What have you got?" Since Mike couldn't seem to ignore Holly for even a second, it was a funny statement. Not ha-ha funny, but…funny.

"You wish you could, mate." Holly was tall, blonde, athletic, and alarmingly pretty. It was hard to imagine any male ignoring her.

"The theory," Miranda spoke up, "that it was remotely triggered."

"But how?" the Chinook's captain asked.

"Jeremy?" Miranda said it so simply. As if she trusted him to have the answer. Which was both cool and unnerving. That she felt he would—

And almost on cue, there it was.

"Databus 4 command. It came in embedded in the satellite telemetry." Everyone huddled around him.

"What is that?" several of them asked at once.

"Data," Miranda answered.

Because of course she could read raw CVDR data.

Wait. She'd once said that she couldn't. Had she lied to him? Maybe like a superpower she wanted to keep hidden and had just accidentally revealed. Or…

Oh. It was data. She'd need him to interpret it, but she knew enough to know it was data. Actual fact.

"Search for anything else that was sent with similar addressing." Which was a pretty insightful thing to say for someone who couldn't read raw command code.

Jeremy started to search…except there wasn't any

addressing. "It reads as if the helo sent the instruction to itself, yet it came in externally."

"What else was addressed that way?"

Right. Of course. He should have thought of that.

It would only make sense that—

There. It...

He froze.

Reading the instruction a second and third time didn't change a thing.

Reading the next instruction only made matters worse.

Very carefully, he looked at his watch.

He double checked the two instructions.

Then his watch.

The bolts on the CVDR would take two to three minutes to remove.

They didn't have two to three minutes.

They didn't have even one.

He hit Save—and waited three painful seconds while the data downloaded to his laptop—dumped the cable to the CVDR, then grabbed his laptop and site pack.

"Run!" he shouted and pointed out into the desert.

Everyone looked at him for a moment in surprise except for Holly.

Without hesitation, as he'd expect from a former Australian SAS operator, Holly had Miranda and Mike by the arm and was sprinting down the ramp.

Jeremy gave the startled colonel a shove.

Campos almost tumbled down the ramp before regaining his balance and his composure. "Let's move it, people."

Jeremy really hoped he was wrong and checked his watch again.

He wasn't.

Praying that the helo was synchronized to atomic GPS time like his watch—a Citizen Promaster Navihawk that Mom and Dad had given him for graduation.

He raced faster.

And counted seconds.

He'd wasted nine full seconds from reading the instruction to starting everyone in motion. He could have shouted for them to run during the three seconds it took him to save the files.

No way to forgive or fix that.

If that hesitation got Miranda hurt, he'd never be able to live with it. If he survived.

No free hand to check his watch, he kept running—five or six more seconds.

About...now.

The emergency fuel dump opened on both tanks. He could hear the splashing fuel puddling on the sand.

The sharp bite of kerosene from the JP-8 jet fuel seemed to burn in his lungs—that stuff really had striking power even at a distance. He wished it was the Navy's JP-5, which had a flash point twenty degrees higher than the Air Force's JP-8, not that it would make a difference. They weren't being extra cautious about highly flammable fuels aboard aircraft carriers here; they were in the desert.

The dumping fuel told him they had ten more seconds. Seven really, because of human reaction time.

He counted to six-one-thousand as evenly as he could against his pounding heart.

"Everyone get down..."

He gave them all another second of sprinting.

"Now!" Jeremy shouted and dove for the sand.

He'd been close behind Holly.

She tripped Mike, then threw Miranda to the ground and lay on top of her.

Jeremy got even more sand down his shirt than when he'd fallen over beside the cargo hook.

Maybe he was wrong. Maybe—

He'd miscounted.

Two seconds after he hit the sand—again his pack sliding up to knock him down hard—a sharp crackling noise sounded behind them.

It was easy to follow the command sequence in his head.

Fuel release at minus ten seconds.

Gravity fed. Hard to estimate volume of the dump into the sand.

Didn't matter.

At zero, a belly flare—used for distracting a heat-seeking missile attack—released.

It sounded like a whole cluster of fireworks and sparklers.

The Fourth of July had been four months ago.

Microsoft threw one hell of a bash, and even though he was the black sheep for not following his parents and over-tall little sister there, they'd brought him along. Even that felt wrong because of that one unforgivable sin that had made him turn down all their attempts to recruit him.

At the moment, he wished he'd pretended he was innocent and gone to work there.

"Faces in the sand!" Holly shouted.

The explosion wasn't as loud as a sonic boom. More of an angry roar of a jet engine at very close range.

Then the heat blast washed over them.

For an instant, Jeremy lay on the hot sand being flame-broiled like a July Fourth hamburger.

But the heat wave moved on.

Jeremy looked up when there was a massive thump in front of them. The heavy rear cargo ramp that he'd been sitting on less than a minute ago had been blown off by the force of the fuel explosion under the helo and landed *beyond* their small group.

If he hadn't "wasted" the three seconds of running time while he made a copy, the whole NTSB team would be under that slab of metal.

He rolled over.

The helicopter was surprisingly intact.

Completely engulfed in flame, but mostly intact.

The dumping fuel continued to feed the raging fire.

"Maybe we should get farther away."

"This time," Holly helped Miranda to her feet, "you'll get no arguments from me." She reached over to mess up his hair as if he was a kid brother. From her, he guessed he didn't have any choice but to accept it.

25

MIRANDA INSPECTED THE HINGE POINTS OF THE CARGO RAMP door.

The roughly eight-foot square ramp had survived the explosion and its subsequent flight over their heads mostly intact. The underside hadn't been exposed to the heat for long enough to do more than scorch the paint. The hinges were designed to take a vertical downward load, not an explosive upward load.

She pulled out her camera and photographed the catastrophic stress fractures, before carefully noting her observations in her notebook with sketches.

A light touch on her arm caused her to jolt. No one except Holly typically touched her. And definitely not lightly.

The colonel withdrew his hand. It was a good hand. Rough with hard work. Perhaps hard work*outs*—he was a colonel after all. She liked observing hands...as long as they didn't touch her. The darker skin of his Latinate heritage was so differently toned than her own fair complexion that she wanted to photograph it to think about later. But it always seemed to bother people when she did things like that.

"Why are you recording that? We know what happened to it."

Rather than looking up at his face to assess the intent behind the question, she looked back down and traced a finger along the smoothly warped surface behind the break line. "See how the metal turned ductile as it was stressed under extreme pressure, prior to fracture and failure? This tells me that the hinge experienced a four to eight kilonewton force that—"

"No. I'm asking why does it matter?"

"Because it broke."

"But why?" His voice forced her to look up at him. He appeared...curious?

How else was she supposed to answer him? It had broken. It was her job to understand that breakage. The correlation couldn't be clearer.

He waved a hand behind them. "There's a helicopter burning in the desert right over there, one that almost killed us all. My A-10 lies in a heap of rubble another thousand meters away. My plane was sabotaged and went down right over there. And you're inspecting a ramp's hinge?" His mood had shifted. His voice growing steadily louder. He wasn't yelling yet, but if his current trend continued, he would be in another four or five sentences.

She didn't like it when people yelled at her, so she attempted to preempt his escalation.

"It is clear that there is no other data obtainable at this site. I am allowing others, including yourself, to get over their shock at the chain of events before asking for transport back to Davis-Monthan in your helicopter. The Huey UH-1 has the load capacity to carry both my team and the five members of the downed Chinook CH-47F. Until such time as that transport occurs, I am educating myself with the inspection of this hinge, stressed to catastrophic failure due to an extreme fuel-air explosive event. Is that clear enough for you?"

She didn't usually share her thought processes. Not since middle school when she had once attempted to explain to a teacher the irrationality of attempting to teach number theory when he clearly didn't understand the complexities of code encryption that her father had taught her before grade school. Perhaps she shouldn't have gone to the board and proven how much more she knew than the teacher. Mr. Bantam had not appreciated it.

Colonel Arturo Campos had far better recovery time than her seventh-grade math teacher. He studied her for under thirty seconds—twenty-seven—then pulled out his radio.

"Get a fire control team to Grid One-niner-two," his voice thankfully returned to normal. "I'm returning to base."

Then he offered his arm to Miranda just like in some old movie. "Ms. Chase? I am yours to command."

Unsure what else to do, she slipped her hand into the crook of his elbow though she didn't squeeze tightly. She preferred firm contact when someone did touch her but had learned that most others did not. Or they thought it implied things that she never intended.

"So, what are the next steps?"

Crashes, once they happened, typically remained in the same place until she was done with them.

She puzzled at it aloud as they retraced their path over the ground to the A-10's original crash site and the Huey parked on its far side.

"The timing with which the sequence of events had occurred could not have been anticipated. The sabotage and crash of your A-10 Thunderbolt II," she indicated the divot he had made in the desert with his airplane. "The fact that the crash was not fully destructive, leading to the call for the Chinook helicopter's recovery effort. The release of the hook and the subsequent destruction of the helicopter itself."

"Don't forget the death of an ace mechanic. Moynihan was a good man for twenty years, whatever ultimately happened."

"Yes, I suppose that wouldn't be a coincidence."

Colonel Campos almost walked into the side of his Huey. "Say what? How could you even question that?"

"I don't think about people much. That's something Mike does for me."

Holly kept her safe, as well as being an ace on airframes and destructive forces. Holly had been the one who'd protected Miranda by getting her the farthest away from the helicopter and then lying down on top of her. It was only chance that had placed them in the greatest danger when the ramp had landed less than three paces farther away. Not Holly's fault.

Mike took care of people.

Jeremy did... "Can you trace where the helicopter received those commands from?"

"Me?" Colonel Campos asked in what sounded like surprise.

"No. Jeremy." Except, once again, Jeremy wasn't here.

He was well behind, close beside the female pilot of the helicopter, and talking very animatedly.

26

Senator Hunter Ramson shifted from fooling with his father's V-C knife to flipping the triangular laser-engraved rosewood nameplate Rose had given him as a wedding gift—with "Senator Hunter Ramson" already carved in though he hadn't even been in politics yet.

"You'll think of me every time you see it. Rose in rosewood." He'd thought her charmingly pleasant and perhaps a little simple when he'd first bedded her during the Miss Utah pageant.

"Not President?" he'd asked her when he'd opened the wedding present almost thirty years ago.

"Do you want four to eight years of prestige or decades of legislative power?"

He'd since learned that the former Miss Utah had *never* been simple. And she was always right.

She'd certainly proved her point. And also predicted accurately; he was having trouble thinking of anything other than her while his hand flipped the wooden plaque.

Blank.

Clunk.

Senator Hunter Ramson.

Clunk.

Keep asking! inscribed on the bottom where only he ever saw it.

Yes. Rose Ramson had indeed proved her worth over the years. Even then she'd known that she was the smart one in their relationship—a harsh lesson for him back then was now a simple truth.

When he was truly stuck on a problem, she would sometimes...

He grabbed his cellphone and sent her a text: *Missed lunch. Join me at the Kimpton?* The best hotel within easy walking distance of the Capitol Building.

Top floor?

Only the best for you. They'd caught the premiere of *Pretty Woman* during their honeymoon and it had been part of their love play ever since. He'd never again questioned his wife's tastes for going to "girl" movies—he'd seen a lot of them over the years.

He buzzed his secretary Sharlene. "Clear the afternoon for me. I'm going to cop a squat."

She'd know that meant to set up the reservation for him and that the top floor, champagne, and strawberries were all required. For lunch she'd order whatever the chef had as a special; *Pretty Woman* hadn't been a foodie movie.

Yes, Rose would know what to do about Clarissa Reese.

And when his phone rang this time, even though the number was blocked, he knew exactly how to deal with it.

Rose wasn't the only reason he'd held this office for four successive six-year terms.

He double checked that the office door was closed, propped his feet up on the desk, and answered the phone without saying hello. The bastard on the other end of the call didn't like the niceties any more than he did.

"It's the bitch's fault. She isn't delivering."

He thought about Rose's fine breasts and one of his ties dangling between them—and nothing else on her lovely body—as the other man vented.

"It won't do any good to spew at me, but don't worry, I can handle her. We'll get results."

Imagining Rose pulling his face to nestle between those generous breasts was a welcome distraction while the ranting on the phone continued.

When Mrs. Senator Ramson walked into an event in an evening gown, men were often struck speechless by her remarkable curves—nothing like the slender Julia Roberts. He'd long ago bought her the quarter-million-dollar ruby necklace Julia had worn, using a small percentage of a little oil investment he'd been tipped off to make.

"You need to think more about your blood pressure, you know." He kept his tone pleasant as he debated whether he'd fuck Rose's amazing breasts or her incredible ass. He pictured Clarissa Reese stalking out of his office and decided on the latter—just for comparison's sake.

Actually, today was Friday—their normal evening for sex anyway. Maybe they'd keep the suite overnight and he'd get to do both.

Rose's hair was more shining gold than Reese's viciously Scandinavian white. And Rose had never worn a ponytail.

Maybe...

No. It would be better not to suggest it.

"Look. It's going to happen. It's going to happen soon. So calm down and let me do my job." Hunter hung up the phone without waiting for a final rant.

He pulled on his jacket and strode out of the office. His secretary Sharlene was a stunning woman with tropical skin and a light Jamaican accent. Rose had chosen her because she knew that Hunter liked to look even if he never touched. She was also happily married and almost alarmingly efficient.

He also suspected that she'd instantly report any missteps to his wife, so he was doubly careful at the office.

"Everything is ready for your meeting, Senator."

"I'd be lost without you." Which was true.

He'd have to remember to buy her a particularly nice gift for Christmas. Rose would know what to get. Maybe a shopping spree at one of Rose's favorite boutiques. Because Sharlene, like Rose, definitely believed in dressing to share her visual bounty. Pure class, but with just the right amount of enticing skin.

There was no safe way to suggest that Rose grow her hair long—her perfect coifs were elegance incarnate.

But it would be easy enough to suggest it to Sharlene, who already wore her thick nut-brown hair down to her shoulders.

Yes. He liked that idea.

27

Harry Tallman, who hated being an inch shorter than Tom Cruise, was caught doodling by his boss.

Shouldn't have been.

His subconscious had heard the sharp clack of her high heels on the polished concrete flooring in plenty of time to screen flip.

So few people had clearance to enter the CIA's CAD offices—not Computer-aided Design, but rather Cyber Attack Division. Which was kind of about redesigning the world, but...not.

His boss definitely had clearance—she'd doubled the size of the already substantial team with a single swipe of a perfectly manicured but unpainted nail.

Those sharp heels always announced her arrival with clear authority.

And he'd totally missed it.

He'd been goofing off, looking under the skirts of the CJ-

100's code—China's newest hypersonic, long-range, aircraft-carrier killer missile.

Not that she'd know he wasn't working on *her* project.

The Director of Special Projects didn't know shit about computer code.

"That's not my project!" Clarissa Reese snapped out before he was even fully aware she was standing beside him. Out his open office door, he could see by the number of geeks peeking out of their cubicles that he was the only one being oblivious.

Harry refocused on his screens, not sure what she'd picked up on.

Over on his third monitor he had a video looping—the two deleted seconds of video "leaked," then deleted from social media by the People's Liberation Army Rocket Force. The PLARF wasn't given to making a lot of mistakes. If it was a mistake, someone had just gotten his ass executed.

Okay, the looping vid of the CJ-100's launch test was a bit of a giveaway to what he was working on.

He'd been burrowing around for a copy of the missile's operations code in the months since the video's release and finally punched through yesterday.

It was classic.

For them.

Every step so regimented that he doubted if there was a stray comment or dead-end loop in the entire stack. Chinese code wasn't sexy. Not like Indian code, which had a sensuous flow and life all its own, but it was clean and damnably efficient.

"No." No point in trying to pretend now. "I just cracked the missile's flight code yesterday. Couldn't wait to see what was inside their newest hypersonic navigation routine."

He prepared for the blast.

But instead, she leaned back against the edge of his desk. Her awesome ass was enhanced even more in profile by the desk's pressure on her upper thighs. She was so close that he could smell the clean heat of her and see just how muscular her legs were beneath her silk slacks.

Some women exuded sex appeal just by breathing.

Some women also exuded danger signs bigger than billboards.

"I'd like a report on that as soon as you're done with it," her tone all soft and reasonable. Major weirdness. Director Clarissa Reese was *never* mellow.

"Uh, sure."

"But first—"

"The next one is already in the queue," he checked his watch.

He didn't know what it was and that ticked him off royally. All he knew was that there was a timer running and every six hours an event was injected into a system he'd never heard of.

"Another three hours and twenty-five minutes." It was out of his control, but he'd been told to open a very narrow window into the Air Force Agency for Modeling and Simulation's computer to let the code stack in. Someone else's code stack and he didn't like that one bit. Already compiled and then encrypted. No real way to look at it.

"I know that," the acid slipped out for just an instant... annnnnd the ruthless bitch was back.

Her nickname in the CAD unit, T-X—the female

Terminator from *III: Rise of the Machines*—fit her like...well... her clothes. He briefly imagined Reese as the naked T-X jumping back in time and walking the streets of LA with her long hair dancing over her naked shoulders. Yeah, never gonna happen, but it would be something to see. Kristanna Lokan had certainly rocked that role.

"What I need is different."

"You're the boss."

Her smile was chilly.

He shrugged and reached for the bag of Doritos, but it wasn't there.

Heidi had laid down the law. Down thirty pounds and exercise five times a week—and, no, sex didn't count despite the positions-calorie-counter app he'd downloaded. She'd given him until Christmas, just over a month out. He'd already made it, and hated to admit that it felt great. She also hadn't been kidding about the sex being better. But damn he still missed his junk food.

"Senator Hunter Ramson of Utah."

He tapped a few keys on the keyboard in his lap.

Old guy popped up on the screen, with total babe wife.

He clicked through.

Former Miss Utah and still built like a winner. Lucky fuck.

Back in June, Heidi, his counterpart in Cyber Security, had said she couldn't marry him unless he proved he had follow-through. The project to clean up his act had been her test.

Maybe someday some punk would click on his picture with Heidi in old age and think, "Lucky fuck." Not that it would matter to him—wasn't a woman born more awesome than Heidi.

"Okay, what about the senator?" Harry looked back up at Reese, skipping the chest and going for the eyes just like Heidi had taught him.

"I need a handle on him."

"How fast?" Heidi had promised him a week off his new regimen between Christmas and New Years and then they were starting yoga. She'd promised it would do even more amazing things for their sex life and he was actually looking forward to it. She'd found a class for him called Yoga for Men Who Don't Bend. Perfect.

"Tomorrow," Reese threw the word down like a challenge. As if some senator was beyond what the CIA's best hacker could find. Well, maybe tied for best. Heidi was pretty unbelievable in cyberspace, too.

"Yes ma'am." He began digging even though she was still there, still leaning that fine ass back on his desk. Didn't matter. He wasn't interested, beyond some random hormones firing off where the keyboard covered his lap. But crazy Terminatrix just majorly was not Harry's type.

For one thing she really was a total whack job.

For another, she'd dug up enough shit on his hacker days to shrivel his balls. Any of that came out, he'd be losing his top-secret clearance for sure. Reese had also dug up shit on Heidi, which was the unforgivable sin to him. Then she'd dumped all that info into his lap just to screw them up.

Harry had told Heidi what he knew, just so that it didn't blow up their relationship—though it almost had anyway.

"Our only choice is to quit and lose the jobs we love, or give T-X Bitch what she wants."

They'd agreed to both do the latter.

Sorry, buddy. I feel your pain, he mentally told Ramson's image on the screen as Reese was leaving his office. He didn't even turn to watch the view.

Frankly, he wanted to bleach where she'd been leaning on his desk.

28

HIS ASSISTANT WAS WAITING FOR HIM WHEN COLONEL ARTURO Campos set down the Huey helicopter at Davis-Monthan Air Base.

Not a good sign.

He waved Miranda's and the Chinook's teams toward the debriefing room—not that there was a whole lot to debrief —then walked up to his Number Two.

"Any word on Moynihan yet?" Arturo still couldn't believe one of his most senior mechanics would sabotage his plane unless someone had really gotten to him.

"Other than the massive heart attack, nothing, sir. Autopsy is still a couple hours out."

"Then why the meet-and-greet?"

His assistant looked grim, even grimmer than usual, which was saying something.

"Spill it, man."

"We lost Major Carl Carmichael in the Nangarhar

Province this morning—last night—about ten p.m. our time. Word only just got out to us."

"MC-Squared went down?" Arturo tried to take it in, but he couldn't make sense of the information.

"Catastrophically. The helo crews couldn't even find any remains in the few moments they had. The LZ was extremely hot, but they were able to extract the bodies of the 75th Ranger platoon he'd gone in to save."

"The bodies." Not 'the survivors.' Shit! And they'd lost one of his men. He'd seen MC-Squared in the bar just two weeks ago. They'd been celebrating the promotion Arturo had pinned on the man himself. The next morning his entire squadron had shipped out.

"Plus they lost a Black Hawk and crew in the recovery itself. Five more injured. Twenty-one US and estimated eighty Taliban Afghanis dead. No civilians as it was isolated, but their government is still pitching a fit."

"Shit." It was still the best Arturo could muster. US firepower usually gave a kill-ratio a hell of a lot higher than four-to-one. Even the Mogadishu, Somalia, disaster back in '93 had been at least twenty-to-one. That made yesterday the worst single-day loss in almost a decade.

Now today had a whole lot of suck in it. "Get me his sister's number...and his ex-wife. It's good that his parents didn't live to see this."

"Yes sir. Anything else I can do for you, Colonel?"

They'd been together a long time and it was nice of him to offer, but Arturo couldn't think of a thing.

He studied the pavement beneath his feet. A thousand stains. A long-ago spill of hydraulic fluid had etched the surface. A blue patch of chalk dust that had been part of a recent practical joke that no rain had come to wash fully away. And the memories of a hundred thousand bootheels.

MC-Squared had walked over this stretch countless times just like the rest of them.

Looking at the sky, he wondered who he'd lose next.

Turning to follow the others, he almost plowed Miranda to the ground. Grabbing onto her arms, he managed to save them both from falling. Her arms felt so thin and light, yet he could feel the strength of them as well.

"Do you often lose two A-10 Thunderbolt IIs on the same day?" No exclamation of surprise or alarm at how close she'd come to being flattened. No sympathy for his loss.

He made sure she was steady on her feet, then released her and stepped back as she continued.

"I read the report on the training accident in 2017 that occurred in the NTTR, though I wasn't part of that investigation. Pilot error when two planes collided at 11,400 feet during a training exercise, but I believe that's the exception, not the rule."

"We rarely have two full-hull losses in a decade, never mind a day."

Miranda nodded to herself as if confirming something.

"Wait. My bird and MC-Squared? You think they're related."

"The square of the speed of light?"

That's about how fast his head was spinning. "Major Carl Carmichael. MC-Squared."

"As a captain would he have been C-cubed or—"

"Three C."

Miranda tipped her head to one side, one of her eyes briefly peeking out from under the shadow of her hat's brim.

"Three-C is much slower, less than nine hundred million meters per second. C-cubed is approximately two point—" she barely paused, "six-nine times ten to the twenty-fifth meters per second. A factor of—"

"Yes, a very big number."

"—three times ten to the sixteenth faster."

"Who *are* you?"

"Miranda Chase." She didn't appear to be joking. Though she was still watching him sidelong from the shadows of her cap's brim.

"That's not what I meant."

"It would be easier for me if you asked what you did mean."

Arturo opened his mouth, considered, then closed it again. How had they gotten on the subject of the speed of light? Then he remembered and felt even worse for forgetting for even a moment. Carl was dead.

Just to ram it home, his phone pinged—a message from his assistant with the numbers of Carl's family members. He had to clench his teeth hard to ignore the churn in his gut; he hated making these calls. For the moment, he set those aside.

Ask what he really wanted to know?

Normally he knew everything in a person's file before they even reached his command—part of how he built teams. It wasn't practical with a group as big as the 355th Wing, but he did what he could.

All he really knew about Miranda Chase personally, even after spending the whole morning with her and her team, was that she flew a historic fighter jet and the Chairman of the Joint Chiefs of Staff had recommended her.

She gave every appearance of being utterly scatterbrained, except after twenty years of service he knew how to recognize competence at a glance—a skill honed by observing an entire generation of flyboys ever since he'd taken his first A-10 aloft.

What did he really want to know?

"Do you actually think that the two crashes are related?"

If the subject change bothered her, she gave no sign. "It seems unlikely, but it is a curious coincidence. In crash investigations, coincidence is a possibility. However, it's one that rarely plays out when studied with sufficient care."

She turned and headed to follow the other teams to the debriefing room. He fell in beside her.

"For example, the two A-10s that collided in Nevada a few years ago. Was it coincidence that a well-trained pilot, intentionally pushed to absorb large amounts of dynamic mission information, should accidentally climb twenty-four hundred feet above his assigned operational altitude and then precisely impact his trainer's aircraft, which was flying properly within a hundred feet of the center of his assigned thousand-foot operational zone?"

Arturo had known both of them as well. Good pilots. But it *never* should have happened. "Isn't that why they're called accidents?"

"By the first definition, yes. 'An unfortunate incident that happens unexpectedly, and unintentionally.' However, the second definition, 'An event that happens by chance or that is without apparent or deliberate cause,' leaves far more room for doubt."

It sounded as if she was quoting a dictionary verbatim.

"Was it truly chance?" Miranda continued in that

relentless way of hers. "The cause was 'apparent'—an error by an overtaxed pilot. And the accident report concluded that an unmeasurable element of apparentness was the cause—no method for calculating the overload that was placed upon that pilot as part of the training scenario. Because the pilots both ejected and survived, we know that it probably wasn't deliberate as we have their debriefing statements, but 'accident' is an unclear term under any conditions."

"What would you prefer?"

"Oh, 'accident' is so deeply imbued in the culture memory that I have no hopes to excise its use."

"What would you, Miranda Chase, prefer?" He held open the glass entry-door for her, which she walked through without acknowledging as if doors everywhere just opened for her.

" 'Unexplained crash event' strikes me as more appropriate. It also has the advantage of removing conjecture and focusing on the known facts."

And she began giving orders as she swept into the conference room where the crews were just settling into chairs.

Except they weren't orders; she wasn't behaving like some military commander. Rather, she was giving specific instructions as if everyone was just a natural extension of herself.

29

HARRY BEGAN SWEEPING THROUGH SENATOR HUNTER Ramson's electronic files.

By Washington, DC, standards, the guy was squeaky clean. No known affairs. No public arguments with his wife. Despite being a pillar of the Republican party, even the liberal press seemed to like him—or at least tolerate him.

He lived very comfortably, but not outrageously for a direct descendant of a major Mormon church elder.

Just one wife and they'd been together forever, since he'd joined a law firm and she'd won Miss Utah...at which he'd been a judge.

"Sly dog."

Harry wasn't a fan of the guy's politics, but Ramson was consistent and it matched his highly conservative state—he still had a home up in Park City in addition to DC. Okay, he had a small, but tasteful mansion with an amazing high-mountain view. *Better Homes and Gardens* had covered it, but not *Architectural Digest.*

Ramson's star had been on the rise since the beginning and was showing no signs of abating.

Harry plunged down another layer.

Good buddies with just about every important person there was out there, especially in the armed services suppliers. Be surprising if he wasn't—he was a top player on the Senate Armed Services Committee after all. Chair of Airland had major say in what happened for all the services.

Scraps and rumors, but no smoking guns. Some investments that the SEC might want to look at pretty closely and an oil lease that was a real anomaly in his portfolio. Published his tax returns every reelection.

"Fucking boy scout."

"If you're fucking a Boy Scout without inviting me, we're gonna have a serious talk."

"Christ! Where did you come from, Witchy Lady?" Heidi was leaning exactly where T-X Reese had been just... He checked the clock, a couple hours ago.

"Straight out of the ether, Wizard Boy."

He double-checked that his office door was closed. They really shouldn't be using their past monikers at all.

But Heidi had known he might use her nickname and had silently shut the door. Awesome. The only word for her.

"The ether*net*," he responded. Heidi's brain, at least, *was* born right out of a computer protocol.

"Precisely."

Which was where he'd first met her.

Deep in the code.

Back then Witchy Lady was a Black Hat hacker with a sense of humor.

They'd met when she'd hacked every electronic reader

board in the Shanghai Stock Exchange and uploaded Papa Smurf peeing on Chinese President Xi Jinping's head.

His speech bubble, in Cantonese, "I'm just smurfing."

While she was at it, she'd changed the passwords on all the display control computers. Even scrambled the electronic security locks on the service room so that they couldn't just cut power.

It had taken them a long time to take the images down.

He'd stumbled on her hack and had been the first to unravel her code far enough to figure out who did it.

Not as cool as doing it himself, but he'd been the one who outed Witchy Lady as pulling it off.

In thanks, she'd hit him with a back-looped polymorphic Trojan Horse virus of such magnitude that it had taken him a week to confine and unravel it. When he did, there was a hidden message in the core code that said, "Hi!" with a Papa Smurf smiley face.

He'd slapped her back with an evolved copy of Brain— the world's first-ever virus from way back in the prehistoric days of DOS 1986—a total retro-hack that he'd upgraded for pummeling on Linux systems.

Wondering if Witchy Lady was for Hermione, he'd planned his core signature to match.

Since he and Harry Potter shared first names, he'd signed it Wizard Boy—with an image of Potter and Smurfette totally getting it on.

They'd teamed up and escalated their harassment of China, Russia, and whoever else came to mind, until the day a CIA recruiter had shown up on their electronic doorstep.

It wasn't until they'd both decided to take the jobs that he finally met Witchy Lady in person and found out her real-world name. They hadn't bothered with separate apartments.

"So tell me about this Boy Scout you're fucking without me."

"Not gonna happen, Witchy Lady. Got all I need right in front of me. Though don't go tempting me with grown-up Girl Scouts, especially not bearing those mint cookies. I've got a weakness for those mint cookies. Were you ever a Girl Scout? Still got the uniform? Got any mint cookies?"

"No and no way," she laughed. "But I'll buy you some of those cookies without the Girl Scout."

"Bummer. And I had such hopes." He leaned back and just enjoyed looking at her. She had Hermione's curly brown hair, but wore it short. Which made her look permanently sixteen—they were always getting carded at bars. Heidi was cute as hell—which was where the similarities to Emma Watson ended. She towered several inches over him and was sleek enough to make Watson look voluptuous.

"So who's the Boy Scout?"

"Some guy T-X wants me to trash."

"Some guy?" Heidi did her dubious-Hermione look with that perfect air of superiority.

"US senator."

"Christ but that woman's totally out of control."

"Maybe I should find some dirt on her instead." Harry pulled his keyboard toward him to see what he could find on T-X.

"No! Don't!" Heidi shoved it out of his hands so hard that it clattered against his monitor and his empty can of, God help him, *Diet* Coke. "Someone has a block of alarm code in our system for anything that touches her. Heavy duty shit.

Not just military grade, but way the hell up there. I can't even find a cover to peel back and peek inside without fear of it exploding."

"What kind of alarm?"

"The kind that crawls up your ass and rips your brain out of your skull the long way round. You go after any back info on Reese and you'll get a very nasty visit very fast."

"Serious enough to stop both of us?"

"Unless you have a death wish."

Harry studied his screen. How many people around could write a block of code that would spook Witchy Lady? Maybe twenty in the world.

Though he couldn't think of one who'd do that to them if Witchy Lady and Wizard Boy were the ones cracking it. Unless...

He felt a chill up his spine.

"Daemon?" he barely dared breathe the moniker aloud.

Heidi did a one-shoulder shrug that said, "Yeah, maybe."

Daemon—like the spiritual counterparts in *The Golden Compass*—but more like Nicole Kidman's pure-evil Mrs. Coulter villain.

Daemon, Demon, whatever, had gone dark just about the same time he and Witchy Lady had retired to the White Hat world of the CIA. At least government-sanctioned White Hat—which mostly still felt like Black Hat—except when Reese came around and it felt like slime mold.

Daemon had been pure slime-mold Black Hat since forever.

What the hell had happened to him? Or her? Whoever it was.

Suddenly surfacing to write protection code for Reese? Beyond creepy.

If—

Then he noticed the countdown timer in the corner of his screen.

Four.

Three.

Two.

30

"SUPER FREAKY," TOUCAN WHISPERED IN HIS EAR AS THEY came out of the briefing room and headed for the simulator room.

"Hey, it's more than they told me this afternoon." William "Poet" Blake still hadn't found out what had happened up there. "I whupped ass on a pair of Frogfeets, and then someone fired on my ass."

"At least you got to fly," Toucan sounded testy.

"Not my fault that I'm so much better than you."

Toucan snorted in mock disbelief and seemed happier about it.

The guys hadn't taken it well that he'd been the first of their class to fly in the new simulators. So not well that he hadn't mentioned it more than a couple dozen times throughout the afternoon just to make them suffer.

Having decided that a fellow-Bronxite could do no wrong, Major Ashton had stopped by their group while they were warming up for a training run. He'd told Billy that had been a hell of a piece of flying earlier—right in front of all the others. Even shook his hand.

Ashton's half smile said that he knew exactly what he was doing, and Billy would have to thank him later for helping make the other guys suffer. It was good to, for once, be on the right side of a little superior-officer hazing.

Billy wasn't dumb enough to trust Ashton, but he might have to shed the "Ass-face" tag in his head.

Now Kiley had selected Billy and Toucan and a pair of Lightning II pilots from his class for a crazy preflight briefing, then told them to meet him upstairs at the simulators.

"Ve vant you to untershtand," Kipper started in a terrible German accent for reasons that no one could ever guess. Kipper was from Texas. "You *musht* untershtand," he continued in twangy Germanish, "how der enemy cease der Varthog in ze battle."

"You said it, bro." Preacher—whose pa *was* a preacher—slapped Kipper on the back. Toucan snorted and picked up the theme with an effete British tone.

Billy kept his mouth shut because, if he guessed right…

Sure enough, Lt. Colonel Kiley, who they'd just left behind in the first-floor briefing room, down a not-all-that-long hall, was somehow standing at the door to the sim room before they'd gotten there.

Toucan sounded like he was choking on something painful.

"Sir," Billy saluted Kiley as he entered the room.

Not even a ghost of a smile. Maybe he was twins.

The others followed him in silence.

Once they were all inside, Kiley shut the door with a heavy thud.

"Take the front four sims stations. Lt. Blake on the right, you other three the order doesn't matter. Each station has been set up with simplified controls for four US drones: a trio of MQ-9 Reapers, and Lieutenant Blake will have the stealth RQ-170 Sentinel drone."

"Lucky shit," Toucan muttered.

No argument from him. He couldn't wait. The only thing sweeter would be an RQ-180, but they were still so classified that it was unclear if they even existed yet. Rumor mill said yes, but even inside the USAF the official word was no word at all.

"All of your aircraft are slower and less maneuverable than the simulated A-10s in this scenario. Your task will be to take them out in any way possible."

Yep! One damn *crazy-ass scenario.* But Billy kept that thought to himself as he climbed into his sim.

"You'll be engaging against come of our top pilots from the 40th Flight Test Squadron right here at Eglin."

"Where are they?" Preacher called out.

Kiley didn't bother answering.

Not here, was the only answer that mattered.

The RQ-170 was a stealth surveillance drone, R for reconnaissance, so he'd be the eyes for the other three guys who were MQ for multi-role drone.

That at least made *some* sense.

There was a variation of the Warthog called the OA-10. Its purpose was more as a combat controller rather than an attack craft.

Command versus fighter? He'd always assumed he'd fly

the latter. This was an interesting change he'd have to think about later.

Then he saw that the RQ-170 wasn't *wholly* unarmed.

He so loved this job.

31

BILLY HAD ALREADY BEEN SOARING ALOFT WHEN HE PLUGGED IN and took over his simulated aircraft.

The RQ-170 Sentinel drone floated along comfortably at sixty-thousand feet, three miles above the A-10 Thunderbolt II's service ceiling. From up here he could see from New Orleans to Tampa, The Florida panhandle and Eglin to the north, and the vast sweep of the Gulf below and to the south.

Felt as if he could see the whole world.

He could also see—

"Flight, this is Poet. Three A-10s cruising southwest out of Eglin. Range one-five-zero miles. Altitude twenty thousand."

Toucan, who'd been circling as scout farthest to the east, turned and began racing in their direction as fast as his Reaper drone would allow.

This was too easy.

They had altitude and surprise on their sides.

Three Hellfire missiles and they'd be done.

Training would be over too fast. Billy wanted to stretch it out a little.

Kipper was the closest, flying a mere ten thousand feet above the A-10s.

"Kipper, drop a Mark 81 on their heads."

"Uh, Roger that."

And moments later, a two hundred and fifty-pound bomb was falling out of the heavens on the Thunderbolts' heads. The 81 was a dumb bomb, so it wouldn't blow up until it hit something.

The chances of that were damned close to zero—it was a foot across in the middle of the whole sky.

It should have fallen through the trio of A-10s.

Billy hadn't expected it to even be noticed until it hit the ocean below the A-10s and blew up some water. Drawing their attention downward was what he'd been counting on.

By pure chance, it hit the wingtip of the trailing A-10. The explosion shattered the plane.

Through the length of three heartbeats, nothing else happened.

No ejection—the software probably decided that the bomb fragments had killed the pilot.

No response from the other two aircraft.

By the fourth heartbeat, the two remaining jets both stood on their wings' end and turned away from each other to avoid being a common target. They'd been ticking along at two hundred knots, but now jolted up into the high-three hundreds.

"Kipper, don't let them get an angle on you."

But a Reaper wasn't an A-10—slow but steady was the drone's game, a hundred knots slower than an A-10.

The lead plane, which had circled west, pulled up hard. When its nose angled straight at the sky, it unleashed an AIM-9 Sidewinder missile.

Billy could see the trademark smoke cloud as the A-10 then lit off the GAU-8/A Avenger rotary cannon built into the Thunderbolt's nose.

The cannon shells were faster so they reached Kipper's Reaper drone two full seconds ahead of the missile. Half the shells missed, but the A-10's pilot was good enough that it didn't matter.

The drone stumbled in midair.

Attitude control gone, it twisted like a drunk in the sky and nosed south with an uncontrolled bank.

Then the Sidewinder hit and Kipper's bird was gone from the sky.

Billy forced himself to look away from the unfolding disaster—which the sim portrayed beautifully—to find the other A-10.

"Preacher—" was all he had time to say before the other A-10 had wiped out a second Reaper drone.

Billy could already hear what Lt. Colonel Kiley would say during the debrief. *You never, ever play around when you have a tactical advantage in a battle. You should have hit them hard and hit them simultaneously.*

Because, damn but the A-10s could maneuver.

"Lesson learned, sir. Lesson learned." Billy told himself aloud to reinforce it.

"Toucan. Drop 'em!"

Toucan fired a pair of Hellfires at one A-10 and then targeted and fired at the other.

Both A-10s corrected hard and kicked flares and chaff.

But one of them got close enough to unload a pair of Hydra missiles in Toucan's direction.

A Reaper just wasn't up to evasive action.

The firing A-10 caught a Hellfire in the fuselage for its trouble.

Billy realized that the Thunderbolt pilot had taken his shot at the Reaper *knowing* he wouldn't be able to get clear of Toucan's Hellfire if he did so. Even in a sim, that was a tough choice. It probably meant the pilot would have made the same choice in real life.

Lieutenant William Blake, if it ever comes down to it, that's the standard you want to live up to.

The last A-10 scooted clear with a maneuver that Billy would have to study later. It was masterful. These guys were amazing; no surprise Kiley had said they were the best.

Now it was his lightly armed RQ-170 Sentinel surveillance drone and one very pissed-off Warthog pilot.

How stealthy was a Sentinel exactly?

The A-10 was clearly circling and searching...but it wasn't coming in his direction.

Billy slid his drone down from his lofty observer post, being careful to stay behind the A-10 as much as possible. He might be invisible—or nearly—on radar, but not visually. His paint job was probably a cream-gray, but that only blended somewhat against the light haziness of a Florida winter sky.

To his advantage, the afternoon sun was low to the horizon.

In fact...

He waited until the A-10 had just circled through facing

west into the sun. The moment it curled away, Billy slid the Sentinel down until he was directly in line with the sun as it kissed the horizon.

Now he waited.

The A-10 circled once more, slower this time as its radar and the pilot's eyes reported no threats.

Once the A-10 had missed him and began a long descent to survey the wreckage of his teammates for possible survivors, Billy pushed the throttles forward.

The A-10 was faster only when it wanted to be, so he had to get close soon *and* maintain surprise. If the A-10 put on full thrust, he'd never catch it.

An A-10 was an incredibly tough plane. They had safely returned to base and landed with blown-up engines, shot-off tail sections, and enough holes in them that the pilot would never have survived without the titanium "bathtub" of armor he sat in.

But the laminated acrylic canopy was only so robust.

The designers knew it was a weak point. That why most A-10s had a "fake canopy" painted on their bellies, so that enemies would waste precious moments firing at that supposedly vulnerable spot.

Billy managed to climb up over the A-10's tail at under a hundred meters range with no reaction from the Warthog's pilot.

It seemed unfair. The pilot had flown such a masterful flight in order to stay alive through the surprise attack.

But he'd also taught Billy not to hesitate.

Billy sighted the .50 cal machine gun at the back of the pilot's head, clearly visible through the back of the canopy.

The simulation's resolution was fantastic. He could actually see the flag emblem on the guy's helmet.

He put it dead center in his sights.

Then Billy opened fire.

32

THE CODE ON THE CRAY XC50 SUPERCOMPUTER IN Subbasement 2 of the AFAMS building registered the change-of-state of the R14A10GM3 variable to true.

The subroutine proceeded through the next four steps:

Generate a four-word message.

Deliver the phrase to three separate secure cellphones.

After all three phones provided a delivery confirmation, drop the external connection.

Finally, the subroutine erased itself and the program that had called it.

33

Senator Ramson lay flat on his back.

The top-floor Presidential Suite at the Kimpton George had been available. It was warm and awash in the winter sunlight streaming in through the broad windows.

He was a special customer, so they'd given him a discount.

Yes, he'd definitely keep it overnight.

Rose had greeted him as he'd hoped, in only a tie—his Swoop the red-tailed hawk one, the University of Utah's finally-PC mascot. They hadn't made it to the big bed; she'd already been lounging on the deep blue sofa when he'd arrived.

He'd joined her there.

She now straddled him facing away. So, he had a double handful of her ass while she rubbed her hand down over herself and then him.

Gods but she had amazing fingers.

After some careful consideration—from his very

advantageous angle—he'd definitely take Rose's ass over Clarissa Reese's any day. He hissed in a deep breath as those perfectly manicured nails ran—

His phone buzzed where he'd tossed it on the thick glass coffee table. The sound harsh enough to pull his attention away from where he could just see the side of Rose's breast from behind.

Ramson glanced sideways at the phone for just an instant.

It had landed face up.

Four words.

Not one or two.

Gulf of Mexico three.

About time.

He turned his attention back to where his wife was taking him.

All the ego boost he needed was thirty years of having Miss Utah in his bed.

Or on the couch.

34

STAFF SERGEANT MATTHEWS WISHED TO GOD THAT HE HAD more sense.

He'd had about eighteen too many tequila shots last night.

Okay, maybe eight, but it felt like eighteen.

Worse, he'd started the night with a hot co-ed bar babe —because God in all his blessed wisdom had put North Las Vegas campus of the College of Southern Nevada just four blocks from his job at Nellis Air Force Base—but he hadn't woken up with her. Or any sign that he'd even been with her. No used condom, no nasty note, no wallet emptied in pissed-off vengeance.

He was used to waking up to those signs—never carried much cash for that reason—but not today.

Strikeout on all fronts.

Today he'd woken up still drunk. That had made the entire day a slow descent into the pure hell of a blinding hangover.

Why was everything so damn loud on a flight line?

He'd gotten through the morning okay, but now it was late afternoon. All day he'd been pumping aspirin, B-12, and chugging water, knowing what was coming.

Hadn't helped.

But you didn't let Master Sergeant Neville see that.

Sir. No sir.

Master Sergeant Neville of Nellis Air Force Base had a standard to uphold and the Good Lord had designated him to be the man to do it.

Matthews didn't mind the self-righteous evangelicals. Some of them were damned cute. A surprising number were willing to "momentarily" ignore their morals for a night out. It didn't seem right, but he made a point of never complaining.

If they got a little preachy during sex, it didn't bother him much. As long as they didn't ask him to pray with them before or after.

Not Master Sergeant Neville. Things bothered him a whole lot.

Especially men on his flight line who had lost a battle with that Devil Drink—a particular high horse of his that always had the capital letters. You could hear them whenever he was on a roll.

The other guys had shielded him as well as they could while he'd just put his head down and worked, prepping planes for flight and servicing them when they rolled back in.

Last flight of the day. A couple of A-10s from the 66th Weapons Squadron headed aloft for a training flight. Go out and shoot some guns in the desert for a while.

At least he wouldn't have to be there when they fired off those big Avenger cannons. Loud enough that his skull absolutely *would* split.

He got Number One prepped and all of the paperwork signed off.

On Number Two, his last, he managed to get it prepped in time...somehow.

"Come on, boy. Let's sit in the sun and enjoy the fruits of a good day's work," Neville of Nellis came up to him as the two A-10s lit off their engines and finally taxied out into the cool November afternoon.

Shit!

He'd thought that he'd covered well enough. He'd even sworn off drink, at least for tonight until his brain cells recovered. Though he'd been thinking he might swing by the bar just to see if that hot bar babe was still around.

Bracing himself for the firing squad of one of Neville of Nellis' morality lectures, Matthews followed him out of the hangar and into the sun.

He hauled on his shades, which cut the sunlight down to merely intolerable.

Neville led him to a wooden shipping crate for an A-10 nose wheel landing strut that was pushed up against the side of the hangar like a bench and sat down.

Neville always gave his lectures standing up.

Serious talks were done in his office.

What was this?

Matthews sat beside him.

For a while, as the A-10s taxied down to the south end of Runway 03 Left, they just sat in silence.

The sun's warmth felt good after all day in the hangar's

cool shadows. Like it was finally cooking the last of the alcohol out of his bloodstream.

"You've been doing a good job, Matthews."

"Thank you, master sergeant." He tried to keep the caution out of his tone—carrot before the axe?

"I watch you push hard."

Never harder than surviving today.

"What do you think about moving up to team lead?"

Matthews could only blink in surprise. That meant a rank and pay bump. But...

His current tour would be over in a few months and he hadn't re-upped yet.

Neville would know that.

So, he'd only get the bump if he re-upped.

Air Force wasn't a bad gig. Another two years in wouldn't be a burden at all—he'd already done eight. And to get that extra stripe and do it as a Technical Sergeant seemed like a good deal.

"I like the sound of that, master sergeant." He let it sit a moment longer. "I like that a lot."

They shook on it and leaned back to watch the A-10's takeoff.

Number One came streaking down the runway. Then, with that characteristic "pop," it transitioned from just sliding along the pavement to banging up into the sky. Not like the F-14 Tomcat—which had always looked like magic the way it climbed—but no slouch of a machine either. He'd grown rather fond of the old Warthogs.

Next in line, Number Two rolled onto the active the runway.

No lecture in sight, Matthews relaxed and rested his hands on his thighs.

Maybe he should believe in miracles...good news after a miserable day.

It took him a moment to notice that his hand was resting directly on his thigh...instead of on the screwdriver he usually kept handy in his right thigh pocket.

Damn it! He liked that screwdriver.

He tried to picture the last place he'd seen it.

Then he remembered.

He'd set it down for a moment after checking a couple of fittings, so that he could pump some more aspirin and B-12.

And he hadn't picked it up.

He'd set it on...

The leading edge of Number Two's wing!

He jolted to his feet as the second A-10 Thunderbolt II passed down the runway directly across from him.

Please God! Let it have just fallen to the ground!

He swore he'd take up prayer and follow in Master Sergeant Neville's footsteps the rest of his life.

If only—

The second A-10C Thunderbolt II did its characteristic "pop" into the air.

The quarter- by six-inch flat head screwdriver with the hardened-steel square shaft, bounced loose from where it had been nestled at the joint of the wing and fuselage. The leading curve of the wing gave the screwdriver an upward impetus to its own flight—one now following a different trajectory from the A-10.

It managed to gain three feet in altitude before gravity

broke its upward travel and began pulling it toward the ground.

It fell three inches before it impacted the leading edge of the left engine's cowling.

The air current created by the General Electric TF34-GE-100A turbofan engine, spinning at seventy-five-hundred rpm for takeoff, made the final decision.

The screwdriver was swept up into the engine.

The impact of the hardened steel cracked four separate titanium fan blades. Eighty-three rotations later, less than three-quarters of a second, the first of them separated. As it was slammed around inside the engine like a howitzer shell, eight other blades were broken free.

The engine barrel and cowling did their job and contained the catastrophe to within the engine itself.

However, the A-10 Thunderbolt II lost half its thrust less than fifteen feet from the ground.

The left wing dipped abruptly.

Not high enough yet to clear the twenty-eight-and-a-quarter feet that the left wing extended from the side of the fuselage.

However, the A-10 had flown just high enough to try to fly rather than flopping back onto its wheels.

But the wing tip didn't just skid along the pavement.

It caught the runway like a pole vaulter planting the foot of his pole.

The pilot pulled the ejection handles.

The rocket-catapult fired immediately, as did as the reel gas initiator.

Because the pilot was already leaning back against the seat for the takeoff, he sustained no injuries as the slack take-up reels on his harness made sure he was secured tightly against the seat to minimize spinal injuries.

The seat launched through the acrylic canopy.

As designed, the two steel canopy breakers at the top of the seatback made sure that the pilot didn't impact the canopy directly—instead punching out through a wide hole.

Two-hundredths of a second before the STAPAC pitch-and-control stabilization system was programmed to fire its rocket and correct the seat's orientation to launch it upward prior to parachute deployment height, the pilot and the seat impacted the ground traveling at two hundred and ninety-four miles per hour.

The pilot's neck broke instantly.

Then, with both the catapult and STAPAC rockets firing but no longer gyro stabilized, the seat spun end-over-end, igniting a long strip of sagebrush and creosote plants.

Meanwhile, the plane planted its nose—hard.

Banked almost vertically to the left, with the right-side engine still firing at full takeoff thrust of nine thousand pounds, the A-10 Thunderbolt II also became a pinwheel shedding body parts just as the pilot was.

The debris field ultimately scattered for over a thousand meters down the runway.

35

COLONEL CAMPOS' PHONE RANG LOUDLY IN THE QUIET
conference room at Davis-Monthan.

Everyone but Miranda jumped in surprise.

Miranda was never surprised by loud noises herself.
With everything in the world seeming so loud and fractious
and unpredictable all the time, what difference did one more
sound make?

She and the others waited through a predictable series of
"Uh-huh" and other sounds one makes when receiving bad
news.

While she waited, she wondered why they were still
here, two hours after they'd first sat down.

The helo pilots were able to offer no new information.

All her team had to inspect was a broken elevator trim
motor that should never have been attached to an A-10
Thunderbolt II and a download from the Chinook
helicopter's flight recorder that Jeremy had salvaged.

It hadn't been informative.

A modern helicopter had a minimum of twenty distinct databus architectures in operation. Flight control computers spoke different protocols than weapons control computers. Infrared mapping, terrain following, and visual were all distinct—then another protocol was necessary so that they could interact with a single screen. Communications swallowed at least five more. GPS navigation was a separate system from VOR, TACAN, and inertial nav. The more capable a system became, the more complex it became.

The FVDR recorded all that it could from each of these channels—and their marginal cross-integration—with no ability to cross reference except by the factor of time.

The spurious commands had entered the helicopter on a satellite communication bus, been transferred to a clock mechanism in the Chinook helicopter's HMUS—Health Management and Usage monitor—where they had access to both storage space and timing from the helicopter's master clock.

When the helo had reached a thousand feet, it sent a signal to the emergency release on the cargo hook via the shared HMUS tracking software.

The system had then waited fifteen minutes.

Was the saboteur expecting the helicopter to be safely back at base by that time, in which case everyone would have been safely clear? Or had they anticipated that more people would have gathered to figure out what went wrong, thus creating more collateral damage?

Jeremy's one other discovery, in copying the file the moment before the helicopter was destroyed, was the final two instructions: first, to dump the gas tanks before igniting it, and second, to erase itself in the last few milliseconds that the recorder would have remained active.

Plenty of time.

If Jeremy hadn't made a copy of it first.

Campos ended the call as another buzzed in.

Miranda began gathering her things. There wasn't anything else to do here.

This time he slumped back in his chair and hid his face as he grunted out another series of unhappy sounds.

"This so doesn't look right, pal," Holly whispered to her.

"We've done our bit. Everything we were here to inspect has been blown up."

Holly tipped her head sideways uncertainly as if—

"Is your neck okay?"

"Neck's fine. Except for the hairs prickling up the back of it."

"Why?"

Holly just tipped her head toward Colonel Campos, who had finished his call and was setting the phone down very carefully on the table as if it might explode.

Miranda had heard of certain smartphone models catching fire, but never exploding.

"Chinook flight crew," Campos spoke in a dead monotone. "Your records will be cleared of any wrongdoing in the loss of the A-10 Thunderbolt II airframe or your CH-47 helicopter. You will stand down for one week—"

There was a murmur among the fliers until he held up his hand to silence them.

"I don't want you having a sudden attack of the jitters on your next flight. You're going to chill for a week. Consider it medical leave. You may go home, go surfing, I don't care. Just get out of here for a week. Counseling will be available if you want it. You're dismissed."

After a little uncertain shuffling and a round of salutes that he didn't answer because the colonel didn't look up from his phone, they shuffled out of the room.

Miranda put her hands on her notebook, then looked at Holly.

Holly gave her head a small shake which must mean to wait.

Campos sighed, still without looking up from his phone.

"Anyone have a sledgehammer?"

36

JEREMY REACHED INTO HIS PACK AND PULLED OUT THE TWENTY-four-ounce framing hammer that he'd found useful when trying to beat his way into a particular section of a wreck and offered it to the colonel.

"I was kidding."

"Oh," Jeremy put it back in the bag.

Still no one spoke. He could see that Miranda was ready to leave and Holly was saying not yet. Mike was just watching the colonel with a grim look on his face.

Why would the colonel want a sledgehammer in a conference room?

Oh man.

He hated it when he missed the obvious. The hammer was for the colonel to kill his phone before it delivered more bad news.

A metaphorical joke.

And Jeremy had offered a real hammer. Why was he always doing things like that?

He was the ultimate sucker for a straight line.

He really needed to learn to think first, then—

The colonel spoke up. "Three of our top A-10 instructors at Eglin Air Force Base just disappeared over the Gulf of Mexico and we don't know why."

"Flew away?" Mike asked.

"Bermuda Triangle?" Jeremy had always wanted to go searching for something in the Bermuda Triangle. Then recalled that the Bermuda Triangle was on the other side of Florida from the Gulf—near Bermuda. Maybe he should pull out his framing hammer and try klonking some sense into his own head.

"They didn't fly or descend or anything. They simply stopped reporting in any fashion. A search team over the last known position has identified significant floating debris— none of it very big."

"Seriously?"

Campos just scowled at him.

"Seriously. Okay. Three at once doesn't seem very likely."

"Five," Miranda said with that perfect calm he could never seem to match.

"Five?"

"Those three, the colonel's crash here at Davis-Monthan, and one in Afghanistan."

"There was one in Afghanistan? What happened to it?"

"Shot down. Maybe," Miranda answered.

The colonel swiveled sharply to look at her, "Shot down...*maybe?*"

"I choose my words carefully, Colonel."

"Explain."

Miranda sighed to herself. "What do we actually know?"

"That Major Carl Carmichael was shot down over—"

"No."

Colonel Campos sputtered to a halt and glared at her.

"We know that his A-10 Thunderbolt II was lost during a battle in Achin, Afghanistan."

"While taking on over seventy aggressors."

"Yes. But we have no witnesses as to what actually happened. All of the Rangers he was there to protect died and can't offer eyewitness accounts. I'm assuming that no prisoners were taken during the extraction of the bodies?"

He shook his head.

"Therefore—especially in light of the loss of five other aircraft of the same type in the same twelve-hour period—I would be unwilling to *assume* that it was lost in an attack rather than some failure independent of the attack."

"Well, you better add another," Campos growled. "The second call was that we just lost an A-10 during takeoff for a training flight at Nellis."

"Six. When was the last time you lost six A-10 Thunderbolt IIs in one day, Colonel?"

"Never," Jeremy knew the answer to that one. "The worst one-day loss of jets was the Diamond Crash in 1982 when four planes from the US Air Force Thunderbirds demonstration team flew into the ground. The lead pilot had a jammed stabilizer, and the three jets in close formation were watching their position on his lead like they were supposed to—it meant they followed him in. Four in one day. Certainly never six. At least not since World War II. Did you know that we lost sixty B-29 bombers in a single day over the Schweinfurt ball bearing plants in 1943? Black Thursday they called it. That was..."

Jeremy saw the looks on their faces, eyes glazing over, and clamped his jaws together. No one wanted to know about that.

"Six is a lot," he finished lamely.

37

A PHONE IN AN EDINBURGH, SCOTLAND SELF-STORAGE UNIT jangled sharply once.

A microphone—because it was always good to have a physical disconnect to block an electronic trace chain—picked up the sound and triggered a one-character text message on another phone to a number in Cabo San Lucas.

One that had never been answered.

It simply sat silently, on a small solar charger in an unoccupied hut in a resort that had not survived the American recession, with an auto-forward set for all incoming messages.

Nothing quite like low-tech.

The single letter, F, arrived on a phone in Oklahoma City.

Because nothing bad happened in Oklahoma City anymore.

The recipient smiled. Nothing except her.

Hello, Client F! And what are you wound up about today?

Because that was definitely what Client F seemed to

enjoy doing, getting wound up. It wasn't like this was a rocket science project, it was just jet science and she could totally handle that.

Daemon opened an app on an otherwise unused computer. She—her identity was female today—was almost always female in Oklahoma City. It was nice to actually just be herself here.

But as Mum always said, "Don't get too complacent."

Yes, it would be time to move on shortly.

Oslo had exceptional Internet connectivity, and in midwinter, it was easy to pass as a slightly androgynous male during the winters there. She did love those thick wooly sweaters.

And sex? Daemon mostly used the ultimate in safe sex... online avatars so she could play any role, or roles, she wanted at the moment. Haggador II in the Norse role play was particularly skilled in visual and audio online play— made her breathless every damn time.

He hadn't just slung a massive schlong on his avatar, like most idiots. Haggador II had *serious* skills. Made her wonder if the person behind Haggador II self-identified as male, female, or something other. Didn't matter as long as she/him/they didn't stop.

The app completed loading.

The NSA and others had the Internet fully wired for tracking malefactors.

Something poor old Mum had found out the hard way. She'd started way back, long before the heavy shit ever came online and the security grew around her in ways she didn't see or fully understand.

She'd never have survived today.

Now nothing happened along the electronic superhighway without them knowing. Anyone dumb enough to hack from the Internet totally deserved what they got.

The agencies were close to achieving that same level of scrutiny on the Dark Web. Would have already if they'd focused, but the FBI kept tripping over the NSA's code, the Chinese weren't cooperating, and the Russians thought it was still the Wild West. Mossad was actually doing better than they knew because it was a little personal vendetta of hers to always fuck with them. The CIA's lame attempts were always such a muddle.

Though lately they'd been showing some actual craft in their coding that she really should look into.

However, the old ARPANET—the first harbinger of the Internet to come—had a node right here in OK City.

She glanced out the apartment window at Tinker Air Force Base. It had been one of the original twenty-five nodes of the first-ever national computer network back in the 1970s. And the network connection had passed through an underground enclosure less than twenty feet from her current apartment.

Best of all, the ARPANET security was exceptional.

Not because it was robust.

Because it was forgotten.

Staying on the ARPANET protocols, she slid to Stanford, which had kept it active for historical reasons, then up to Utah because those people deserved whatever was coming to them.

There she surfaced into the Dark Web and, after a few pings off random cities, connected with a computer just down the road in San Antonio. Well, at least *electronically* just down the road.

"What do you, uh, want?" She used an AI trained on movies to alter her voice. Today a bumbling Hugh Grant would do her talking.

Her contact had no such masking. Of course, Client F didn't need it as she knew exactly who he was.

"The Chinook helicopter? At Davis-Monthan? Was that you? Why did you kill a helicopter? That's not what we hired you for." He sounded pissed.

There was no video connection to double-check—the old ARPANET bandwidth barely supported voice, even with heavy compression. How did people ever live like that?

His anger made no sense.

A couple of quick searches clarified the matter. His boy was a combat pilot currently stationed—*aw, so sweet*—aboard a Chinook helicopter at Incirlik Air Force Base in Turkey.

Poppy all worried about Whiddle Baby Boy. WBB's Chinook had an upgraded glass cockpit, which meant it was as eminently hackable as the one at Davis-Monthan. She made a note of the frame number and equipment IP addresses in case she needed some leverage later.

She flipped her voice over to Arnold—not the slightly wry *Terminator* voice, but the dead-serious *Predator* voice.

"You are an idiot," in over-enunciated looming-doom Austrian-accented English.

She ignored the sputtering response.

"I had to destroy the Davis-Monthan A-10 to hide your clumsy mechanical solution. To do that, I had to send instructions through the helicopter's systems. So, QED," not very Arnold-like, "I had to obliterate the helicopter to cover that evidence. *Vas der anyting else?*" That was better.

The silence stretched long.

The dude thought so slow. How was it that he was a fixer, thinking that slowly? Next time one of the big military manufacturers needed some dirty work done, they should skip the middleman and come straight to her.

"You should have killed Campos on the first try," he finally grumbled. "Now he's got an NTSB team stirring up trouble."

"Don't make me laugh."

"This woman is—"

Daemon terminated the connection with what she hoped was Schwarzenegger-level prejudice and *Deadpool* disdain.

NTSB? Ha!

They took years to analyze and conclude that some pilot had been an idiot and killed a couple hundred tourists. Airliners were such simple devices compared to what she did.

The takedown of the A-10s over the Gulf of Mexico had been artful. First she'd had to spoof the 96th Test Wing's training command system to order the A-10 practice flight. Then she'd hijacked real CIA drones, flown them to the right positions in time, and crosslinked them to the Eglin flight simulator with its own set of commands for the sim pilots: *shoot 'em down, cowboys.*

And the sim pilots had used real world CIA drones to off a bunch of A-10 trainer pilots and their aircraft over the Gulf —without even knowing that's what they'd done.

Let's see some NTSB chick do shit like that.

Sure as hell, the fixer for the arms manufacturers, Client F, couldn't do that or he never would have hired her.

And there wasn't a chance of the CIA ever admitting that three of their Reapers had gone missing.

And since they wouldn't even admit that the RQ-170 Sentinel existed, they weren't likely to complain when she'd dumped it in the Bermuda Triangle—which she felt was a particularly nice touch.

The NTSB was the least of her worries.

No, the challenge was how to pull off the next stunt.

That one was still a puzzle.

38

Jeremy spotted Colonel Campos rushing up to Miranda as they were getting ready to leave Davis-Monthan.

Mike was preflighting the Mooney airplane. He and Holly were stowing their gear. Miranda was already done and dressed in her flight suit.

"You don't need to go to Nellis," the colonel called out as soon as he stepped in front of her.

"We weren't going to Nellis."

Which was news to Jeremy.

"But you don't need to go to Nellis," Campos sounded confused.

"We aren't." Miranda, returned to donning her helmet.

"Don't you want to know why?" Campos leaned in.

Miranda sighed and lowered her helmet once more and waited.

"Well?" Campos sounded ticked.

"I was assuming that you were going to tell me, so why should I ask?" Miranda was as cool as cucumbers. "Holly,

Mike, do you know why people are so insistent on stating the obvious?"

Jeremy wondered why she'd left him out. Not that he knew.

Oh, because Miranda knew he didn't know. He tried to figure out how she knew that he wouldn't know, but all that did was loop him back around to not knowing why people stated the obvious.

He actually hadn't noticed that, until Miranda pointed it out. She was right.

Holly raised her hands in denial, "Not a clue, pal."

"See? That right there. Your hand gesture had already communicated that prior to your speech. Mike?" Without even pausing, Miranda turned to Mike.

"I think it's twofold, Miranda. One level is perhaps communicating in multiple modes as Holly just did to amplify or reinforce a particular message."

Miranda tipped her head to the side for a moment and then nodded for him to continue.

"Most of the time, I think the real reason is community. If I state something that others already know or believe, I become a member of that community. Through confirming of a shared belief, I'm joining in the same side."

"So the fact that I don't spend my time reiterating the obvious is what makes me the outsider?"

"No, you're *not* an outsider," Jeremy cut in.

"No more than you," Holly patted Jeremy on the head and he pushed her aside. "Well, more than you, but we like you both anyway. Right, Mike?"

Jeremy didn't give him a chance to speak, "Miranda belongs more than any of you people."

"More than you, too?"

Jeremy opened his mouth...and closed it again. He'd only ever "belonged" in two places. Graduating high school two years early hadn't helped him fit in there. Just like Miranda, he'd gotten a double masters, but it had taken him two years longer at twenty-two.

In college he'd always been too young and in grad school too driven.

He fit in with his parents. He was their "little genius" and had given everything to live up to that. At least until he'd betrayed them in a way that could never be fixed.

Jeremy had broken trust with them—something they could never know.

And he'd belonged in the online gaming world.

Unlike most people he wasn't into the roles and the battles, he was into the tech. Not how to kill a charging knight, a demented wizard, or a spell-casting pink dragon with a taste for the heads of Ken dolls, but rather the most efficient way to do each of those—that the code allowed.

But he'd left both of those behind and he was never, ever going back.

And...

"Hey!"

"What?" Campos had been talking, but Jeremy had no idea what about.

"I fit in a new place."

"Congratulations," Mike shook his hand as if he'd just won the lottery, or a goldfish at a county fair.

"Where?" But Holly's smile looked as if she already knew.

Jeremy risked stating the obvious and pointed at the ground. "Right here. Right now."

"Welcome aboard, mate." It sounded like a tease, but Holly's smile looked sincere.

If he belonged here, he'd better start acting like it.

He turned to Campos.

"Why aren't we needed in Nellis?"

"Because—" Campos growled through gritted teeth.

"Because," Miranda spoke right over the colonel. "It doesn't fit the pattern."

"No," Campos didn't look happy at being interrupted yet again.

He took a deep breath, but Jeremy could see that his calm was shredding.

"Because it was caused by a flight-line mechanic accidentally leaving a screwdriver in the wrong place. He confessed immediately to his section leader, who he was with at the time of the crash."

"And it doesn't fit the pattern," Miranda repeated.

"What pattern? And if not Nellis, then where are you going?" Campos turned on her.

"Eglin Air Force Base. I'd appreciate it if you would set up a clearance for our arrival."

"Why Eglin?"

"Because the loss of the three pilots there fits the pattern," Miranda sounded as if she was talking to a three-year-old. She began pulling on her helmet.

"What fucking pattern?" Campos snatched the helmet out of her hands, banging Miranda's head with the edge of it in the process, causing her to yelp in pain.

Jeremy and Mike moved in at the same time, but they were far too slow.

Holly, who'd been standing mostly behind Miranda, shifted sideways and stepped through the gap Mike's movement had opened.

Three gliding steps forward and her fingers closed around Colonel Campos' windpipe.

He made a surprised gurgling noise.

In her other hand, she held Campos' sidearm.

"Jeremy," Holly held out the sidearm.

He reached out to take it, and she ejected the magazine, which dropped into his palm. Then she rested the weapon on top of it.

After that, she took the helmet from Campos' hands and held it out to Miranda without ever releasing the colonel's throat.

The colonel was beginning to really struggle. His face was bright red.

Then there was a long, slick sound as Holly withdrew the big knife from her thigh sheath. It glimmered in the afternoon sunlight as she held it close to the colonel's nose.

"If I let you go, will you be calmer and listen to the lady?"

The colonel gurgled.

"Was that a yes or a no?"

The colonel managed a microscopic nod.

Holly let him go, then steadied him as he wavered on his feet.

Jeremy made a mental note to never tick off Holly Harper.

39

MIRANDA SIGHED AND TRIED NOT TO LOOK AT HER WATCH.

She could feel time slipping away from them. She held out her helmet and someone, Mike, took it.

While she struggled for calm and focus, Holly did something with the colonel's gun. It fell into pieces, which she proceeded to tuck separately into each of the colonel's pockets.

She patted his breast pocket after she slipped the barrel into it. "Just bein' sure, mate."

Miranda held up a finger.

"First, the loss of the A-10 in Afghanistan at 9:30 a.m. Afghanistan Time, because Afghanistan chose not to follow a simple hour zoning. That's midnight Eastern Time."

"Second, the loss of your aircraft at 4 a.m. Mountain. That's 6 a.m. Eastern," she held up another. "Continued through the loss of the helicopter, but that was still related to the disposal of whatever evidence was attached to the A-10."

"Third, the training flight over the Gulf of Mexico." Three fingers. "Ten a.m. our time, noon Eastern."

"Every six hours," Jeremy breathed out in surprise. "You're right, the A-10 at Nellis happened approximately half an hour later than the Gulf of Mexico, so it doesn't fit."

"Right. Each event happened by itself. In isolation," Miranda nodded to him.

"It's so obvious," Jeremy thumped his palm against his forehead and Miranda was suddenly glad that he wasn't holding his hammer.

"Three's not much of a pattern," the colonel's voice was weak as he protested.

She waited for Colonel Campos to stop massaging his neck and really look at her.

And he wondered why she didn't want to explain things during an investigation.

"There's a secondary pattern. There is also a trend of increasing severity. First, the death of a single pilot in combat in Afghanistan. Second, the intended death of the commander of the largest A-10 Thunderbolt II Wing, the 355th, you. Third, the downing of three trainers over the Gulf of Mexico."

"But still—"

Holly slapped a hand down on the colonel's shoulder hard enough to stop him.

Miranda continued. "There is no evidence remaining in the first and third events. It is only because of your exceptional piloting skills that this wasn't also true of the second event. The likelihood of identifying an extra trim control motor among the wreckage after a major crash and fire would have been very low. However, the takeoff at Nellis was most likely a simple FOD—foreign object debris—case. As it indeed turned out to be. Again it didn't fit the pattern."

The colonel just blinked at her.

"I can't afford more time explaining this, Colonel." She retrieved her helmet and climbed up into her Sabrejet, then called down to him, "Each event occurred precisely six hours apart. Eglin and Nellis occurred just twenty-three minutes apart. I have less than six hours to get to Eglin and prevent the next event if the pattern holds. I expect it will be much worse."

"There will be another attack?" Colonel Campos voice was still husky and still stating the obvious.

She climbed the ladder and strapped herself into her seat.

The ground crew already had her plugged into external power so she checked that her gear lever was indeed set to Down and throttle to Idle. She signaled she was ready and they turned on the power. Her starter motor began cycling up the jet. She flipped the pressure gauge switch to Alternate for alternate power. Once the pressure hit three thousand psi, meaning the engine was fully engaged, she flipped to Normal and flagged the ground crew to disconnect.

She focused on bringing the various avionics and radios online.

Flashing her thumbs outward had them pulling the chocks away from her wheels.

Perhaps she'd been too abrupt with the colonel.

Had she hurt his feelings?

How was she supposed to tell?

She looked down at him and the others backing away from her jet as the engine noise continued to climb. Barely noticeable through her helmet, more felt through her seat as she was sitting directly above the intake fan.

Colonel Campos had been nice to her, despite starting his day with ejecting from a crash and ending it with Holly choking him.

For lack of anything better to do, she offered him a salute.

It was a civilian one, but she gave it.

He saluted sharply in return. Then he may have smiled as he waved her forward.

Two hours to Eglin.

It was time to hurry.

40

"SHE LIKES YOU," HOLLY TOLD COLONEL CAMPOS.

Jeremy twisted around in surprise, "She who?"

"Miranda," Mike nodded toward the departing jet, "likes him," he nodded toward the colonel.

"Really?" Jeremy spun back to the departing jet as if he could somehow see what Holly had seen.

"When was the last time you saw her thinking about anyone else once she was in her plane?"

Jeremy tried to think, but he couldn't remember her even waving goodbye except with a waggle of her wings when she blew by them on the way home from some investigation.

Then he studied the colonel, who looked surprised as well.

At least Jeremy wasn't the only one in the dark.

"What's she like when she *doesn't* like you?" Campos was watching Miranda's plane as it raced along the runway and headed aloft with a roar that was almost comically small compared with the heavy two- and four-engine aircraft that swooped in and out of Davis-Monthan all the time.

"You're invisible," Jeremy had seen her do it to any number of onerous officials. Not just officials. Once a team member was assigned a task, it was like she ticked some checkbox in her brain and they no longer existed until that task was complete.

Why the colonel? Because he'd been nice to her? At least up until the moment he'd banged her head while grabbing her helmet.

Most women scared the crap out of Jeremy. He was always finding out too late that someone had been attracted to him—after he'd missed every opportunity.

Mom often accused him of being too much like his father. "I finally had to drag him by his nose to go on a date with me. He never caught a single hint."

Was it really as easy as a woman waving at him?

God he hoped not, or he was even denser than he'd thought.

Then he thought about the female helicopter pilot. Was that why she'd been sticking by his side and talking to him? Because she liked him? The more he thought about it, the more certain he was. Again he considered whapping himself on the head with the hammer now tucked deep in his pack.

"Jeremy," Holly jostled his arm. "Come on. By the time Mike gets us to Eglin, her deadline will almost be here."

"Past," Mike shook his head. "The Mooney is quick, but it's still five hours away."

"We'll take a C-21A Learjet," Colonel Campos strode away into the hangar where the Mooney was still parked and called out for assistance.

"I guess he's going with us," Holly was watching after the colonel.

Jeremy had never been in a Learjet, so that would be good. And getting there in half the time was excellent. The C-21A was fast. Not as fast as Miranda's Sabrejet, but they'd only be about twenty minutes slower across the country, rather than three hours.

"The commander of the 355th Wing is flying with us..." Mike echoed Holly's thoughtful tone.

"Does that mean that he likes Miranda?" Jeremy guessed.

Holly rolled her eyes at him and Mike laughed a little as he slapped Jeremy's shoulder.

He'd take that as a yes.

Jeremy wasn't sure how he felt about that.

41

CLARISSA HATED WAITING.

Almost as much as she hated the *Kryptos* sculpture that perched in the CIA headquarters' courtyard—a sculpture garden between the New and Old Headquarters Building.

But ever since that Miranda Chase bitch from the NTSB had forced a meeting in front of it last summer, it had become the best place to get some hard thinking done. And while the courtyard was a popular summer lunch spot, cold November evenings she had it all to herself.

If she went inside to her office, there would be messages, emails, project leads, and more, all wanting a slice of her time. Here it was just her and this stupid sculpture.

The eight-foot-high and sixteen-foot-long folded S-shape of thick copper had stumped cryptanalysts for decades. Three of the four panels built by James Sanborn had been solved, but the last eluded everyone despite the three separate clues given by the artist over the last fifteen years.

Damn him to hell.

But the location *had* helped her solve any number of problems.

So, here it was, falling evening with the temperature already nearing the thirties and she was pacing circles around the damn thing.

Clark still wasn't back from the White House.

Harry Tallman still hadn't given her dirt on Ramson.

With her last major project scrubbed, despite its successes that really should have earned her—

Clark was right. She really had to let the MQ-45 Casper drone project go.

But she needed a win and she needed it badly.

Her phone buzzed with a message.

Not from Clark.

Nor her pet programmer.

When she unlocked her phone, she saw that she'd missed an earlier one as well.

The first one was because of that former Casper drone project; she was still on the notification list for any status changes or mishaps with CIA aircraft.

Three MQ-9 Reapers and an RQ-170 Sentinel had gone missing.

How in fuck-all did forty-five million dollars' worth of Reapers and another thirty for the Sentinel just go missing?

A sudden chill froze her in place.

The three Reapers had been stationed in the southeastern US. The Sentinel always flew out of Groom Lake in Nevada, but with its range, it could be anywhere in the country within hours.

She tapped for the older, missed message—thirty-four minutes ago.

Gulf of Mexico three.

Three A-10 Thunderbolt II Warthogs had just been scratched from the list. Lost for no apparent reason. Perfect. The contractor she'd told Client F to hire was finally doing their job well. It bothered her that she didn't know who the hacker or Client F were. Some pal of Ramson's.

If the contractor had taken out the three, forty-year-old jets worth a lousy sixty million *before* they'd been worn out, but killed seventy-five million dollars' worth of CIA drones to do it, then—

CIA drones! That was a traceable lineage back to—

The chill ran even deeper.

How in the world was she going to create deniability on this?

First, pray that Clark wasn't on the aircraft losses list.

And second—

An arm slipped around her waist with an easy familiarity.

"I thought I told you, never at the office," but she let herself lean back against Clark because she knew he wanted it. Besides, the CIA's inner courtyard was only lit from window-spill in the descending dusk. On this chilly night it was otherwise deserted.

"You're so soft in this coat. Can't help myself."

"You should see me out of this coat." She did love her new Max Mara cashmere trench coat. A splurge, but a very worthwhile one.

"How about *only* wearing this coat."

Clarissa smiled and leaned back against him a moment longer. He was learning. She'd make a good lover out of him yet.

Time to move things forward.

"How was the White House?" She slipped out of his grasp, then tucked her gloved hand around his elbow and led him on a slow promenade around the courtyard so that they could talk privately.

"Roy Cole's a sharp guy. He asks the hard questions and doesn't mind hearing the hard answers."

"You like the President."

"More than I used to. He's a tough man, but he's one I can absolutely respect."

"Good, I'm glad." Clarissa debated for a moment but knew the answer was "no" before she even thought about it.

No, Clark definitely didn't need to know that she was placing him in the vice-presidential slot of the next election. All she had to do was sweep VP Mulroney out of the way. With all her grooming over these last months, Clark would be the obvious choice to replace him.

The opposition party was already running their campaign for next year, but Cole was popular enough that it wouldn't amount much. The two other contenders in his own party? Well, one was a joke and the other had just had a stroke—with no assistance from her.

Cole was a good bet. He had the nomination of his own party fully secured and a very high probability of reelection.

How to get Mulroney out of the way?

Her programmers hadn't come up with anything nearly damning enough...at least that was published anywhere. She couldn't exactly requisition the Vice President's FBI file without triggering a lot of flags.

Who knew where the skeletons really lay?

She couldn't ask Clark, even though he would know. He

had too much integrity—a surprising trait in a former field agent turned CIA Director.

One more turn around *Kryptos,* listening to the details of Clark's meeting with Cole, and something vague about both Clark and herself going to an event at the White House. Right on plan: social first, business later...

Yes. Social first...tonight. But first she had to take care of Clark.

Damn that Chase women for doing this to her—she didn't like being cold any more than she liked Kryptos—*but there was something about it that forced her to think more clearly.*

She stopped Clark in the deep shadows inside the curve of the *Kryptos* sculpture.

Leaning her back against the cold copper, she nudged him to face her directly, but kept him a step away with her fingertips on his chest.

With her other hand, she undid the belt and three buttons of her coat.

She shouldn't have worn slacks, but it was too late to help that.

Clarissa undid the single button of her Brooks Brothers wool crepe suit jacket.

Hooking a finger through his tie, she tugged him forward into the shadows until she could wrap one leg and then the other about his waist.

She reached up and hung on to the sculpture where the letters had been punched as holes through the thick copper. As if she was bound to the sculpture. Let him think her trapped; she was the one holding on to the power.

Exactly as planned, he moved in the rest of the way and

pinned her against the hard copper. One strong hand cupped behind her and the other clutched her breast.

Slacks to pants, she began to move against him as he drove against her.

Kryptos at her back. Its secrets clenched in her hands as Clark took them both upward—their breath making misty clouds in the night air.

Codes within codes.

Games within games.

Yes, she had a *very* good idea.

And Clark would never need to know until he was elected. Perhaps not even then.

Yes. *Kryptos* was a *very* good place for many things.

42

At the knock on the Presidential Suite's door, Senator Hunter Ramson grabbed a plush terrycloth bathrobe off the warming bar behind the door, eased the frosted glass sliding door to the bedroom mostly shut behind him, and answered it.

He'd been expecting dinner a bit later, but this was fine. He wanted to surprise Rose by serving it to her in bed.

The woman was gloriously insatiable today and he looked forward to just how long it would take them to eat a Trout Amandine and one of the Bistro Bis' fine Angus strip steaks...with each other as a palate cleanser between courses.

He opened the door with a flourish, but wasn't ready for what was waiting in the hall.

"Good evening, Senator," Clarissa Reese breezed in. "I'm glad I'm not interrupting anything."

"You are!" Goddamn bitch of a woman had him traced.

Not that it was all that hard. He wasn't trying to hide some secret affair, so there'd been no need to be circumspect.

"You may want to close the door."

"Not until you're on the other side of it, Reese."

She waggled her fingers at him as if shooing the door closed. Then she sat on the couch, exactly where Rose had been waiting in just his tie when he'd arrived this afternoon.

Somehow it felt as if she knew even that and had been purposeful in her choice of seat.

Out of options, he let the door swing shut. A quick glance toward the bedroom revealed no changes. He'd left Rose sleeping. "We'll need a nap now to regain our energy for later, dear." And they had, until the soft knock had woken him. Hopefully, she'd stay that way.

Out of options—short of calling the hotel detective to remove a Division Director of the CIA—he let the door swing.

He chose a narrow loveseat that would keep Reese's back to the bedroom door.

"We have a problem, Senator."

"What have you screwed up now?"

"Touchy. Touchy. Touchy. Perhaps I should say that we *each* have a problem."

"What's yours other than being a manipulative bitch and a—"

She raised a hand palm out. "This is probably not the moment to say something that you might regret later, Senator Ramson."

He could think of a lot of things to say, but she was right, none of them were nice.

"I'm in a position to help you with a problem and I'm

hoping that in exchange, you can help me with a problem of my own." Reese made a show of re-crossing her legs.

Rose had long since taught him most of the little tricks that women used to grab a man's attention. Subliminal until you learned to see them, then they became laughably blatant.

The bikini girls at the beach who had learned to throw one shoulder back to emphasize their chest.

Bar babes crossing their legs at the ankles before leaning their elbows on the bar to emphasize their asses.

A woman who began speaking normally, but gradually spoke softer and softer to drag you in until you were practically nuzzling her neck to hear her.

Reese's obvious move had no power over him. Instead, he wanted to smile.

So he did.

It earned him an uncertain frown.

Just *let* her try to read him. Rose had taught him better than whoever had trained this bitch.

But then she shrugged ever so slightly. Not enough to shift her breasts enticingly, but more to herself.

He waited her out, but she didn't make him wait for long.

"You want something. You want it badly. Not only can I help you get it. I can help keep you there. But I need to know what you have in exchange for me."

"Could you be a little less cryptic, Ms. Reese?" He turned to inspect the mantlepiece clock, an elegant example of Swiss woodwork and engineering. "My dinner should be arriving shortly."

"I can. And can you shove your dismissive impatience up your ass long enough to actually listen?"

He made a show of considering. Actually, he did consider.

Stupid people weren't put in charge of CIA divisions, no matter who they were screwing.

He hadn't been able to discover much about her online, before a virus had irrecoverably eaten his computer.

Ah!

A virus that may have been launched *because* he'd searched for her background. He'd finally just had a friend at the FBI send over her file. It was thick. And had included her time as a baby agent running one of the CIA rendition sites in Afghanistan. Not working at, but "running." Agent in charge of torturing information out of America's enemies right at the beginning of her career.

Driven, ruthless, *and* not stupid.

He wondered what demons drove her. Those hadn't been in her file.

But she was apparently desperate enough to talk frankly.

Swimming in shark-infested waters could be very dangerous, unless you were a bigger, badder shark yourself.

Hunter Ramson waved for her to toss the first bit of bait.

43

THE OLD ARPANET WAS TOO SLOW FOR SERIOUS RESEARCH. It was a precision tool. For just looking around, Daemon knew that her standard layers of security were plenty sufficient.

She'd spent a few hours earlier fooling around with the GPS satellites...but nothing satisfactory came of it.

Her mandate was to make the A-10s appear faulty and ineffective.

Hacking and shifting the satellite signals wasn't hard.

All pretty standard military code once you ducked through the Air Force Space Command's firewalls. No frills. No prettiness. Just "I'm going to do *this* task and I'm not going to look at anything else." She wondered why they didn't all shoot themselves for writing such boring shit.

Major yawn.

They fully documented their code though, which was mega-handy. Saved gobs of time.

But there was no way to localize the effect of GPS

distortions. The twenty-seven active satellites were always on the move. And location receivers aboard aircraft or in cars were constantly recalibrating across the ever-shifting array of visible sats. That meant, to misroute an A-10, she'd have to misroute everything in the area. She tinkered for a few minutes with the five backup satellites, but they were of no more use than the primaries.

Daemon had cut the connection to reduce pingbacks and traces while she considered other possible approaches.

Mum had always said it was better to think of something else and let an idea cook away in the background. Sometimes they'd hack something stupid, like a Walmart. Other times they'd just play *Adventure*—the original text-only version.

Mum had always been the best to hang with...until they caught her.

She'd grown up as Mum's "Little Daemon," especially after the movie came out with Nicole Kidman cast as the lead in *The Golden Compass*—Mum looked a lot like Nicole. She'd even dyed her hair to match.

Daemon herself looked more like Taylor Swift, except in need of a few more inches of height...

And a few less pounds.

And blonde looked stupid on her.

Daemon briefly considered tracking down Haggador II and having some serious cybersex while they ransacked a village of Irish maidens or French monks or something.

But she was getting itchy for the real thing and that would just make it worse.

Never having met Haggador II in the meat world, Daemon was left to wonder how much of that prowess was real and how much imaginary. With her luck, it would be some snot-nosed fifteen-year-old or a prepubescent girl. Definitely not worth bursting the bubble to find out.

Time for a different kind of distraction.

Maybe...

She slid online again and went looking.

There was some code she'd been meaning to look into. A churn-and-burn job she'd done a couple years back. She'd left a hidden alarm on the outer shell folder, which had pinged her a couple of times. But since the core had never squawked, she'd ignored it.

Time to go see who was being nosy.

Tinker to Andrews, up the coast and into Wall Street. A satellite jump to the London financial market, which was already showing the severe stresses of the last few years' political chaos and were bound to crack soon.

She made a mental note to go back and lay down some buckets to pick up a few bits of the inevitable falling pieces. Nothing much, just a few million pounds here and there when it finally broke.

A right at Stockholm and a left a Geneva.

Crimea had always been a wide-open gateway even before the Russians swept in. A pal had spent a couple summers programming games there...and come away with a very sultry Ukrainian wife.

He'd clued her in.

Now it was a total playground so snarled in the conflicting code of gamers, Ukrainian spammers, and Russian hackers ghosting IP addresses that if you could dump someone in it, they'd never find their way back out.

After laying a trap deep in the maze, she punched once more across the Atlantic on undersea fiberoptic.

Back in Washington, DC, Daemon made a small mistake, not that it would matter. She'd shot straight into the backdoor she'd left at the CIA's Langley computer without laying another disconnect trap.

Three directories before she reached the folder that had been pinged, a trace latched onto her.

A total shitstorm of pingbacks, sniffers, and code imagers latched onto her signal.

What the fuck?

Her attempts to retreat back across the ocean to Crimea didn't work.

This couldn't be happening.

The sniffers were already there ahead of her, tracing her signal backward through the snarl. They barely slowed down for the one trap she'd set.

So not possible!

No other cutouts on this signal.

The attacker was on the move and chasing her ass.

And not in a good way.

Rather than trying to salvage her original link, she jumped onto another terminal and sent a course-correction command to the initial trans-Atlantic satellite that had gotten her from Wall Street to London.

It fired all of its yaw thrusters and spun the antenna out of alignment with the ground stations.

Twenty-two thousand miles above the equator in geosynchronous orbit, the satellite tumbled, cutting the connection.

It also threw billions of dollars of international market

trades onto a significantly slower backup connection, which would take hours to clear. Significant price changes were going to be sabotaging several fortunes before the day was out.

It would be hours, perhaps days before they got the satellite restabilized and back online. Didn't matter as she'd only needed a few more seconds to finish collapsing her back path.

She spent half an hour double-checking that nothing had gotten into her system, or even traced back to Tinker Air Force Base.

Nothing.

She was clean.

Daemon blew out a breath and slumped back in her chair.

Shit but that had been close. She held up a hand and watched it shake, before dropping it back in her lap. *Damn* close.

Is that what it felt like when they tracked you, Mum? So sorry.

What had she seen?

No code grab, there hadn't been time to do that, so she had nothing to inspect.

Something might have been caught by the Crimea trap, but they'd have that staked out now. It wasn't worth the risk to go check.

But there *was* a signature to it: a style.

Which meant it wasn't military—they were always so forthright.

Definite Black Hat tactics.

Tactics that she'd seen before, though not in a long time.

Oh... Oh, yes!

The aggression. The flair. The unmitigated speed of the thing meant that the security counterattack code had been very small, very lean.

Wizard Boy.

He always coded clean and efficient, nudging every tick of the processor clock for all it was worth.

And wherever there was Wizard Boy, there was Witchy Lady.

This was going to be fun.

She needed to let them cool down for a while before she came back at them. But when she did, it would be from so far sideways they'd never see it coming.

In the meantime, they'd given her the answer she'd been looking for.

Small. Lean. Fast.

Keep it simple.

She logged back in across the ARPANET, because speed wasn't essential for this task.

This was gonna be awesome.

She'd toss it in as a bonus.

Mum had always said that the beauty of being predictable—like her attack every six hours—was that it made it so much juicier when you were unpredictable.

Once she had it set, Daemon popped a soda and sat back to watch the show. Tapped into the OC-3 Internet backbone at Tinker Air Force Base, she had a hot feed to a front row seat.

44

"WHERE THE HELL YOU GOING, CHASER?" FLIGHT LEADER "Tomahawk" radioed him.

Lieutenant Tom "Chaser" Stevens had certainly earned his tag last night. The other guys just didn't get the power of speaking Korean in Korea. Some guys had learned Japanese before shipping over, but A-10s weren't stationed in Okinawa; they were at Osan Air Base in South Korea.

F-15s? Sure, learn Japanese because your butt would be in Japan along with the rest of the 18th Operations Group.

America wanted its A-10s close to the DMZ and he had no complaints. And Korean women were always intrigued by five-ten of blond-haired blue-eyed corn-country American, fluent in their language. Fluent enough anyway.

Last night he'd landed a very chic pair of hipster twins— a first for him. Un-be-lievable! Koreans had a thing for thigh-high skirts with knee socks that he completely approved of. Matching cable-knit sweaters. Short purple hair matching purple Converse, and long silver hair matching silver

Converse. Both even had that weird flat-brimmed flat-top hipster hat that seemed to be required for indie music lovers.

He'd gotten to chase both those tails all night and had been sure to rub it in all morning during preflight.

"Where are *you* guys going?" Because indeed the rest of the four-plane flight was veering away from him toward the DMZ itself—a major no-fly zone.

"We're following protocol. Two kilometers off the zone."

"I show that's where *my* ass is."

"Hold. This is Flight Lead. Check in position by the numbers."

"Flight Two. On flight plan. Confirmed GPS coordinates and inertial tracking."

"Flight Three. On flight plan. GPS and inertial tracking confirmed."

"That's three to one," Tomahawk came back. "Your plane's busted."

"Roger that. All else appears functional. I'll form up on you." He prayed Tomahawk didn't kick him back to base for a malfunctioning nav system. It was too beautiful a day to miss flying.

The ground team had pulled his own plane for scheduled maintenance, so he was flying a backup bird this morning. Looks like it needed some maintenance too.

"Roger, take the four slot."

They were flying a simple diamond; except he was no longer the right-hand part of the diamond because he'd vectored away from the group even before they'd formed up. "Big Boy" moved up to the Number Three position and he slid in behind.

Now Chaser's plane was bracketed between two

functioning A-10 navigation systems and following the flight leader from a position just a little high so that he didn't get wing-tip turbulence or engine exhaust off the lead plane.

"This is Chaser, deep in the tail slot."

"Roger that." It earned him a background chuckle, but no more.

There was no room for joking once they came up to the DMZ. More landmines per square meter than anywhere else in the world wasn't the Demilitarized Zone's only line of defense. North Korea also had the largest number of anti-aircraft guns in the world. You didn't mess with that, but you had to let them know they couldn't just get away with shit.

Today was a standard show-of-force flight.

Four A-10 Thunderbolt IIs buzzing the entire, curving length of the DMZ at two kilometers to the southern side. Visible to the North, but clearly obeying the rules.

He flicked a finger against his GPS map on the screen display. It insisted they were approaching the Zone.

More than approaching, passing into it.

"Stupid electronics."

Chaser looked around to double check. Not much to see from here though. Just a lot of rugged mountains on both sides of the Zone.

The harsh terrain lay less than five thousand feet below —no point in having a show-of-force flight if they were too high for everyone to see.

They were flying over Yeoncheon County...

Except the Imjin River was wrong.

It took a very distinctive massive double-S curve through the hills that he'd flown over at least a hundred times.

If they were two klicks off the DMZ, the S should be directly below them.

Except it was off to their right.

Well off to their right.

More than just two kilometers.

"Tomahawk, this is Chaser."

"Go ahead."

"The river doesn't look right, sir."

There was a long pause. North of Yeoncheon, the DMZ followed the west bank of the Imjin in a long curve to the southeast.

Which also lay off to his right.

Which meant—

"Bank hard right!" Tomahawk snapped over the radio.

As if they were a single aircraft, the diamond formation banked south.

But it was too late.

The North Koreans didn't send up interceptors to escort them back to the south.

They didn't fire their anti-aircraft guns at the American formation. The A-10s were tough enough to probably survive that.

Instead, a local commander, who'd been dying for an excuse to test his newest weapon, unleashed four KN-06 surface-to-air missiles.

Seven meters of missile—each fully half the length of an A-10C Thunderbolt II and half a meter across—went rapidly supersonic.

As they were fired at close range—from almost directly below the straying aircraft—it was less than two seconds before they reached the aircraft.

The KN-06 wasn't some little Stinger with a three-kilo warhead or even an AIM-9 Sidewinder with ten kilos of high explosive packed into its warhead.

Each KN-06 delivered two hundred kilos of nitramide RDX explosive.

The A-10s weren't hit—they were disintegrated.

Three of the missiles turned the four aircraft into a rapidly expanding cloud of burning gases and metal shrapnel that would litter several kilometers of the rugged mountainsides—some north of the DMZ, but most in the heart of no-man's land.

One missile missed.

The missile's comm package received a destruct signal.

A connection in the electronics, weak due to poor soldering during assembly, had broken during the shaking and high g-force of takeoff.

The signal never reached the warhead-ignition trigger.

The KN-06 flew on, continuing to accelerate past Mach 5.

It covered three hundred and ninety-four kilometers—a hundred and forty-four kilometers farther than Western sources had estimated as the extreme limit of its range—in three minutes and fifty-seven seconds.

By chance, it impacted on the island of Iki in Japan's Nagasaki Prefecture.

The KN-06 missile's two hundred kilogram warhead of high explosive destroyed a section of a highly valued paleolithic archeological site, shattered all the glass windows within half a kilometer, and killed a herd of grazing cattle.

In under five minutes, Japan had scrambled six alert fighters—all F-35B Lightning IIs.

Ten minutes from the death of twenty-four head of cattle, another eight F-15 Eagle jet fighters were aloft.

By that time, automated alerts recalled all military personnel from leave.

Two minutes later, the fifty-six thousand additional reservists were called to duty.

Within the hour, three of Japan's four helicopter destroyers were away from the dock and driving into the Sea of Japan.

The two Izumo-class craft shifted the bulk of their helicopters ashore. Even as they departed, more F-35s were en route to the destroyers to be forward deployed.

Two of the country's four KC-767J refueling tankers pulled aloft to service the F-35s.

No parachutes had deployed over Yeoncheon.

45

"YOU ARE PRESENTLY THE CHAIRMAN OF THE SENATE ARMED Services Subcommittee for Airland."

Not at all where he'd been expecting Clarissa Reese to start as she lounged back in the sofa even more.

Senator Hunter Ramson nodded carefully.

"Clint Howards is presently the Chairman of the Senate Armed Services Committee itself."

He tried breathing, but couldn't seem to find any air. Even a nod was beyond him at the moment.

"Yes, he is," Rose swept into the room wearing a bathrobe that matched his own, but only in its material. On Rose it was breathtaking. Her blonde hair was perfect—she had paused at least that long before joining them.

Her well-toned and tanned legs swished through the front overlap. Where he had pulled his own bathrobe tight to cover his chest, Rose's ample cleavage was on display well past the lower bra-line—except she wasn't wearing one.

She scooted onto the small loveseat beside him, offering

him an excellent view. There really wasn't room to sit side-by-side, so he raised his arm and placed it across her shoulders.

When he went to flip one of the lapels over her barely concealed breast, she patted his hand, then brushed it aside.

He stopped trying to cover her.

"Dear Clint," Rose was saying in a pleasant tone. "He's been a good friend for *so* long." Her tone said, "far, far too long."

"As I thought," Reese said politely and seemed to relax, stretching an arm across the back of the sofa the way a man would. It emphasized her chest quite splendidly.

"Perhaps you heard that he's announcing his campaign for reelection on Monday."

"I had heard," Reese smiled. "I was curious that the senator..." she nodded at him but she continued speaking to Rose.

As if he wasn't sitting right here!

"...has never sought higher office."

Rose responded before he could open his mouth.

"Oh, no. Not my Hunter. Hunter has no aspirations beyond serving his country—year after year."

Ramson could only blink at her. It was exactly as she'd recommended all along. Power for six-year term after six-year term as senator. Perhaps the presidency at the tail end...

But Rose had said no every time he brought it up.

He waited, sometimes years, then tried again.

Each time she would point out that Ted Kennedy had served forty-seven years in the Senate and Strom Thurmond forty-eight. Robert Byrd had been a senator for fifty-one after a four-year stint as a congressman.

Perhaps Rose was right, though he liked the sound of President Ramson.

The last thing blocking his path to getting control of the Armed Services Committee was...Clint.

And Reese thought she could sweep him aside?

In next year's election?

He tried to keep his heart rate under control, but was having a very hard time of it.

"Of course..." Reese waved a hand negligently.

"Yes?" Rose asked politely as she crossed her legs and the robe slid aside to expose her perfectly toned musculature almost to her hip.

That's when he figured out what she was doing. Rose was showing her that Reese wasn't the only savvy woman in the room.

"There are many people wishing to serve their country, in various roles," Reese offered with a chilling smile. Snake was too kind and shark was too understated.

Ramson wondered what role Reese wanted.

Why had she asked if he was interested in the presidency?

And why had Rose been so fast to assure her that he wasn't?

Oh, God save them all!

Reese wanted the presidency!

But how? No one knew who she was.

It would be laughable...if she wasn't sitting here so casually in the room playing power games with his wife.

"My dear friend Clark, for one," Reese said easily.

And Ramson felt far better. Clark might be a crafty power broker, but he wasn't a twisty devil like Reese.

"He has developed such a fine working relationship with President Cole these last months. It is such a pity that they can't work more closely together for the next election."

Rose smiled radiantly.

It was the Miss Utah smile.

The Top Ten Miss USA smile.

It lit up cameras to this day. Always demure. But always at just the right amount, close beside him when the moment came. He'd witnessed the power of that smile on far more poor sods than himself.

"Ms. Reese," Rose said pleasantly. "I'm sure that you and Hunter can help each other in this matter." Then she patted his thigh.

Help her? Help her get Director Clark Winston the vice presidency in next year's election?

That would mean knocking Ricky Mulroney out of the vice presidency. To do that...

Oh! No, that wouldn't be hard at all. It was the same lever he himself had used to get on the Senate Arms Committee to begin with. Mulroney had a weak spot, the exact kind that someone like Reese would know how to leverage.

"Won't you stay for dinner?" Rose asked every so politely.

Reese inclined her head in polite acceptance.

"Dear," Rose turned to him. "Why don't you call down and have them add the Sea Scallops to our order? They sound simply delicious."

As Hunter reached for the phone, he knew that the rest of his evening wasn't shaping up at all the way he'd planned. They were a long way from getting back to the bedroom.

46

Daemon hadn't quite expected that.

A little straying.

Three bad nav computers. Would have been four if the fourth jet hadn't gone in for service at the last moment—she hadn't noticed the airframe changeout. Too late to reprogram the replacement's onboard systems.

A North Korean Shenyang J-5 or J-6, just as old and primitive as the A-10s but much less well maintained, should have come up and chased them back out of the territory. The report should have been about failing equipment on the aging Thunderbolts.

Instead, North Korea had just sent five million dollars' worth of missiles aloft to kill four pre-historic jets.

It was quite the show.

She played it back again from a different angle—the US had a vast array of surveillance cameras along the entire DMZ. It only took a moment to find the right one that provided the best angle.

Definitely dead.

But it didn't give her what her client needed.

She tapped into their radio logs, which had been automatically recorded back at Osan Air Base.

Yes, this time she had proof that it was the A-10s' failing and not some supposed pilot error or Taliban lucky shot.

She took a moment to sync the two together. Then, to make sure word got out, she dropped it into the anonymous drop sites for CNN, Fox, and Al Jazeera.

Finally, she forwarded the change-value command to a phone in Singapore. It dialed a number in Manhattan, which...

47

THE CODE BLOCK LOADED ONTO THE CRAY XC50 supercomputer in Subbasement 2 of the AFAMS building. She had preset the value of the R14A10DMZ variable to true before loading it.

The subroutine proceeded through the next four steps:

Generate a short acronym.

Deliver the phrase to three separate secure cellphones.

After all three phones provided a delivery confirmation, drop the external connection.

Finally, the subroutine erased itself and the program that had called it.

48

DMZ.

"Jesus Christ, lady. What did you just do?" Senator Ramson was staring at his phone.

Clarissa looked at her own phone again. It didn't make sense. "Nothing was planned there."

"It damn well better not be. That place is a goddamn powder keg with the fuse already lit," Ramson found the remote and turned on CNN.

"The news wouldn't have had time to get..." she tapered off as an unsteady fireball filled the screen. Shot on someone's phone from the south side of the DMZ.

"And this just in," the news anchor flipped to another video. "We're just seeing this for the first time ourselves."

This time the image was rock solid, with high resolution.

Three jets flying in tight formation—and one well off to the side.

The fourth one rejoined the others in a tight diamond.

They shrank into the distance for a long minute.

Then, four bright streaks rose from the bottom of the screen.

A massive fireball erupted.

"And here it is again, with the pilots' actual voices." The anchor sounded harried, as if the control room had only just found out there *was* an audio track.

"Where the hell you going, Chaser?"

"Where are you guys going?"

"We're following protocol. Two kilometers off the zone."

"I show that's where my ass is."

"Hold. This is Flight Lead. Check in position by the numbers."

"Flight Two. On flight plan. Confirmed GPS coordinates and inertial tracking."

"Flight Three. On flight plan. GPS and inertial tracking confirmed."

"That's three to one. Your plane's busted."

"Roger that. All else appears functional. I'll form up on you."

"Roger, take the four slot." The straying jet rejoined the others and slid into the base of the diamond formation.

"This is Chaser, deep in the tail slot."

"Roger that."

A long pause as the flight continued to shrink with distance. Someone in the control room did a shaky zoom, losing the jets twice before getting their blurry images centered on the screen.

"Tomahawk, this is Chaser." The transmission remained clear and ungarbled.

"Go ahead."

"The river doesn't look right, sir."

A much shorter pause.

"Bank hard right!"

Seconds later, while they were still banking, all four jets disappeared in a brilliant explosion.

Hunter turned to Clarissa. "That certainly sounds like us."

It did. Client F had gone completely out of control. She'd take the bastard down right now—if she knew who it was.

CNN started reporting on the alarming mobilization of Japanese aircraft and warships.

Rose stood slowly to her feet and drew her robe tightly closed.

"Hunter. What have you two done?"

49

"WHAT THE HELL IS GOING ON OUT THERE, GENERAL?"

Chairman of the Joint Chiefs of Staff, four-star General Drake Nason wished to God he knew what to tell the President. All of the information that should be flowing into the White House Situation Room—wasn't.

Just a damned CNN feed that he hoped to God was part of some bad movie.

His assistant was feeding him reports from the Pentagon over the secure phone. Drake was repeating them as they came in.

"We got an unannounced North Korean missile launch, Mr. President. A smaller surface-to-air one, not the big ballistic missiles he's been launching lately. A flight of A-10 Thunderbolts were on a routine show-of-force flight along the DMZ when they were targeted and downed."

"*Downed?*" President Roy Cole leaned forward abruptly.

"Yes sir." Even now, his assistant Bart was confirming that in his ear over the phone.

"I'll have imaging in a moment," Lizzy spoke up from her seat at the Situation Room table. The three of them had been meeting about the changes to the US Air Force Space Command when he'd been alerted to an incoming priority call. Which meant that his information was only seconds ahead of the President.

A hazy satellite image flickered on one of the side screens as Lizzy tapped furiously at her keyboard. Another, sharper image replaced it moments later.

"What are we looking at?"

"Nothing useful. Please give me a moment, sir." Lizzy didn't even look up.

Not "Lizzy." Drake had better be damned careful. She was General Elizabeth Gray, Director of the National Reconnaissance Office in this room—not Lizzy sitting beside him at the Metro 29 Diner's counter last night.

He'd wanted to have an atypical date and going to a *Diners, Drive-Ins and Dives* location seemed like a good first choice for two members of the Washington elite. It should never have taken him so long to follow up, but her recent promotion had overwhelmed her and he'd foolishly waited to give her time to settle in.

What took you so long? General Gray had asked him over a shared appetizer of Buffalo chicken wings.

Unable to dodge her questions for very long, he'd finally confessed to being an idiot over her crab-stuffed filet of flounder and his own boneless ribeye topped with onion rings. And it was true. She was as smart and charming as he remembered. Also, out of uniform and wearing a casual blouse and jeans, she was equally impressive in such a different way.

Most would just see the slim, pretty Eurasian woman with the bright laugh he was dining with. But that, combined with being the head of one of the most powerful and clandestine agencies in the entire government, was just head spinning.

The counter waitress had teased him and Lizzy (because she was definitely Lizzy by the end of the meal) into splitting a massive three-scoop banana split with patriotic strawberry, vanilla, and blueberry ice cream. He'd still been able to taste it when she'd kissed him as he had his driver drop her off.

We aren't teenagers anymore, you know? definitely-not-General Gray-at-that-moment had whispered before slipping out of the car.

He knew. But after last night's dinner and kiss, he felt like one.

Not teenagers anymore. If he'd been thinking faster, he'd have taken it as an invitation to tell Lamont to just keep driving until they reached his silent home. With the kids grown and gone and his wife buried five years ago, the house was echoingly empty...

The image on the Situation Room screen stabilized.

"Is this the crash site?" Drake squinted at the screen, but didn't see the normal scorched marks of a crash.

"It's their last reported radar position. I'm now scrolling backwards in time."

She didn't have to go far.

The image was unchanging as she manipulated the controls with the ease of the image analyst she had once been.

Back until...

The bright flash was unmistakable—a massive fireball on the satellite image.

Li—General Gray hit pause, then rolled forward slowly.

By the time the explosive cloud disappeared there was no sign of debris or... "No parachutes."

The President cursed.

General Gray headed back in time.

The fireball compressed moment by moment until it finally resolved into four planes.

"You said missiles. Where are the missiles?" President Cole was still straining forward.

"If they're what we think they were, they were traveling in excess of Mach 3.0," and Drake prayed he was wrong. Even knowing he wasn't.

"Mach 5.0. A mile a second," Gray confirmed. "Our satellites are not movie cameras; they form an image every sixth of a second. So, within eight hundred feet..." She was zooming out.

The jets shrank at the center of the image until they were barely the length of his finger.

"There," he and Gray said in the same breath.

Four sparks of light appeared from the top edge of the screen.

She zoomed in.

They were blurred, but there was no mistaking their direction of travel—straight at the jets.

"Why would the North Koreans be shooting down our planes on a standard patrol? An attack over South Korean soil is asking for war. I need to speak to that bastard Kim Jong-Un right now." The President called the last out to the room which was constantly monitored by the Situation Room staff.

"Uh, Mr. President, you may wish to hold off on that call," Gray spoke softly.

"Hold that," he called out to the room. "Say it like you mean it, General. That's why we gave you the job. You're the Director of the NRO now."

"Yes sir, Mr. President." And General Elizabeth Gray was the only one in her chair—Lizzy was suddenly nowhere to be seen.

"There's something you need to know first." She dropped a red circle around the jets and then kept zooming back.

And back.

And back...until their final position was indistinguishable except for the marker.

Then another red line came into view at the edge of the screen and began moving onto it from the lower right edge.

"Is that—" Drake's throat closed on him and he couldn't speak.

President Cole collapsed back into his chair.

"That, Mr. President," General Gray announced, "is the Korean Demilitarized Zone. The northern edge of it. Our aircraft were almost ten kilometers into North Korea."

50

"THE JAPANESE," DRAKE LISTENED WITH ONE EAR TO HIS VICE chairman as Bart fed him fresh updates from the Pentagon, "threw the switch to an offensive war footing at 19:43 our time."

It was well known that the Japanese were imminently prepared for the moment, if they felt that was necessary. Or rather *when*.

And nuclear weapons?

Everyone said a year, but he'd bet they had everything worked out to make it happen within twenty-four hours— assuming they didn't already have a couple sequestered away.

"Why the hell did they do that?" President Cole was not happy.

"A North Korean missile impacted Iki Island. At the moment the fatalities appear to be—"

His surprise stopped him from echoing Bart's words into the room.

"It *what?*"

The President and General Gray were both watching him closely.

Bart repeated himself, though Drake still couldn't quite believe it as he repeated the words, "A herd of cows."

The President shook his head. "For the first time since 1945, in direct contravention of Article 9 of their constitution—"

"Which we wrote for them in 1947," Drake couldn't help putting in.

"—which we wrote for them in 1947," President Cole conceded, "Japan is on a war footing over a herd of cows?"

Gray had been tapping at her keyboard while they'd been speaking.

"Here's the real reason why," she spoke softly.

On the screen, Gray—no goddamn it, she could be Lizzy in his thoughts, a Eurasian named for Elizabeth Bennet out of some romance novel that he really should read—had set her software to track the missiles rather than the jets.

The flight of missiles swept rapidly up to the jets and the white-out fireball happened. But the view kept tracking and the explosion slipped off the screen.

Now a single missile was highlighted on the display.

She zoomed in on it. It was a nasty piece of work, at least seven meters of flying death, still burning rocket fuel at a prodigious rate. It was their first clear view of the KN-06 and it wasn't going to make anyone in the West happy. Launching four of those monsters against a flight of A-10s was definitely swatting flies with a howitzer.

The background switched from mountains to the dark blue of ocean.

"It's a runaway," Lizzy stated.

"But they didn't destroy it."

"Maybe they're so clumsy that they don't know it survived."

Drake hoped that Lizzy was wrong.

A scary thought to have a nuclear power that was also incompetent.

"Maybe it just broke," Drake liked that idea better.

"Maybe they used *our* planes as an excuse so that they could test Japan's reactions," President Cole offered a thoroughly depressing suggestion.

Whatever the reason, the missile continued flying over the sea. Finally, the engine cut out.

"It's in ballistic fall now. An unpowered, unguided supersonic descent."

They all watched in silence.

At the very last moment, ocean blue background became land green, and then the missile landed.

Lizzy scrolled back to the final image before impact and, sure enough, it would land at the center of a herd of black-and-white cattle.

"Two seconds more, or less, flight time and all it would have killed was some fish underwater. Instead, a North Korean missile impacted on Japan's terra firma." Drake put his phone back to his ear and spoke to Bart, "Why didn't our Patriot missile interceptors fire?"

"With no launch notice, they were too slow to react. The KN-06—which we've now confirmed—was also faster than expected. By the time they tracked the lone missile, it was out of range of our batteries. Our Patriots are lined up at the border, not anywhere south."

"Make a note to get on with US Forces Korea and the South Koreans to rethink that...assuming we all survive whatever happens next."

The President picked up another phone.

Drake eavesdropped.

"Mr. Prime Minister Kagawa? Yes, this is President Roy Cole... Yes sir...I know about that, sir. I'm going to ask you to stand down until we know more... Yes sir. I know about the cows, sir."

Drake knew from experience that Roy Cole appeared affable when it suited him, but could use anger with equal facility.

"I'll pay for the goddamn cows myself, Mr. Prime Minister, *if* you stand down immediately... They were Wagyu beef?"

Drake couldn't help smiling.

"Worth *how much?*"

He could see Lizzy covering her mouth to hide her smile.

The President rolled his eyes at them. "We'll talk about the damned beef later, Mr. Prime Minister. Just get back off war footing before North Korea really does launch... No, he wasn't shooting at you. He was shooting at us and he missed. Let me deal with him... Thank you, Mr. Prime Minister... Yes, I'm sorry about the cows, too... Uh... I understand."

He hung up the phone and slumped back in his chair.

"They've been experimenting with the flavor effects of Wagyu cattle raised outside of the Kobe region, including a small test herd on Iki Island. It seems that the US government is going to own a great deal of flash-seared beef. Either of you want to come to the picnic? Maybe you can both bring a date."

Drake knew it was a mistake even as he was glancing over at Lizzy, who blushed instantly.

President Cole looked back and forth between them, then sighed. "Please, no more bad news today. Just keep it to yourselves."

"Yes sir." Drake kept his voice as serious as he could.

Lizzy's blush had colored her lustrous skin and he could see her struggle to regroup herself. She was doing a better job of it than he was.

51

Miranda rolled to a stop at Eglin Air Force Base by the designated hangar.

Night had descended while she'd been en route. San Antonio, Houston, New Orleans, and Mobile had lit her way to western Florida.

"We have a briefing room set aside for you, Ms. Chase," an Air Force Captain Bell greeted her at the hangar as she deplaned.

The ladder was a stepladder, not the proper Sabrejet service ladder like the one that Colonel Campos had arranged for her. This time she left her helmet in the cockpit before climbing down because she needed both hands to steady herself.

"The rest of your crew is less than thirty minutes behind you."

Miranda blinked in confusion. Again, they were arriving impossibly quickly. She looked around to make sure they hadn't already arrived and the captain simply hadn't noticed.

But she didn't see them anywhere.

The Mooney was fast, but should be three hours behind her.

"Who arranged for the briefing room?" She hadn't asked Colonel Campos to arrange anything more than flight clearance.

"General Drake Nason, Chairman of the Joint Chiefs of Staff," the captain spoke with a certain awe. "We're supposed to call him as soon as your crew is fully assembled."

"Okay. Can I get something to eat while we wait?"

The captain looked at her as if she was supposed to have said something else, though she couldn't imagine what.

Some food and a quiet place to make the world stop. She'd been on the go since seven a.m. Pacific Time, flying from one corner of the country to the other.

Technically, that wasn't correct. Cape Flattery, the northwestern most point of the continental US, lay a hundred miles west of her island, and Key West lay six hundred miles to the southeast of Eglin. Not corner-to-corner, but more than she wanted to ever again fly in a single day. Her Sabrejet had covered the distance in under four hours, but it was a jet meant for sorties, not crossing countries.

Miranda did pause at the hatchway, through which the Sabrejet's six .50 cal Browning machine guns used to be reloaded, to extract her NTSB vest. She felt better when it was on and she'd checked that everything was in place.

"You're with the NTSB?" Captain Bell looked confused as he led her to a waiting Chevy Suburban.

She felt that the six-inch-high, fluorescent-yellow letters

across her back would confirm that sufficiently, but apparently they didn't, so she answered in the affirmative.

She never liked the Suburban. It was easier to climb into her airplane than into the high ground clearance vehicle. There were never pitons or climbing ropes around when she needed them and the Suburban always made her feel as if she did.

"The NTSB is not what I was expecting." Being six feet tall, he stepped into the vehicle easily and sat behind the wheel.

"And what were you expecting?"

"At least a major general by the way General Nason issued the order. Picking up NTSB agents isn't exactly a typical job for a captain."

"I spent the entire morning being escorted around Davis-Monthan by a colonel. It didn't seem that unusual to me."

As he pulled away from the hangar, two Security Forces cars that had been parked nearby fell in with them—one leading, one behind. Did they think she was a terrorist of some sort? Or were the eight thousand military personnel of Eglin Air Force Base on high alert because they thought they were being attacked by a Korean War-era jet?

Maybe they were just going her way.

In a little three-vehicle convoy, they drove toward a brightly lit building. Through the windows she could see a crowded area of personnel facing each other across tray-laden tables.

Yes, food would be good. Holly would approve.

"Please have my team brought here as well."

"But the general—"

"They haven't eaten in just as long as I haven't eaten. Our

last meal was interrupted by two rather significant explosions—one in alarming proximity—and a cross-country flight. Is that somehow unclear, captain?"

He harrumphed as he pulled up to the door of the DFAC and she prepared to climb down. "Not unclear. No. Just...unusual."

"How is it unusual to want to eat?"

"No ma'am. It isn't, ma'am. It's unusual to ignore the CJCS. And the order itself that he gave, ma'am, very unusual."

"Which was?" At this rate they'd still be here talking by the time her team arrived.

"He made it sound as if I'd be court-martialed if anything untoward happened to you, ma'am. That's why we have the SECFOR escort." Indeed the two Chevy Tahoes had pulled to a stop.

Confirming his statement, two airmen with heavy arms stepped from the forward vehicle and began scanning the area rather than watching her. She looked in the side mirror in time to see a handler release a military war dog from the trailing vehicle, then they both stood ready. Also waiting for her to step out.

"Do you think they're hungry too?"

"Who?"

"Your policeman and the dog."

"Why?"

"If they feel such a need to protect me on your own military base, it would seem to make sense if we all ate together. Or do they need to go and escort the others from my team?"

"They have their own escort, ma'am."

Miranda was out of the vehicle and halfway to the door, at the center of her towering escorts and the dog ranging along ahead of them sniffing the air, when the oddity began to make sense.

"You say that Drake asked for this level of security for me?"

Captain Bell turned to her so abruptly that he stumbled. "You call the Chairman of the Joint Chiefs of Staff by his first name?"

"He asked me to. Is there a problem?"

"Ma'am. No ma'am. I've never even *seen* the CJCS."

"He's a good man. He gets very upset when bad things happen to his pilots."

"Even though he was an Army Ranger?"

"He was?" She hadn't known that about him. "And he has a thing for Krispy Kreme donuts. I saw a large empty box on his desk one night."

The captain just looked at her wild-eyed for a moment.

That had been a very long night and she was sorry now that she'd remembered it. Too many people had died before she'd solved the cause behind those losses. She hoped that she never had to deal with the CIA ever again.

Some instinct told her that she should knock on wood as a safety precaution. As surreptitiously as she could, she rapped her knuckles on her head. The captain didn't notice, but one of the SECFOR troops grinned at her.

Her stomach growled. She was becoming as bad as Holly —now she craved several slices of pizza rather than her usual salad.

52

JEREMY SPOTTED MIRANDA FIRST AS THEY CAME OFF THE EGLIN chow line with their trays. She was almost invisible at a corner table. He might not have noticed her at all except for the three military police standing along the wall behind her.

And they had a war dog.

He rushed over, but stopped abruptly when the dog snarled at him.

"Not friendly?" He set his tray beside Miranda's but turned to face the handler.

"Surprised him a little is all. As long as you don't piss me off, you're safe."

"Good to know," Jeremy slipped a piece of bacon out of his bacon cheeseburger as an apology.

At the handler's nod, he held it out for the big German Shepard.

"Viktor," the handler said.

"Viktor. Good doggie," he offered the bacon.

The dog looked to the handler for permission. At the

man's nod, Viktor snapped it so fast the Jeremy was left holding only the tiny bit still pinched between his thumb and finger.

Two chomps and it was gone.

Then Victor gently wrapped his teeth around Jeremy's fingertips and scooched the last bite free.

"Lucky to still have your fingers. Viktor likes bacon," the handler grinned.

"Me too. Maybe I'll just sit down." There were a ton of questions he'd like to ask about the dog and how to handle him, but with Holly and Mike headed their way, he felt it was better to sit down. Mike might not push his tray aside to sit beside Miranda, but Holly definitely would.

He slid into his seat beside her.

Miranda sat across from a Captain Bell, but neither was speaking.

"Can you believe we're at Eglin?"

Miranda looked at him with some surprise.

"This is one of the big sim centers."

"Like the card in my phone?" Mike asked as he sat down beside the captain.

"Flight simulators," Holly corrected him.

Holly sat on Jeremy's other side, which was awkward. Now he could either face Miranda or keep an eye on Holly, but he couldn't do both.

"Oh," Mike sounded bored.

Colonel Campos arrived last, hesitating at the head of the table for a long moment before moving down to sit by Mike across from Holly. If he *did* like Miranda, did it bother him to be forced to sit kitty-corner from her? It definitely worked for Jeremy. During the flight, he'd decided that he didn't like the way the colonel might be thinking about Miranda.

But Mike's indifference didn't let Jeremy focus on that.

"No, Mike. Seriously. This place is super cool. These sims aren't those clunky multi-million-dollar boxes on hydraulic legs. They're fully networked systems capable of large-scale battle scenarios with tons of simultaneous players."

The Air Force captain had stopped eating and was eyeing him strangely.

"The Army has CAMTT—Combined Aircrew Mission Task Trainer—over at the Air Maneuver Battle Lab in Fort Rucker, Alabama. They play these massive helicopter wargame scenarios there. The Navy has one too, though I forget the name. The Air Force pretends that they canceled their sim program, but no way. For beginners, they've just launched the Pilot Training Next program in the last few years, but that's just simple scenarios. One of their biggest simulator setups is here at Eglin, all part of the Air Force Agency for Modeling and Simulation. Their primary development site is just over in Orlando. You can bet Disney has a couple of big contracts in there."

He took a bite of his burger and felt a bit like Viktor when he only chewed it twice, then swallowed it down so that he could keep going.

"Between the three main services, they can now run wargames with literally hundreds of aircraft, main battle tanks, helos, destroyers... You name it, they've got it. All without burning a drop of fuel or shooting a single round. I've always—"

"Hey!" The captain across the table snapped out. "That's classified."

"Oi, mate," Holly wrapped an arm around Jeremy's shoulders, but she didn't *seem* to be about to attack him.

Jeremy kept his shoulders braced just in case.

Instead she leaned toward Captain Bell.

"Haven't figured it out yet, have ye? Think we should tell him, Jeremy?" Like he was on the inside of some grand secret.

"Why don't *you*?" He wasn't sure where she was going with this, but he decided to be on the winning team—which meant being on Holly's team.

"Captain Bell. Like Tinker Bell?" she asked.

One of the SECFOR guys snorted, then whispered none too softly, "His call sign *is* Tinker. Like the little fairy."

"I got it while flying the big tankers out of Tinker Air Force Base. Besides, you telling me Julie Roberts wasn't hot as Tinker Bell in *Hook?*"

"Your point, sir. She's old, but she is *always* hot," the SECFOR acknowledged.

"Well, Captain Tinker, buddy, pal," Holly drew it out. Maybe because she could see it was really bothering the guy. "The person at this table with the lowest security clearance is the one in your shaving mirror. Closely followed by your buddy there," she hooked a thumb at Colonel Campos.

The captain glanced over at the colonel.

"Nothing would surprise me at this point, Captain Bell," the colonel said mildly as he dipped another piece of fried fish into his tartar sauce.

"The top of the stack?" Holly picked up a piece of pizza, took a big bite out of it, then pointed it over at Miranda.

Jeremy watched Holly closely, but still missed how she managed to smear a long line of tomato sauce across his vest

—like a slash through his heart. It wiped easily off the nylon, but still, she was sneaky.

"You were saying, Jeremy." Holly took another big bite before she finished chewing the prior one.

"Uh..." What had he been saying? And how much more could he say, not knowing the captain's security clearance?

Not much.

Though what he knew hadn't really come in the front door. Most of it had come from Dad. The *Microsoft Flight Simulator* game that most people saw—and that Dad was a lead programmer on—was only the tip of the iceberg. It was also the deep core of the US military simulator systems: Air Force, Navy, Army, and Coast Guard. Which probably meant he should mention even less rather than more.

He knew far more than his security clearance allowed. And if they ever found out, his security clearance would be gone.

Then Miranda wouldn't be able to use him on any high security investigations.

He'd be off the team.

And then he'd just die.

No, keep his mouth shut. That was the ticket—the *only* safe choice.

"Anyway, I'd really like to see the Cray XC50. I've never seen one in person before."

"The...what?" The captain's eyes appeared to cross.

Holly leaned forward again.

Jeremy checked, but both of her hands were clean and now empty.

"It's a ruddy big computer."

"Oh."

Jeremy wondered how Holly knew that.

Once the captain had returned his attention to his next forkful of meatloaf, Holly whispered in Jeremy's ear.

"Did I get that right?"

They shared a grin and he whispered back, "Yep. A *ruddy* big one."

Yes, belonging was a very good feeling.

53

Clarissa had always wondered how a man like Hunter Ramson had become such a significant force in the Senate. Nothing about him stood out. Even less now, wrapped in a Kimpton Hotel bathrobe with his thin chest hair just starting to go gray. She'd never liked chest hair and was glad that Clark was smooth-chested.

Hunter had done nothing truly underhanded or Harry her pet hacker would have found it, and he hadn't.

Though she'd wager that he could find a lot more on Ramson's boss, Senator Clint Howards, Chairman of the Senate Armed Services Committee. And if he couldn't find it, she wasn't above fabricating it.

Now she could see exactly how Hunter had risen so high —and that meant that she knew how to read him. Clarissa had been looking for his hidden strength, and not finding it.

Now she had.

Rose Ramson commanded the room. It was irrelevant that she'd walked into the living room from bedding her

246

own husband in one of *the* luxury hotel suites in a town known for them, wearing no more than a bathrobe herself. She had walked in just like the beauty queen she'd once been.

A simple statement, *here* is the power.

So why had Ramson tried to slip this operation past his wife?

Rose was asking exactly those questions.

Not that Clarissa cared. Though she'd definitely have to make sure that Clark didn't think he could get away with that around her.

The more she listened to Rose Ramson—*not* fists on hips and ripping Hunter a new asshole—the more Clarissa shifted her thinking on that. Rose didn't ram her power down Hunter's throat. Instead, she had sat back down on the love seat beside him, but kept her robe tightly closed. She proceeded to make it clear that she was an asset, but only if she knew everything that was going on. *Everything.*

Rose treated them like a unified team, even if she was clearly the one in charge.

Clarissa had always stood alone.

After her abusive father's sudden and unexpected—at least to him—demise, she had been on her own.

Her tall, blonde-and-built looks had started as a burden.

Then she'd cultivated that power and ultimately weaponized it.

Men were distracted by the body as she ferreted out their secrets. Then they either did her bidding or she destroyed them.

By the time the opportunity of running Black Site interrogations was offered, she'd made herself the obvious choice. Extreme rendition to extract actionable information from fucking Taliban and al-Qaeda slime? No problem. She never even got the shakes.

Taking down the A-10 Thunderbolt IIs that should have been retired a generation ago? So what if it there were some losses to make it happen?

As Hunter slowly explained the project to Rose, Clarissa thought about how such a scene would play out with Clark.

He wouldn't like it. *Really* wouldn't like it. So, she wouldn't tell him.

No, she couldn't tell Clark about this project, but maybe it was time she let him really know just how much more she was worth than for fucking against the *Kryptos* sculpture.

Yes.

It was time for the next step.

"Rose?"

Rose broke off with Hunter and turned to face her.

"If I remove Clint, what word do I have from you that Vice President Ricky Mulroney will be gotten out of the way —without damaging President Cole? It needs to happen soon." Before someone else saw what she was up to and tried to supplant Clark's rightful place as the next Vice President.

Or attack *her*. She just might need the protection of being D/CIA if this operation went too far sideways.

"Well, that will be up to you, my dear." Smoothly professional, Rose Ramson didn't miss a beat.

"To me?" Clarissa allowed the question to sort of hover between them. Casual, but not too much so.

"Oh yes, completely."

"And Clint's reelection announcement is this coming Monday?" Clarissa knew she'd have to pay the price first.

"Oh, I think that timing would work very well. Perhaps right after that. Hunter dear..." Rose turned, her bathrobe slipping partly open once again.

Clarissa wanted to laugh.

Hunter's hindbrain would know his transgression was forgiven, but she wondered how much longer Rose would keep his forebrain on tenterhooks.

"...you should invite Ricky to join you on your inspection trip to South America next week."

"I should?" Hunter pretended to look surprised, but wasn't. He wasn't a complete idiot.

That meant the answer to taking down Mulroney was right there on the table. Not revealed yet, but promised in that invitation to the VP that there was indeed an answer that could be delivered quickly.

Rose leaned back on the loveseat beside her husband.

I am a woman in command in every way.

Clarissa liked meeting another elemental force. Perhaps she'd ask for some advice from Rose in Clark's upcoming campaign. Or maybe reserve that weapon for after Clark had served his time as VP and it was her own turn to run as *his* VP.

Hunter might not want the presidency—or rather not be *allowed* it by his wife. But perhaps Rose would enjoy being Vice President when Clarissa ultimately reached the top.

For now, Clarissa simply nodded that Clint's campaign was doomed to a disastrous launch.

Rose smiled that million-dollar smile of complete satisfaction.

"I'd prefer if you're the one who arranges things," she said with all the sweetness of a debutante pit viper. "When he's traveling out of the spotlight, Ricky likes his girls dark and very young."

Clarissa felt her gut wrench. Her father had once maintained an avaricious taste for her own youth.

A taste she'd killed him for.

Ricky Mulroney?

Him, she'd merely ruin. And it would be a pleasure.

54

JEREMY *HAD* MADE MIRANDA CURIOUS ABOUT THE CRAY XC50 supercomputer.

However, now that she was standing in front of it, she was disappointed—though Jeremy didn't seem to be.

After Jeremy's descriptions of high-tech simulated warfare and advanced pilot training, even modeling of future control methodologies, she'd expected more. Jeremy had made it all sound so exciting.

Instead, they'd stood together in an underground room of stark white. White plastic floor tiles. White ceiling tiles. White walls. Air conditioning cool enough that she was glad she still had her coat.

The computer itself was four lines of six-foot-tall cabinets. It had a long blue swoosh logo across the cabinets —much simpler than Nike's swoosh.

Clean lines.

She liked that at least.

And it was a nice color of blue. Not soothing, but giving

confidence that the computer behind the cabinet was very high tech and definitely knew how to do its job.

Across the face of the line of cabinets, it declared "Cray XC50" in foot-high letters, so there was no doubting what it was.

A Lt. Colonel Kiley had tried to explain it to them, but he knew less than Jeremy and barely managed to insert a word in edgewise.

"It runs a petaflop per cabinet," Jeremy stood at a cabinet that had been opened for him and couldn't seem to look away even as he spoke. "That's a thousand-thousand-billion floating point operations per second, a million times faster than the average home computer. IBM didn't really break the one petaflop barrier—a peta is a one with fifteen zeroes after it, you know—until 2008 with Roadrunner, which filled six thousand square feet and had almost three hundred computer racks. Now here it is in a single cabinet."

Miranda looked down the four rows of three computer cabinets each. So, twelve computers all hooked together into one.

"See these?" Jeremy pointed at the narrow cabinet attached to each main computing one. "Water-cooled electronics because the air can't dissipate heat fast enough."

But seeing the computer was a little like seeing the inside of the crash before the outside. It was the wrong layer. She was still pursuing the pattern and causes of the crashes, nowhere near ready to consider the cause of the overall calamity.

Observing the crash first...

The crashes...

"I need to see the tape of the DMZ incident. Actually,

everything on any simulations run through this particular computer in the last thirty-six hours." Only after she'd turned and walked to the exit did she realize that Jeremy had still been talking.

Lt. Colonel Kiley rushed to catch up with her. "This system is involved with between fifty and five hundred simulations at a time—all the time."

"Narrow it down to simulations including any A-10 Thunderbolt IIs. I need to see them all now."

55

MIRANDA WAS HALFWAY THROUGH THE LIST WHEN THE SCREEN at the head of the conference room table lit up.

"Hello, Ms. Chase. It's good to see you again."

Drake Nason was on the screen. Along with General Lizzy Gray.

She didn't have time for them and kept working.

Mike said something nice and she continued to ignore them.

The standard flight training programs were easy to dismiss. She swiped them off the screen one by one. A few she had to watch, but often only briefly.

"Ms. Chase?"

"Later." She kept working.

"Miranda?" Drake repeated much more forcibly.

She turned to the screen.

"Drake, you've lost ten A-10 Thunderbolt IIs in the last twenty-one hours. There appears to be a break in the pattern or I would have said that you have approximately three hours and forty-two minutes until you lose the next one, or more."

"Until I *what?*" Drake shouted the last of it.

"Remember, Drake, there's a reason you called her," Lizzy Gray reminded him.

"Ten? And you think they're all connected?"

"Nine of them almost for certain," Miranda considered. "I don't have proof..."

"And we all know how you like your proof."

Miranda paused.

Drake did like to tease people.

Is that what he was doing now? How was she supposed to know?

Unsure how to respond, she ignored him and returned to her queue.

And ended up with nine possible scenarios involving over twenty aircraft.

"Jeremy. Can you tell me what these have in common?"

"Miranda?" Drake again.

"Later," she called out.

"What are we looking at?" Drake was insistent.

"If I knew that, I wouldn't need Jeremy's help, would I? Now be quiet for a minute."

There was a muffled laugh. Female. Holly or Lizzy Gray.

Together she and Jeremy—and probably everyone else as Jeremy had routed the playbacks to the main screen—watched each event.

A combat loss in Afghanistan. Yet it was logged into the *simulation* computer, which was decidedly unusual. At least a final mission report of it was. More than should be for a mission flown nine-and-a-half time zones away.

Colonel Campos' A-10 crash at Davis-Monthan was there as well. Except it appeared on the data falsely as a simulation, not a real flight.

"Look, something *did* take control of my plane. From here! What the hell are you up to, Kiley?" Colonel Campos yelled across the table.

"Quiet!" Miranda hated when people shouted. The emotions seemed to charge into her and bounce around like a bullet fired inside a steel room, ricocheting unpredictably until she didn't know where it would land.

"But—"

"Colonel. Do *not* disturb Ms. Chase." Drake snapped out a sharp command.

She could hear Campos sputter, but he otherwise kept his silence—which was all she cared about.

Miranda played another simulation, two A-10s in a dogfight with Chinese PLAAF jets.

She played it twice, then looked at Jeremy.

He shrugged.

Holly shook her head.

Whatever Miranda was looking for, it wasn't in this one. She deleted it.

The next was a simulated airplane battle in Syria.

"Hey," Kiley spoke up. "I recognize that scenario."

"Damn good pilot," Campos observed.

Miranda ran it again and watched the lone A-10 take on a pair of Su-25 Frogfoot Russian aircraft, as well as dodging an AIM-9 Sidewinder missile. Yes, it was a *very* good pilot.

"Trainee named—"

"Irrelevant," Miranda cut him off.

It also had a different feel than the partial simulations she'd watched.

"This really happened."

"No," Kiley insisted. "I saw the flight in the simulators myself. Lieutenant William Blake flew that scenario."

Miranda turned to face him. "No. That really happened."

"But—"

"There are a dozen flight characteristics that the simulator doesn't have yet. There's buffeting from air pockets. Control slippage. Unpredictable behaviors in adversarial aircraft. Colonel Kiley, please check action reports for Syria at the same time as your simulation."

"But—"

"But what, Colonel?"

"That means..." he sounded as if he was choking. "Select the next simulated flight, two more down on your list."

"Skipping ahead isn't orderly."

"Lady, just do it."

Holly rested a hand lightly on her arm. Holly must think it was okay to review them out of order, even if Miranda still didn't like it.

She took a deep breath and skipped over the next one she'd selected to highlight to the one the lieutenant colonel indicated.

It *really* wasn't orderly. Order. It was in the very meaning of the word: this one, then the next.

Still, she clicked Play.

56

THREE A-10S FACED OFF AGAINST THREE MQ-9 REAPER drones and an RQ-170 Sentinel in the replay from Eglin's simulator.

"The first two Reapers were very sloppy," Jeremy observed as they watched.

Miranda almost looked away to inspect him. Mike was the pilot—though only of small, general aviation planes.

Jeremy wasn't a pilot at all. Yet he could see that the Reaper pilots had indeed been sloppy.

The cat-and-mouse game of the final Warthog and the lone Sentinel played out across the screen.

"Again, a very fine maneuver," Campos concluded as the A-10 spiraled out of sight into the ocean.

Kiley cleared his throat again. "Same trainee pilot, Poet Blake. But again, that wasn't all a simulation. We lost three of our top trainer pilots this afternoon in the same area. Less than five hours ago."

Jeremy let out a low whistle. "Someone actually interfaced the simulation and the real world."

Miranda actually felt relieved. Aircraft losses at sea were very hard to explain. The loss of her parents' 747 at sea had taken four years to solve and be finally reported by the NTSB. She'd been dreading the analysis of these three aircraft since the moment Colonel Campos had reported them back at Davis-Monthan.

Now they knew the answer with no dredging of the seabed and piecing together infinitesimal clues.

Miranda rolled the video back and read off the tail numbers on the A-10s. All three had "EG" tail codes—for Eglin AFB.

"They check," Kiley whispered.

"Would someone explain what the hell is going on?" A small window in the corner of the screen showed Drake leaning toward the camera. Close enough to luridly distort his features.

"Yes," Miranda focused on the playback because Drake looked scary. "We've just identified the cause of three A-10 losses. They were shot down during a simulation run on your Cray XC50 computer. Four pilots, thinking it was a simulation, unknowingly flew real-world drones in an attack that killed three trainer pilots of the 96th Test Wing based here at Eglin."

"Oh, Christ." Nason dropped back into his chair. Which was a relief.

"Hey! Run that again," Jeremy pointed at the screen.

"But we still haven't looked at the one before it."

"I saw something."

57

Jeremy watched the simulation screen closely.

He was missing something.

Someone? No, something. He just had no idea what it was.

The first A-10 losing a wing and plunging from the sky.

An MQ-9 Reaper going down, and then another.

A pair of Hellfire missiles aimed at the remaining A-10s. Then, just as the final A-10 shot the final Reaper, the view from the RQ-170 Sentinel caught a sideview of the last drone.

"Freeze it!"

Miranda did.

"Zoom in."

Miranda manipulated the controls. The image was a little blurred by distance and air currents, but one thing was clear.

"Who flies an MQ-9 Reaper with no markings on it?"

58

Drake's blood ran cold.

The Army, Air Force, and Navy all flew with tail numbers.

The only people who didn't were...he looked across his Pentagon office desk at Lizzy and she nodded confirmation.

The CIA.

"Whoever it is," Jeremy was saying, "just lost three Reapers. And who flies the Sentinel? That's gotta be the CIA, doesn't it? I mean, who else would have that cool a surveillance drone?"

"What makes it so cool?" Mike asked from Eglin.

"It's a flying wing. Super-stealth. Ultra-classified. That would explain why the last pilot never saw what hit him. And the simulator pilot knew it. He just slid the Sentinel in sweet as could be and Ker-pow! Down goes the A-10."

"Real people, Jeremy," Holly this time.

"Right. I knew that. But it was still amazing." Though he did sound a little sorry for his comment.

Drake pulled himself together. Though it was damn hard. He was losing planes all over again. If he got proof of that Clarissa Reese woman being involved, he'd have her taken out and shot—even if he had to pull the trigger himself.

"Miranda. What about the flight into the DMZ?"

"I still haven't reviewed—"

"Miranda," he cut her off, then cursed himself. He hoped it didn't stop her thinking as he'd seen it do before. "Please. I have the Japanese ready to start World War III in North Korea. Can you tell me what happened there?"

There was a long silence.

"Miranda?"

"I haven't watched that one yet, Drake. I don't know anything about it."

"Let's watch it together, okay?"

Again the long pause.

"Miranda?"

"There's a problem, Drake. I have a record here, but it's empty. There's nothing inside the record. Jeremy and Lt. Colonel Kiley are working on it."

He signaled Lizzy, who spoke up, "Watch your screen. We have the satellite files of the flight."

She hit Play.

Together they watched the broken diamond formation reform. Lizzy had synced the pilots' crosstalk with the satellite image.

"But the KH-II doesn't record audio."

"No, Liz— General Gray synced it from their actual broadcasts."

"As long as you didn't corrupt the original files."

"They're stored separately," Lizzy assured Miranda.

"Oh, okay. Play it again."

This time the viewing passed in silence except for the pilots' voices.

"That would appear to be real world. Which doesn't explain why there was any record at all in the AFAMS simulation computer. However, we can likely conclude that the aircraft were tampered with."

"What makes you say that?"

"We can either hypothesize that three of them had both GPS and inertial tracking failures, or that that those three aircraft were tampered with. This flight remains an anomaly."

"Why do you say that?"

"The other four flights—Afghanistan, Colonel Campos, Syria, and the Gulf of Mexico—occurred within minutes of six-hour intervals. This one occurred nineteen hours and twenty-eight minutes after the initial known event. Nineteen hours and twenty-eight minutes is not evenly divisible by six hours. It's now nine-oh-one Eastern Standard Time. There's two hours and fifty-nine minutes until the next expected occurrence."

Drake hit the mute button.

"What do you think, Lizzy?"

"Uh..." Lizzy fooled with the keyboard, aligning it with the edge of the desk. "There's a reason you called her. We hadn't even connected the events. She not only connected them, but she found a pattern as well."

He unmuted the phone.

"Two hours and fifty-nine minutes—"

"Fifty-eight now," Miranda replied.

"Any theories?"

"There is no pattern of East to West or North to South, even discounting the event in the DMZ. I'd say that the answer either lies in the computer here, or in Washington, DC."

"Here?"

"Commands have been issued. CIA drones were either used or stolen. A highly secure supercomputer here at Eglin appears to have been hacked. That speaks to CIA, NSA, or someone else at the Fort Belvoir, Virginia, intelligence complex. Unless we can capture the next action, we won't know about it until after it occurs. We must be ready for that."

Drake cricked his neck.

No way to stop it until he knew what was going to happen next.

And no way to know what was going to happen next, until it had happened.

"Ms. Chase. How fast can you get to DC?"

"I have my jet. Which places me a little over an hour away."

"Go."

He cut the connection and looked at Lizzy.

"Another person for the Wagyu beef barbeque?" Lizzy's tone was painfully dry.

"Maybe we can get her to bring a date. That will just make the President's day."

Lizzy actually smiled despite all the grim news.

"What?"

"The image of Miranda Chase with a date. I don't know. It just seems...funny."

Sadly for Miranda, that was true.

As much as he hated to, he hit his intercom to his assistant, "Find me CIA Director of Special Projects Clarissa Reese. Give her an *official* escort to my office."

"Sir?" His assistant clearly remembered how much trouble the woman could be.

"No cuffs. But get her here." He disconnected.

"Do you think she'll cooperate?" Lizzy's questions weren't always the most comfortable.

"No, probably not. Does that mean that we need Director Clark Winston as well?"

"Might help keep her in line."

Drake sighed and picked up the phone to place the call.

"Do you think she likes missile-fried beef as well? I mean, since you're already inviting her date."

He hung up the phone without calling.

Drake really should have retired while he still had a chance.

Unless...

"Come on, Lizzy. We're going back to the White House Situation Room. There's more than one way to control the renegade."

"Here she'd assume she's under attack. There she might think she was called in to help," Lizzy nodded her agreement.

He notified his assistant of the change of plans, to notify Ms. Chase's escort and call for his car to meet them in forty-five minutes.

"You going to come along, Lizzy?"

"Wouldn't miss it for the world, General Nason."

He sighed. If only he could.

59

DAEMON HAD DECIDED TO SCRATCH THE ITCH WITH HAGGADOR
II.

And things were just getting good.

He and her avatar, a harpy of sensuous female with an eagle's wings and talons, were helping the Mongols shred the Chinese at the Great Wall. There really was nothing like a good pillage to stir up the hormones. She was just about to have a mid-battle tryst with a remarkably virile Kublai Kahn —whose avatar looked like a pumped-up Leonardo DiCaprio—when a whole cascade of alarms went off.

She flipped out of the sim to see what they were...

And completely forgot about the Mongol hordes.

ACH, DAVIS, SYR, GM3, even DMZ had all been opened on the Cray XC50.

That was seriously bad. No one should have even looked for them.

And they'd been deleted.

There had to be some other backup running that she'd missed.

Shit! The supercomputer had a massive memory cache to service repeated access of information more quickly. She'd deleted the original commands and the backups, but she hadn't thought to flush the cache.

Even now, someone was scrabbling down into time stamps and user signatures—not that they'd find anything, she wasn't that sloppy.

But no one should even be looking. Especially not this fast.

Haggador II pinged her.

She shut him down.

He pinged again.

She blocked his address.

He could walk around that easily enough—Haggador was good enough—but he didn't.

Didn't matter.

Daemon stared at the screen and thought back to when the trouble had begun.

That A-10 Thunderbolt II that should have died at Davis-Monthan. Then that stupid helicopter dropping it should have been enough.

But it wasn't. It hadn't returned to base; it had been called back to the crash site for inspection.

That had meant she'd had to destroy the helo.

Whoever had investigated the Davis-Monthan incidents was apparently now at Eglin prowling through her computer code. Code that was supposed to have been erased.

Oh well, no use beating herself up about the past.

Who had called back a helicopter that should have been forgotten? Or flew to Eglin?

She didn't like anomaly. Anomalies...

Two of them.

What if it was a pattern?

It took almost an hour to find it...

An F-86 Sabrejet had arrived at Davis-Monthan. Then from there to Eglin Air Force Base in the exact time window between the helo crash and the folder pings.

And now...

It was approaching Washington, DC.

Well, clearly the folks in DC needed a distraction.

Too bad an F-86 was so primitive. It limited her options from doing something truly spectacular.

60

HARRY AND HEIDI WERE SET UP IN A SMALL, AND VERY SECURE CIA conference room at two facing terminals.

"Nothing here, Wizard Boy."

"Nothing here, Witchy Lady." But he knew that patience was the key to this game.

Well, the first key.

He hoped.

Between them they'd gotten a glimpse of Daemon's trail a few hours ago. A query had come in, dipping toward that protection code that Heidi had discovered wrapped around Clarissa Reese's name.

Per agreement, Heidi had slow-hacked Daemon—fast enough to keep her moving, but not so fast as to make her cut and run—while he'd unleashed a suite of tracking tools to race ahead. They'd gotten a clear footprint.

"Same structure as Reese's protection," Heidi had gasped out.

As close as you got to a positive ID in the Black Hat world.

When Harry had gotten mired in the Crimean nightmare of anonymous directories and failed passwords, Heidi had leapfrogged to look for what came out the back of the snarl.

The instant the hacker had emerged, Harry had abandoned the trap and they'd both chased her back through a satellite broadcasting station.

But there was no way past the destabilized sat.

"That was a brilliant move."

"Major," Heidi agreed.

Their boss had hired the craziest Black Hatter of them all to make her protection code. Then she'd brought Daemon on board for this project.

Whatever the hell it was.

For now they could only wait and watch...and watch.

And watch.

And...

A new packet arrived for insertion into the AFAMS computer.

Only after he watched it slip in did he connect the two.

The packets that had been dropping through the backdoor must be part of whatever the hell Reese had hired Daemon to do.

"Oh shit."

61

JEREMY HAD BEEN DELVING INTO THE XC50 FROM ONE OF THE sys admin consoles since the moment Miranda had rushed out of the room.

Lt. Colonel Kiley had called in the lead programmer and together they'd taken apart each event Miranda had initially identified.

Jeremy's stomach clenched hard. And then it started to *really* tighten up.

It was a world he used to live in. And one he'd almost ruined his parents' careers in.

He'd played a lot of shooter-games for Mom. He'd been the first beta-tester on a lot of versions of *Halo*. Because he knew the code, he could even usually tell her roughly where the problem was.

But on Dad's *Flight Simulator,* he didn't play—that's where he learned how to code. All the way down. And he'd leveraged that for hacks—and his dad's secure login—out into some strange chunks of cyberspace that were very, very classified. Today wasn't his first time in a top-secret supercomputer.

But at eighteen, he'd been cocky and stupid—and triggered a whole series of alarms. The only thing that had saved him was all of the Air Force's anti-attack code at that time was outward facing. It had all gone looking outward for the origin of the attack rather than sitting right there inside the firewall.

He'd come from inside, right up the developer's pipeline from Microsoft down to the Air Force Combat Command's main computer.

If he'd been caught, Dad's top secret clearance would have been stripped. Guaranteed that he and Mom would have been fired and Sis' first internship would have been canceled.

He'd just turned eighteen and would have been tried as an adult.

Thank God no one had caught him.

When they'd installed the XC50, had anything been preserved from...

Oh man! There it was. He'd left a hidden folder of code, thinking he'd come back for it someday.

Right there!

Like a grenade waiting to land at his feet before it exploded his life, then his entire family's lives.

Jeremy didn't want anything to do with any of it.

Shut it down.

Erase it.

Set a real grenade off *inside* the computer.

But it would be backed up.

Maybe he could excise it without anyone noticing.

There'd been a worm in that toolkit. It wouldn't take much to make it hunt itself and its brethren that Jeremy had dropped in there so long ago.

If he could burn it out here, then find where the backups were... He had access to at least one, the cache where he'd found the deleted simulator logs.

He'd wipe it from in there as well. Then maybe he could poke around and—

A hand grabbed his shoulder and Jeremy's nerves did everything in their power to leap out of his skin.

62

"What's going on?"

"Shit, Holly! Don't do that!" Jeremy looked around, but no one else was paying any attention to them.

"You're looking mighty freaked, young Padawan."

Great! Now he was a junior Jedi knight. But he'd watched *Star Wars: Revenge of the Sith.* Anakin Skywalker consumed by the dark side of the Force until he'd become Darth Vader destroying friends, family, everyone who mattered, then—

"Hey! Jeremy!" Holly shook his shoulder. "Breathe, goddamn it. Breathe!"

"I don't want to go back to the dark side." He'd been there. Gone there voluntarily. Gleefully disregarding all consequences. Almost been ensnared and almost ruined his family.

"What?"

"The light side. I chose the light side of the Force. Years ago." He was babbling but couldn't stop it.

"Yeah, and the Force is powerful. Now what the hell are

you talking about?" She kept her hand firmly on his shoulder, but more as if to keep him from exploding than anything else. Keeping the pin in the grenade—barely.

He looked back at the screen. It was there. He could see it. Hundreds, thousands of hours of work. Powerful hacker code. Probably massively outdated now, but there. Staring at him.

Highlighting the whole folder, he tapped in the command for a complete scrub delete. And hit Execute.

No alarms went off.

"Jeremy." Holly's voice was an irritated growl.

"I don't want to mess up Miranda."

"Good thing or I might have to beat on you. What did you just do?"

"Erased my past. I hope." Or at least the evidence of it.

"What are—"

He faced her and whispered quickly. "I was Anakin becoming Darth. Years ago. Black Hat hacker. That's some of my code. If anyone ever finds it, traces it back to Dad, or to me and links me to Miranda... I'll just... I'll just die."

Holly didn't look away. She didn't look angry.

"Is it really in your past, Jeremy? Are you truly done with it?" Holly leaned in so close that all he could see was the intense blue of her narrowed eyes.

He could only nod.

"Is that all of it?"

He forced himself to look at the screen.

Supercomputer data was typically too big to store to any fixed media anymore. Now it was simply stored on another, slower computer.

Slowly, feeling his way through the darkness, he found a

second local backup, one in Orlando, and one more in an archive in Fort Knox—where there was a lot less gold than there used to be, but a lot more computers.

"Wipe it all."

He did. "You're not going to tell? Please don't tell Miranda."

"Cross my throat and hope to die," she made a severe chopping motion at her throat.

So over dramatic that it almost made him laugh, but he didn't because he was afraid he might cry instead.

"One thing."

"Uh-huh," he said cautiously.

"Now you've got to go in and use those same skills to help Miranda."

She was right. He hated it. It was like his Dark Force palm prints were all over the insides of this computer just waiting to be found. And if they were... If somehow they were traced back to him, it would bring disaster.

"So, let's go through the remaining events."

"Okay, I can do this." *He could do this.*

It was hard to put his fingers back on the keyboard, but he slowly found the rhythm again. He began with the simulation playback file that Miranda had skipped over before her departure.

They watched it together.

When Holly shook her head, he struck it from the list. Yeah, something about the feel of it was wrong. The next was obviously just a pure simulation...an uneventful one at that. With Holly's approval, they were soon down to a core of six events.

There was a footprint to them—well, to five of them. A

footprint he recognized from the Black Box code he'd copied from the CH-47F Chinook helicopter seconds before it blew up.

The sixth one hadn't involved a crash.

Instead, it was a solo simulated flight by a Lieutenant William Blake. He was in the simulator even now reworking the Syrian scenario over and over again.

Jeremy had finally moved it into the "unlikely" pile.

He glanced at the clock.

Fifty-six minutes had passed. Scrubbing his old codes and analyzing the rest of the scenarios had taken a lot of time. Miranda would be in DC soon.

He began delving into how the Gulf of Mexico scenario had been run through the computer using real aircraft and a compilation of real and simulator piloting. The code to that was far beyond anything he'd ever done.

He was showing it to the lead programmer. It was *way* out of that guy's league and Jeremy had to do a lot of explaining, which helped him get the full structure of it in his head.

It was truly an elegant hac—

Jeremy spotted a new item just entering the Command stack.

63

THE FILTER FOR A-10 SIMULATIONS WOULDN'T HAVE grabbed it.

But the system administrator for the Cray XC50 had placed an alarm on any new data coming through the firewall from a non-US Air Force source.

This program had tripped that alarm.

Jeremy grabbed a copy and plugged it into an isolated simulation environment so that he could run it without interfering with the computer's normal operations.

The XC50 loaded up the scenario on his station.

No unusual weather settings.

Clear air space—busy but nothing dangerously close.

Just like Miranda approaching a wreck, he approached the simulation in spheres from outer to inner layers. Following her methodologies had been a big part of his climb to the light side of the Force.

The simulation environment—a brightly lit airport not far ahead.

Ronald Reagan Washington National Airport in DC.

Then he glanced down and saw the simulated aircraft console.

He knew it right away.

It was—

"Holly!"

His scream made everyone in the room jump.

"I need a radio. Now!"

Too late! He was too late!

The dark side was here!

64

GUIDING THE SABREJET INTO A LONG FINAL AT DC's REAGAN
National airport was easy. But after her third long flight on
an already very full day, Miranda focused on being
particularly careful.

The approach path was sandwiched in between
Arlington, Virginia, and the P-56A Prohibited Airspace over
downtown Washington, DC. All traffic slithered along—
flying southeast directly over the Potomac—making it one of
the busiest aircraft corridors in the nation.

General Drake had arranged a landing window at
Reagan National for her, despite the late notice of her flight,
as the airport was just a mile from the Pentagon.

She was on a three-mile final, second in line to land after
a United Express Embraer ERJ145 fifty-passenger jet.

The Pentagon was two miles straight ahead. The
National Mall of downtown DC stretched off to her left,
marked at this end by the prominently lit Lincoln Memorial.

She dropped from twelve hundred feet to nine hundred

at the Georgetown Reservoir. At Key Bridge from nine hundred to five hundred.

And then everything went haywire.

Her radios and NAV computer scrolled random frequencies.

Then they all turned off.

The Fuel Pressure gauge dropped to zero.

Miranda switched on the emergency fuel system, but nothing changed.

Her instincts had her attempting to transmit to the tower, but her radios were out.

She tried turning the radios on again.

Nothing.

Breakers were all in.

She drew parallel with the northern edge of the P-56A Prohibited Airspace zone.

Entering there was asking to be shot down.

Even as she watched, the temperature of her fuel-starved engine plummeted.

The altimeter showed her falling through four hundred feet.

Her ejection seat was good only above a thousand.

Time slowed strangely.

For an endless moment she was seated beside her parents in Flight TWA 800.

It was after the fuel-tank explosion had ripped the plane in two and their nose section was tumbling in its long, eighty-three-second fall toward the Atlantic Ocean off the Long Island Shore.

Mom in Seat 2A. Perhaps holding hands with Dad in 2B just as they had so often in life.

It felt as if she could look across the aisle and see them to her left from Seat 2D—not from the cockpit of a fighter jet built twenty years before the 747 that had killed her parents.

She didn't have the glide to reach Reagan Airport.

Even as her hands worked to restore the fuel system and restart the engine, she knew it was futile. As futile as yanking the ejection handles at the end of her chair's arms.

She really should have gotten the upgrade.

Her father smiled at her in that way he always did after hours of code work had proved to be yet another futile attempt to break a cipher.

"Only has to work once, sweetheart," he always told her. "Start again."

No engine restart so no airport.

No safe ejection.

Landing in the Potomac wasn't going to be survivable, even if she could miss all of the bridges.

Through her father's imagined visage, Miranda saw Lincoln sitting there, much as Sam Chase would have been. Calm. Upright. The rock of her childhood—shattered when she was thirteen.

She passed him by. The back of Lincoln's memorial. A long row of columns shining in the night.

Two-fifty and falling.

And right there...

A chance...

A chance to start again.

65

Very quietly, so quietly that Harry didn't even dare speak aloud to tell Heidi what he was doing, he watched the auto-launch of the tracer he'd built years ago. The same tracer that a young Wizard Boy had used to locate Witchy Lady as the attacker on the Shanghai Stock Exchange.

He'd never brought it inside the CIA firewall. It was as if that was the one true proof of who he was before the wild jungle of national security had swept him up. His one proof that Wizard Boy still existed in some form.

It was the finest block of code he'd ever written. It sucked to know that in some ways he'd peaked when he was seventeen, but he'd always loved it. It had taken him a year to build his "Missile In Cool Kode Extra Yowza!" Another year waiting for the right test.

He probably could have come up with a cooler name: Super Hydra, Multi-fanged Terror...something.

Seventeen-year-old Harry Tallman had called it Mickey and the mouse's name had stuck for him.

No one knew about it.

Partly because he'd only used it that one time to find Heidi. But even she never knew what had caught her.

Mickey wasn't just fast, it was also extremely stealthy.

It launched where he'd tucked it away, a low-security Netflix server. He'd chosen a frame used for storing old Jimmy Stewart movies, as it had pretty low traffic, which meant that most of the server's bandwidth was his.

Mickey would only need it for less than a minute, but every Jimmy Stewart movie streaming south of the Mason-Dixon line was going to be hit with the spinning loading symbol. In a race where milliseconds counted, Jimmy's "Well, I don't rightly know about that" drawl was going to take even longer than usual.

It fired out from the IXP's server farm in Atlanta, GA. As it flew, it called other elements of itself from nineteen other servers within the US alone—thirty-three more worldwide. That's what made it impossible to trace, and so fast. It went from nothing to everywhere as part of its launch.

Mickey punched through the gap he'd pre-built in the CIA's firewall—precisely one Mickey wide—without even slowing.

High-bandwidth fiber from here to Eglin and in through that gap that he'd pried open for Reese.

Latching onto the object that had just dropped into the Air Force Cray XC50, the trace started running backward along the object's load path.

Like a MIRV—a multiple independent reentry vehicle nuclear warhead that could bomb twenty cities at once—Mickey appeared from every direction at once, and attacked.

66

"Won't you get that, dear?"

Hunter headed for the suite's door. Dinner was finally here. He didn't want any more surprises tonight and maybe food would stop the flow of unnerving revelations.

Clarissa Reese might be insanely dangerous.

She might even be insane.

But if so, she was brilliantly insane.

Hashing out a mutual trust between the three of them had been tricky. Clarissa and Rose had appeared to like each other—and appeared ready to fight just to see who won.

That was Hunter's strength in committee. He could always get different groups aligned and he thought they were close now.

Opening the door, he started with, "You can just use the..." But he never got to mentioning the table. Didn't even complete the gesture toward the suite's mahogany dining set.

Two US Army sergeants were standing at the door. At

least they were in dress uniform rather than battle fatigues, but they were definitely both armed.

Not just sergeants. Sergeants with 75th Ranger Regiment badges above their stripes, tan berets, and an impressive array of combat metal on their chests.

Oh god. I'm screwed.

The A-10 replacement operation was the riskiest undertaking he'd ever made in thirty years in office.

Now it was blown.

They found me.

They were going to string him out to dry in front of the whole senate. Trials. Jail. *Media!*

Maybe he could—somehow—just put on a brave face and get through this?

"Can I," Hunter had to swallow hard...twice against a scratchily dry throat, "assist you gentlemen?"

Clarissa and Rose were out of sight behind the half-open door.

"We're looking for CIA Director of Special Projects Clarissa Reese," one of them announced formally.

Oh, thank God!

This wasn't about him.

"It's for you, Clar—" time for a little distance, "Ms. Reese."

She rose from her seat and came to the door. Clarissa wore austere like a second skin. It was the one look that Rose could never pull off. Sexy, powerful, friendly, charming...but his sweet Rose didn't have austere anywhere in her system.

"Yes?" Her voice was less steady than she'd like to pretend.

"We've been asked to escort you to a meeting. We would appreciate it if you'd come with us."

"Well, that's a fair amount more civil than last time," her voice had a mean edge.

The two sergeants didn't look at each other and their tone matched their words, "We wouldn't know anything about that, ma'am." But Hunter was close enough to see that they were hard pressed not to laugh.

He recalled the scene just a few months ago. A team of Rangers carting Clarissa off the Georgetown streets with her wrists locked in plastic zip ties. It had been nationally televised—he'd kept it on the DVR for quite a while for whenever he needed a laugh.

He didn't feel like laughing right now.

Hunter was now in bed with Clarissa in every way except physically, far too deep to back out cleanly if she went down for something.

"Where's this meeting?" Her voice had none of the smoothing tones that Rose could use to calm down any situation.

"At the White House, ma'am."

"Oh, well that's fine then."

Hunter could only look at her in surprise.

"Clark mentioned something but didn't know the specifics yet."

Hunter inspected the two US 75th Rangers standing outside the Presidential Suite's door at the Kimpton George and guessed that this had nothing to do with CIA Director Clark Winston.

67

"Are you sure that we need her?"

Drake drummed his fingers on the console folded down between their seats as the driver crossed the Arlington Bridge. He'd left the Sit Room shortly after the DMZ-Japan fiasco this evening to work from the Pentagon. Now, past ten p.m. he was headed back to the White House.

"Yes, Lizzy. I'm sure. If Reese isn't involved, she'll know how to get us the answers."

"And if she's already involved?"

"Then she'll already have the answers and we just need to beat them out of her stubborn hide."

"I love when you get all stern and soldierly." Her tone was definitely mocking him.

"Hey, they didn't make me CJCS just because I look good in a uniform."

"You do look *very* good in a uniform, Drake."

"So do you, Lizzy."

"What do you say, once this is over, we see how we look out of our uniforms?"

Drake struggled for his next breath. They had taught him a lot of things during his forty years serving in the military. But they'd taught him *nothing* about how to field such a question.

His driver was watching him in the rearview.

"Eyes front, Lamont."

"Yes sir. Can't help having ears though, sir. Just saying. Lady says something like that, a man oughta answer right quick."

"Go to hell, Sergeant Lamont."

"Quite likely, sir."

Drake turned to Lizzy, who was watching him with that patient thing she did: eyebrows slightly raised, no readable expression.

"I'd like that a lot."

"Good for you, sir."

"You're still here, Lamont." But he didn't look away from Lizzy's smile either.

"Sorry, sir. Hell didn't have no openings for a sweet guy like me."

Drake ignored him.

Then just over Lizzy's shoulder, he saw a flash of silver.

A small jet, descending fast beneath the Arlington Bridge off-ramp into DC and the Lincoln Memorial.

Not following the river, but headed straight into DC where no jet should ever be.

It was unique.

"Lamont! Follow that jet!"

Lizzy twisted around, but missed it as it slipped below the trees.

Lamont hadn't.

Though he'd already taken the right-hand off-ramp that would take them under the bridge and north toward the White House, Lamont turned sharply left.

He shot through a narrow crosswalk under the trees.

A hundred feet later he twisted right onto 23rd Street Southwest and, with a hard squeal of tires, managed to miss a late-night bus by half a car-length.

At Independence Avenue he turned sharply east and put the accelerator to the floor.

The jet was out of sight behind a line of trees but Lamont drove like he was in a race with it.

Drake was glad that he hadn't gone to hell. He was the best driver Drake had ever had.

68

MIRANDA RECALLED THAT THE REFLECTING POOL WAS ONLY two thousand feet long—the same length that her runway on Spieden Island had been.

Had been, because she'd had to extend it by half again to safely land the F-86 Sabrejet once it was given to her. Then more than that, in order to take off again.

Nothing was working right.

Time to trade maximum glide slope for minimum landing speed.

At a hundred and eighty knots, she extended the speed brakes and the flaps.

Then the battery failed.

Or switched out of the circuit.

She tried the Alternate Power switch with no luck.

Lowering the gear wasn't happening.

She could try for a belly landing. But just this morning, Colonel Campos—with far more experience than she had—

had chosen to eject a second time rather than ride his plane all the way down.

Miranda yanked on the Gear Emergency Release lever and held it for several seconds.

She heard the two clunks as gravity pulled down the main gear.

Unable to hear or feel the nose gear lock, fired down by a one-time hydraulic pressure accumulator, she could only hope that it was in place.

The Reflecting Pool was now a stretch of darkness off to her left. The row of trees to either side were lit from below. The lights beneath the southern trees illuminated the grass field she was targeting.

Empty.

That had been her one fear, but there was no event there tonight so the field was all hers.

Think like a space shuttle.

Think like a space shuttle.

They do their atmospheric braking by putting their belly into the wind, using most of the surface area as an air brake.

There was no peep from a stall indicator as she raised the nose higher and higher for air braking. No electricity to make it peep.

The F-86 Sabrejet was *very* unforgiving in a stall, but she held it on the edge of the buffet zone for as long as she dared.

Lincoln Memorial on her left.

A flash of asphalt and upturned faces of late-night tourists along Lincoln Memorial Circle where thousands had gathered for so many different events.

How many would see her die if she couldn't make this work?

Past the last walkway and out of time—her airspeed down to a minimal hundred and twenty knots—she sank toward the grass field along the south side of the Reflecting Pool...

Impact!

She fought her instincts to reach for the ejection handles. That was a near certain death warrant.

The main gear held.

No time for more air braking.

She nudged the joystick forward and the nose dropped.

The nose gear clanged loudly against the piston stop on the oleo strut. The hard impact slammed her against her harness.

But the strut didn't fold.

The wheel didn't catch in the rough ground.

Brakes.

Brakes.

More brakes.

She was down under a hundred knots when she reached the JFK Hockey Fields. She'd seen one of the last major Field Hockey Tournaments there in 2003 while training at the NTSB Training Center.

No war or presidential memorials had been built over the three fields yet—still just swathes of grass, hard with the chilly November.

Three field lengths and she was down under fifty.

But the grass strip was running out.

The tall spire of the Washington Monument towered

ahead like a beacon, but a long line of trees that would tear her plane apart was coming up much faster.

At the last moment, she saw an out and veered right, still going forty knots.

She cleared the tree on the left, but clipped off the right wing-tip navigation light on the corner of the concrete restroom.

Across a sidewalk, off a curb with a hard bounce, and she was rolling the wrong way along a bus parking area that thankfully had no busses.

The F-86 Sabrejet finally ground to a halt less than ten feet from a pair of trees even her small, thirty-seven-foot wingspan wouldn't have fit between.

69

DRAKE HAD NEVER SEEN ANYTHING QUITE LIKE IT.

He was first to arrive at the downed Sabrejet, by only seconds.

It was eerie.

He was leaping out of the car even as the jet stopped, but it was completely silent. No noise of a winding-down engine. No noise of any kind.

Then, with a loud bang that made him duck for cover, the canopy slammed backward on its rails. Emergency canopy release.

There was nothing else, so he moved up closer to the plane.

He was pretty sure who the pilot was.

"Miranda?"

The pilot pulled off her helmet and looked down at him.

"Are you okay?"

"I need to order a new ejection seat."

"What happened that you landed here?"

As she climbed down, eight or ten police cars raced up with their lights and sirens going.

Officers piled out of their cars, weapons out and aimed.

Close behind them, four black Chevy Suburbans rolled up and disgorged black-suited Secret Service agents.

Drake stepped forward to calm them down—and all of the guns twitched to aim at him.

He froze.

Shouting out his name and rank didn't do any good, because no one could hear him as a pair of F-18 Hornet alert fighters flew by less than a hundred feet overhead.

By the time of their second pass—after a hard turn around the Washington Monument—a trio of Black Hawks arrived and out poured US Army Rangers and National Guard.

While the fire trucks, ambulance, and SWAT team arrived, he gave up and waited to see who would take charge so that Drake could talk to him.

Miranda looked around them. "Apparently they take Prohibited Airspace P-56A very seriously here." Drake could barely hear her over all the shouted orders and the hovering gunships.

"Yes, they do. So, why did you violate it?"

"Oh. Someone sabotaged my plane. In flight. Let's go find out who." And she just walked away from all of the armed personnel, headed for his car.

"But," he waved a hand at her plane straddling the bus lanes.

"Oh, I'm sorry I couldn't park it any better. They can

move it to the side, but it will need a mechanic to reset all systems and rearm the canopy release. I'll also need more fuel before I can take off again. I believe Independence Avenue doesn't have the runway length that I'll require, but Constitution Avenue from the Lincoln Memorial to the Ellipse should do nicely."

"That's not gonna happen."

She looked up at him as if he was the one not making any sense.

The head of the Secret Service team had apparently decided he was the one in charge. He made it halfway to Drake before recognizing him and calling for everyone to stand down.

Meanwhile, Miranda slipped into his car. In the slowly descending silence, he could hear her say, "Oh, hi, Lizzy. What do you think about the technology necessary to cause an F-86 Sabrejet to—"

Within minutes, he had organized everyone and come up with a plan to deal with Miranda's jet—at least for now.

Drake stood outside his car and watched over a hundred servicemen and women, First Responders, gunships, Secret Service, and a fully activated SWAT team, trying to shift gears away from terrorist attack.

He waited to make sure they got it.

But what to actually do about Miranda's jet?

Take off along Constitution Avenue? Fly right past the White House in a fighter jet? Not a chance that was going to happen.

He'd be damned if he knew how to explain it to her or everyone now facing him.

A pair of television vans rolled up. Reporters jumped out and the vans began extending those big rebroadcast roof antennas that the major setups carried. Time for him to get out of there.

"I'm betting," Lamont said by his elbow, "that telling them all to go to hell wouldn't be the best choice?"

70

"TOLD YOU SHE'D BE FINE."

Holly had said no such thing, but Jeremy was too relieved to complain. If she hadn't been sitting there, he might have broken down and wept with relief.

He'd followed every step of the simulation on the screen as it took over Miranda's jet and he'd been helpless to stop it.

But she'd done it. Miranda was so amazing that she'd saved the Sabrejet despite no fuel and a complete systems failure.

Besides, Holly had switched into full-on soldier mode, ordering Kiley and the others to get information out of DC. Once Colonel Campos ordered the others to do what she said, chaos became a smooth chain of command...from Holly Harper.

"You'd have made a good officer," Mike teased her.

"Couldn't pay me enough, mate. I work for a living," Holly had answered before issuing a new slew of directions.

They'd started with radar, flight path tracking.

When the area P-56A perimeter alert was triggered, they soon had the alert fighter camera feeds going.

Moments later, the display screens had filled with feeds from DC police car cams, SWAT team shoulder cams, and ultimately several Black Hawk helicopter infrared feeds.

"See?" Holly's hand rested on his shoulder, but it didn't set off his alarm flags.

It was comforting.

With her other hand, she tapped the screen showing a heat image of someone climbing out of the Sabrejet's cockpit. "That's her. She's fine."

After reassuring himself that she was indeed okay, Jeremy reran the radar feed that show her landing.

Mike whistled an impressed sound.

Lt. Colonel Kiley harrumphed, "Whatever assholes were keeping women out of combat flight for so long never saw that kind of a landing. Textbook says that wouldn't work."

"Now," Holly sat down beside him and Jeremy felt he could finally think again. "What alerted you and how do we find out what happened?"

71

DAEMON CONSIDERED KICKING THE SHIT OUT OF HER television.

What it was showing was just so damn *wrong!*

Hi-res, full-color, with running commentary—it was breaking news on a dozen different channels.

"Korean War fighter jet attacks White House" was far from the most lurid or inaccurate.

Some enterprising producer tapped the EarthCam at the top of the Washington Monument, then highlighted the Sabrejet from the moment it came into view.

Daemon could see it stumble in the sky.

It lost altitude abruptly as the engine power had failed.

It wavered as the pilot fought to restart all the things Daemon had made sure wouldn't restart.

Then, less than a hundred feet left to fall before it plummeted into the Potomac, it carved a hard turn straight toward the camera high atop the Washington Monument.

For an instant, Daemon thought it might plow into the back of the Lincoln Memorial, which would have been cool.

Or maybe plunge into the Reflecting Pool, which had a certain awesomeness.

No such luck.

Instead, it flared and straightened out at the last second and landed on the grass.

What was up with that?

The plane was too old. It hadn't had enough electronics for her to sabotage. No fly-by-wire. No munitions aboard. Nothing.

Still, she'd taken out enough systems through the lame radio and targeting computers that it should have gone down.

Whoever the pilot was, they would definitely be a problem.

One of her alarms beeped. Something had probed her outer defenses.

She checked, but it was just some search engine's robot spider indexing the Internet.

Nothing here, junior.

Her defenses automatically delivered some nonsense about a law firm promising you top dollar for your accident claim, "Just call 1-202-456-1414." She hoped the White House switchboard enjoyed fielding those calls.

Daemon replayed the code that had triggered the alarm, but still didn't see anything strange in it.

Still, the itch told her it was time to get moving.

Had Mum listened to that itch and just been too slow? Or had she not heard it at all?

Didn't matter, she'd been too late.

All Daemon knew at first was that Mum's superuser password had suddenly popped up on her phone. A final gift from hacker-mom to hacker-daughter.

Turned out Mum's Delta flight out of Tel Aviv had been delayed at the gate. Mossad tried to grab her. Very bad people to be grabbed by.

Emergency exit had been a good play, Mum always sat right over the wing for that reason. Sliding down the front of the wing instead of the back had been a bad choice, as the engine was already spun up. She'd dodged around a baggage handler and gotten too close to the engine.

No more Mum, except a bloody splatter out the back.

Daemon wouldn't be caught loafing around.

She'd deliver this one last thing for Client F, then climb on the plane he'd left at her disposal and get the hell out of OK City, the US, maybe even the Western Hemisphere. She hadn't done anything in Macau for a while. That could be fun.

72

Harry had finally called over Heidi to watch what Mickey was doing.

"Oh my god, Wizard Boy," Heidi had whispered once she understood what it was doing. "That is sooo sexy! Is that how you found me?"

He could only nod.

She grabbed his face, turned him from the screen, and kissed him really, really hard.

Then, as she rested her head on his shoulder and held his hand, they turned to watch Mickey sneak along as quiet as a mouse.

Its work had only begun.

Now it called up his MiNi code—Miniature Nibbler. MiNi was designed to map the edges of influence by a programmer independent of IP addresses (because they were too easy to spoof or mask), multi-terminals (because of course you'd do that), or any of a dozen other masking techniques.

MiNi was only interested in two things: programmer's signature (their style in the code), and their actual electronic and physical location.

"Oh," Heidi gasped out a happy sigh and put her free hand over her heart as MiNi moved in, "Happy as two mice together."

73

"WHAT IN THE *HELL* WAS I DOING IN THE PEOC?" PRESIDENT Cole roared into the Situation Room. He was beyond furious.

Drake considered hiding under the table. Not seemly for a four-star general, but he considered it.

Lizzy's tiny bit of squint said that she knew all too well what he was thinking.

It was typically a prelude to possible war that caused a forced evacuation of the President into the underground Presidential Emergency Operations Center. Not a straying NTSB investigator. Especially not one invited to DC by the CJCS.

"The old one under the North Portico or the new one next to the West Wing?" Miranda asked completely calmly.

"The new one under..." Cole sputtered to a halt. "Who the hell are you and what are you doing in my Sit Room?"

"Listening to you at the moment."

Drake watched Cole, but he was looking just as confused by Miranda Chase as Drake always was.

"To your other question: my name is Miranda Chase. I'm an investigator for the NTSB."

"The NTSB? The National Transportation Safety Board? That one? Was there a crash in my Sit Room?"

"Yes. Yes. Yes. And no," Miranda replied without even blinking.

To Cole's credit, he didn't have to pause to reconnect the answers to the questions. "Oh my god. You're the one they shot up a house over. The one in Georgetown."

"No sir, Mr. President. They blew up a front door, kicked down a bathroom door and a gate in that order, and tore off a rain gutter. There was no shooting."

Cole looked at him and Drake waited.

"I'm told there was an invasion of DC's airspace," the President finally ventured.

"Yes sir. My plane was sabotaged while I was on short final into Ronald Reagan National Airport. I really need to purchase a new ejection seat."

"Why is that? Didn't yours work?"

"It's the original model, sir. Technically rated to a hundred meters, but practically it's unsafe below three hundred meters. My plane was sabotaged at an altitude of less than a hundred and fifty. It seemed that my presence was important to General Drake's ongoing investigation, so I thought it would be better to land at the Lincoln Memorial rather than die in the Potomac."

Cole blinked at her. "You landed by the Lincoln Memorial? Like that Cessna 172 that flew into Russia and landed at the Kremlin?"

"No sir. Like an F-86 Sabrejet fighter aircraft on the JFK Hockey Fields. Apparently some people found this alarming. Do you wish to keep discussing this or would you rather I return to pursuing why you've lost nine A-10 Thunderbolt II jet fighters in the last twenty-three hours, and will be losing one or more in…" Miranda checked her watch despite the row of red-LED clocks clearly labeled by their time zones: Eastern, President (which matched at the moment as he was in DC), London, Moscow, and Beijing. "… fifty-seven minutes."

Cole dropped into his chair and waved a hand helplessly for them to proceed.

Drake knew exactly how he felt.

74

Clarissa's escort stopped at the lobby entry door.

She went to turn for the Navy Mess. It seemed likely that Clark would meet her there, though she'd been hoping for the Presidential Dining Room by the Oval Office.

They redirected her to the Situation Room entrance through the adjacent door.

Not a social gathering—though nothing was ever just social in DC politics. She was going to be in a *real* meeting.

Yes! She'd been right to accelerate Clark's nomination to the Vice Presidency. Things were happening fast.

Per usual Situation Room protocol, she left her coat, purse, and cell phone at security before entering. The Sit Room always surprised her. A conference table for ten people, and barely enough room for chairs lining the wall. Four large monitor screens on the far wall, and not much else to recommend it. Always dark and mysterious in movies, she was always surprised at how corporate and beige it was in real life.

Two steps into the room, she hooked a heel and almost fell flat on her face.

She'd expected President Cole and Clark to be waiting for her.

Except there was no Clark.

Instead, that awful Miranda Chase woman was there with goddamn General Drake Nason. She only vaguely remembered the Eurasian woman in the general's uniform... Gray. Elizabeth Gray. Newly promoted to head up the National Reconnaissance Office.

Perhaps they needed her help on... Clarissa couldn't think of a thing.

"Now we're all here, we can begin," Nason announced. "Though didn't you need to be somewhere else, Mr. President?"

"No more interesting than this. Please proceed, Ms. Chase."

"As I had already mentioned, you've lost nine A-10s. At least eight of those are clearly sabotage and—"

"Sabotage?" Clarissa's knees went soft and the last stage of sitting in a chair didn't go smoothly.

This *was* about the A-10s.

And no one, but no one was supposed to know that it was sabotage.

How the *hell* had this weasel of a woman gotten in the middle of one of her projects again?

Then Clarissa realized that she'd started in exactly the right place to gain deniability. "Wait? What? The A-10—like the big highway north out of London? I presume we're not talking about that."

"Yes, you can presume that," Miranda replied in that flat,

sexless voice of hers. She was the most unreadable woman Clarissa had ever encountered.

She nodded for Chase to continue.

Clarissa was going to kill that hacker if she ever laid her hands on him.

Her.

It...

Whoever.

They were going down hard. She didn't care that Client F had done all the hiring, and it had been her recommendation. Clarissa was going to beat Client F's identity out of Ramson, follow the link to that hacker, and absolutely commit some murder.

"I can only assume that the saboteur is the same one who attacked my plane," Miranda was rambling on.

"You were attacked?" Maybe she'd shake the hacker's hand before she cut it off. Or maybe not. Miranda Chase was still alive after all.

Miranda's look either said that she didn't like repeating things or that Clarissa should go straight to hell.

"There have been a series of cyberattacks: either originating in or reported through the Cray XC50 supercomputer at the US Air Force Agency for Modeling and Simulation's branch at Eglin Air Force Base."

As if on cue, a phone rang in the room.

Clarissa spotted Drake Nason's quick glance at President Cole.

"Your meeting, Drake," Cole waved for him to answer it. "I'm just slumming."

Clarissa had started to think she'd dodged a bullet with

Cole in charge. But with Nason running it, she was suddenly much less sure.

He punched the speakerphone, "Nason here. You're on speaker."

Before he'd even finished the sentence an over-excited young male's voice sounded from the phone.

"Are you okay, Miranda?" He didn't wait for response before continuing. "We saw the code come into the XC50, but it was sent right back out. By the time I opened the code it was too late, you were already under attack."

Drake was watching Clarissa across the table, for reasons she couldn't fathom, as he asked, "Jeremy, I assume?"

"Yes sir. Is Miranda—"

"She's fine. She's right here with me. Were you able to trace the origin of the instruction?"

"Not very far, sir. It has an IP address of Tijuana, that's in Mexico."

"I know where it is, Jeremy."

"Right. But they aren't set up at all for a serious attack. I mean Tijuana just isn't a hotbed for computing infrastructure. So we looked at the prior inputs that Miranda identified as suspicious and they come from a wide variety of odd origins, but none within the US. That makes me guess they're somewhere in the US. Kind of a natural thing to do as a hacker. I mean, I think it would be. You know. If I knew about that kind of—"

A woman's voice, with a thick Australian accent cut him off. "That's all we know, sir."

"Okay, thank you, Jeremy. Holly. We'll be back in touch if we need anything."

"Okay. And, Miranda?" Jeremy was back. "Whoever is

doing this knows a lot about aircraft. Each attack has been different, leveraging a different aspect of the aircraft. We can presume from the reports coming out of Afghanistan that the plane was destroyed in midflight—perhaps an explosion. A mechanical override on Colonel Campos' plane. A miscalibration of GPS and inertial guidance in Korea, and two mixed simulation-reality scenarios."

Clarissa again found herself being impressed by the hacker she'd sent to Client F.

"The attack on my plane was hasty," Miranda finally spoke up. "The hacker didn't have time to study my plane sufficiently. Perhaps it was the age of my aircraft. There were any number of systems shut down, but I can think of several other choices that could have been made, which I would have been less likely to survive."

"Ms. Reese?" Nason turned to her.

Here it came. The attack. The accusations. If he uncovered that she was the one who—

"I know that your focus is legally overseas..."

Did Nason stress "legally" or was that her imagination?

"...but based on your prior experience with the MQ-45 Caspar drone, I was wondering if you had any insights? Or know of someone who might be able to help us quickly?"

"Especially as the CIA lost four drones in one of the scenarios," Miranda Chase added.

"The CIA lost what? And didn't see fit to report it?" Cole glared at her.

Nason and Gray clearly knew about it. Probably from Chase.

"I'm sorry, sir. It's not my department. I'll have Director Winston find out why it wasn't reported properly. However, I do have some people already investigating that. We don't know yet how it happened."

She needed to get away and collect herself. For half a moment she considered calling Rose Ramson for advice, but knew it was too soon for them to trust each other. She'd have to figure this out fast on her own.

"If I could perhaps place a secure call?"

Nason waved her toward one of the phone booths lined up outside the Situation Room, then turned to Miranda with some other question.

Clarissa hurried out into the white-carpeted hall. The three phone booths stood in a line. Circular, three feet across —not made for fat men, with a brass-trimmed curved plexiglass door that swung on a circular track. The booth included a small shelf and both standard and secure phones.

She selected the secure one and dialed.

75

"SHIT! IT'S T-X," HARRY PUNCHED THE CONFERENCE ROOM speaker. "Yes ma'am?"

"Why am I on speakerphone?" Reese's voice snapped out.

"I've been conferring with Heidi about my search for information on Senator Ramson. We aren't coming up with—"

"Forget about him. He's clean."

"Well mostly, but he also—"

"He's clean," Clarissa insisted. "Wipe anything you found on him. No, better yet, send it to me, then wipe it. I just met with him and he provided hints that the problem I was pursuing actually lies higher in the Senate Armed Services Committee. I will need everything you have on Senator Clint Howards of Arkansas."

Now she's after the chairman? Heidi mouthed at him.

Harry could only shrug. Nothing would surprise him.

"But first, there seems to be another problem that I need your assistance on."

Heidi looked at him in surprise at the sudden smooth-and-calm act that Terminatrix T-X Reese was putting on.

Told you, he mouthed at her.

Wild.

"What do you need, Ms. Reese?"

Heidi made a simpering little face at him.

"I need you to show a little spine, Mr. Tallman."

Heidi made a show of a big laugh, silently.

"You too, Ms. Geller," Reese snapped out, though Heidi hadn't made a sound.

Now it was his turn to laugh. But he stuck his tongue out at her instead.

"You know the passage that you opened through our systems into the simulations supercomputer at Eglin Air Force Base?"

All the humor of the moment died like *Alien*-monster acid dripping down from above.

"I know it."

"We're done with that. Close it. Erase it. It never existed. There's a bonus for you both if you can find out who completely overstepped their mandate. If you do, shut them down so hard that they'll never recover."

"Can we ask what they—"

"No. Just let me know when you've closed the hole and when the contractor is permanently silenced."

Harry tapped a quick string of keystrokes. "Hole's gone."

"Oh. Okay. Well, it pays to hire the best. Now go do what you do."

Harry tipped his head until his neck cracked audibly. He

raised his eyebrows to Heidi, who shrugged back. Then he stared at the information they'd both been watching Mickey and MiNi accumulate about Daemon.

"Um, They're domestic," Harry knew that much.

"On US soil," Heidi added. "The CIA's mandate is foreign only."

"Welcome to the games, Harry and Heidi. Just make sure they're never found here. Or anywhere else. Message me on my phone when it's done. Or in the Situation Room if I don't answer right away."

And the connection was gone.

"Welcome to the games?"

"Yeah," Heidi slumped. "First competition, swimming in shit."

"No, first competition is being better than Daemon when we take him or her on."

Now Heidi was the one trying to get a kink out of her neck.

76

"MY PEOPLE FOUND THE SECURITY GAP AND ARE CLOSING IT. IT seems they'd already picked up suspicious activity and were taking care of the situation." Clarissa sat back down at the Sit Room table, much calmer than she'd been before.

Yes, people. The CIA knows exactly *how to do the hard tasks.* Like chopping off the initiative that had included so much planning, effort, and money.

Convincing the establishment to finally mothball the A-10 Thunderbolt IIs in favor of thirty billion dollars' worth of F-35 Lightning IIs just wasn't going to happen this way. It was too bad. It would have meant an immense amount of money for Ramson and decades of ongoing foreign intelligence for her.

This effort had failed.

Time to pretend it never existed and move on.

"The source of the attack?" President Cole looked impressed. This could be turned into another point in favor with the President for the Clark-Clarissa team. So not a complete loss.

"They're working on it. It's coming off a Ukrainian server, but we think the origin is the Far East. I'll make sure that Clark has all of the final details for you as soon as we have them." Extra point nailed.

"China or Russia. We should take them both down," President Cole grumbled.

Now there was a mandate she could live with.

"Working on closing it," Miranda said quietly as if speaking to no one in an empty room.

"Yes. My people are very good." And she would reward them...if they got that hacker.

"*Working* on closing it," Miranda repeated. "I don't want to be investigating another A-10 crash in forty-eight minutes."

Clarissa was about to say that she wouldn't be. But that might expose her hand too much. Especially if she was wrong.

The hacker—who sometimes sounded like Madonna and sometimes like Michael Jackson—might not be stopped by the Wizard twins shutting off access. Reese had gone to a lot of trouble to hire the best—both in and out of house.

Thankfully, Client F had picked up the costs. No CIA money—traceable or not. He was a fixer, hence the F she assumed, for the US defense industry. Lockheed, Boeing, Raytheon, Northrop...maybe Thales out of France or BAE from the UK.

Clarissa didn't know or care who had hired him.

The demanded price from her and Ramson? Get the A-

10 Thunderbolt II out of service for the close air support role. Lockheed Martin and all of its subcontractors would benefit immensely if the A-10 was retired and replaced by the hundred-million-dollar F-35 Lightning IIs. Three hundred aircraft would make them thirty billion dollars.

Then there were the real monetary gains for them. An F-35 cost thirty thousand dollars per hour to fly versus the A-10's six thousand. And a lot of that money flowed back up the pipeline in terms of staff, parts, and expertise.

Yes, the client benefitted immensely.

But so did the military. It didn't cost five times as much per hour for the fun of it. The F-35 was a vastly newer and improved platform—even if all those soldiers and pilots said otherwise.

For her, the hunger to have the newest and "the best" was her leverage into so many foreign governments. It wasn't only the forty-three billion in cash that was generated by foreign military sales each year. The intelligence opportunities escalated directly with the cost per item and an F-35 Lightning II sale garnered far more information than a hundred million in tanks or rifles.

Ramson? No, they wouldn't have offered Ramson money, not directly. Ah, finance his campaigns for life.

It had been a sweet deal, but now it was gone. Or perhaps only gone for now. She'd think about different solutions later. She'd wager that Hunter and Rose might have some ideas on that.

The US Air Force brass had been unable to kill the old plane despite their four-year effort ending in shambles by 2017.

Congress had saved the plane.

And now, if the plan had worked, popular opinion was supposed to damn them for it.

But Miranda Chase had uncovered sabotage as the cause of the losses before anyone outside the military had even heard about the A-10 "failures" that were supposed to break the plane's popularity.

She sighed.

Definitely time to close off this effort.

The Wizard twins would find that damned hacker and shut them down. But would it be soon enough?

Everyone rose to their feet, and Clarissa scrambled to hers. She should have been paying closer attention.

President Cole stepped over to shake Miranda's hand. "Thank you for your fine work on this."

"My team did a lot of it, sir."

"Yes. Of course. Well, now that that's done, we can—"

"We don't know if it's done, Mr. President," Chase cut him off. "We need to move to the simulator and make sure nothing more happens while Director Reese's people are working on it."

"The hole is closed," Clarissa protested.

"And are we sure there isn't another?" Chase looked up at her, though her eyes seemed to be focused over Clarissa's left shoulder somewhere.

"My people are very good."

"I don't see how that's relevant. The saboteur is also very good or they wouldn't have had such a high success rate. What is relevant is that we don't definitively know."

Clarissa became aware of the others watching her. The CIA fulfilled a vital role and her people wouldn't fail.

But she gave the woman a nod that perhaps she was

right. There was a hideous thought—conceding anything to Miranda Chase was just so wrong.

But what if her people weren't good enough?

77

A HIGH-PRIORITY ALARM WENT OFF ON DAEMON'S ALERT system.

The pipeline through the CIA firewall into Eglin had just been closed.

The program that had closed it had come from inside the CIA. Her alarm had also done a screen-and-camera grab from the computer that had issued the command.

They'd closed her hole in, but her alarm code had already been inside Eglin and sent the message back out with perfect ease.

And there they were.

Wizard Boy and Witchy Lady finally had a face.

Weren't they just too cute for words, sitting side by side like that.

With a face and location, it only took moments before she had far more on them.

They'd gotten in her way for the last time.

Fixing them once and for all was going to be so much fun.

Another ping, this time from someone who had direct access to her, and those were few and far between. Well, as direct as anyone ever was allowed—a three-server bounce with two heavy firewalls.

From Haggador II. He'd come in around the block she'd thrown up before, which was kinda sweet. He was much more a gamer than a hacker, so it must have been hard for him. It meant he cared.

She opened the message.

"Want to come play?" His big avatar was bare-chested and sweaty.

"Busy now." Rather than her fierce Harpy, she sent back her semi-cat sylphlike avatar clothed only in soft fur, every sexy curve almost showing. It had taken a lot of work to make the fur flow naturally, sometimes stirred by a passing breeze.

"Ever in LA? Want to come play for real?" This time rather than his avatar, he sent an actual photo.

The same face as the avatar—hers wasn't. But it was a good face. And while his bare chest wasn't over-muscled Viking warrior, it was very, very acceptable.

"Maybe soon," she sent back a faked nudie of Taylor Swift...because Taylor's body seriously rocked. "I'll keep you posted."

And maybe she would.

Before playing with Haggador II, she needed to cut a new path into Eglin's supercomputer.

But first...

78

Harry groaned.

"Food. Must have food."

"And distance," Heidi agreed.

Time to clear their heads. Get out of the secure conference room in the goddamn CIA building's basement for half an hour, stoke up and chill for a bit. They'd have to be sharp to take on Daemon.

"Rocco's?"

Harry shook his head. It was the closest pizza place to the CIA's Langley headquarters—making it like spook central even if the pizza was first rate.

"Amoo's?"

He nodded. The kebabs were excellent and it was away from Langley's main restaurant cluster without being too far away. They had some serious work to do, so he didn't want to go far. To save time, Heidi called in their order to get it cooking. They always got the Combination III—Koobideh ground beef, Barg tenderloin beef, and saffron chicken with black cherry rice.

Heidi had been a New York City gal, and hadn't owned a car. His old second-generation Toyota Prius from Seattle had made her laugh at its practicality, but not once had she complained that it wasn't some hot Beamer or sports car. Nor had she argued when he bought this fourth-gen one new last year. She had a key...that she mostly used for opening the rear hatch. She rarely drove.

He rolled out the north gate and looped onto the George Washington Parkway.

At the speed limit—yes, he was that square—he eased his foot on the gas, but the car kept accelerating. Foot off the pedal. Harry even hooked a foot behind it to pull up, but it wasn't stuck.

"What are you doing, Harry?" Heidi braced herself. She was never really comfortable in a car.

"It isn't me." As if to prove his point, the wheel jerked in his hands and he jumped into the other lane despite trying to hold it in place.

"If it isn't you..." Heidi didn't finish the sentence. Instead she looked around them. Then up through the moonroof.

When she didn't look back down, Harry risked a glance himself. A small drone was keeping pace with them from above. Its high buzz was just audible.

"We've been hacked."

He punched the Start/Stop button, but it wasn't working.

Shifting the car to Neutral did nothing.

Daemon—because it had to be the Daemon—kept accelerating and weaving them from one lane to another. The other traffic on the George Washington Parkway was starting to blow their horns as they veered and swerved through the late evening traffic.

"The Route 123 interchange," Heidi warned him.

Less than half a mile ahead.

It would be easy for Daemon to ram them into a bridge abutment. All the airbags in the world wouldn't save them from a ninety-mile-an-hour head-on with a concrete wall.

If Daemon just wanted to mess them up, there had already been plenty of opportunities to slam them into a guard rail or another vehicle.

No. Daemon wanted their destruction.

Harry drove this road every day. It was far too easy to picture the heavy supports for the Route 123 bridge over the Parkway.

Again he tugged on the wheel. He could redirect them for an instant, but Daemon jerked them back into the other lane just to prove his helplessness.

It wouldn't be enough.

Then he remembered something he'd read in the manual, because he was one of those weirdos who actually read manuals.

"Give me your key! Quickly!"

As Heidi dug through her purse, he tried to roll down the window.

Nothing.

Open the moonroof?

Still no luck.

The door wouldn't unlock at speed.

Daemon had trapped them in a box.

He reached down for the small hammer he'd shoved along the left side of his seat.

A lot of drivers around Seattle's Puget Sound had them because there was a lot of water to fall into, off bridges and ferries. In the handle was a seatbelt cutter, but the hammer had a special steel tip for smashing car windows.

"Here," Heidi shoved her key into his hand.

He let go of the steering wheel, since there was no point in fighting Daemon, and fished out his own key fob.

Harry slammed the small hammer at the glass as hard as he could without any room to swing.

The carbon steel tip did exactly as advertised and shattered the window. So easily that he lost his grip and it flew out the window.

"Harry...." Heidi was pressed back hard in her seat staring at the upcoming bridge.

He tossed the two key fobs out the missing window.

As the keys fell behind, the car shut off.

That's what he'd remembered from the manual. Toyota had learned that it was too easy to spoof a key fob sitting on a shelf by the front door to start a nearby car. Most keyless cars could then be driven away; they'd run until the engine was stopped or they ran out of gas.

So they'd made a change.

The new Prius stopped running the moment both key fobs were too far away.

He grabbed the wheel and braked hard.

No power assist, but also free from Daemon's control.

The car was dead.

He steered for the shoulder and eased it to a stop under the bridge.

Heidi inspected the massive bridge support just inches outside the passenger window.

Harry looked ahead and spotted the drone that had been transmitting Daemon's hacking signal.

For five long seconds it hovered under the bridge with its camera aimed at them.

Then, in what he hoped was a fit of pure fury, the drone slammed sideways into the next pillar down and shattered into hundreds of pieces.

"I thought Reese was wrong," Heidi said softly, still watching the pillar. Better blocking her door than having their car wrapped around it.

"About what?" Harry's hands would shake if he took them off the wheel, so he just kept them there.

"Daemon has to go down really, really hard."

79

"YOU'RE SURE ABOUT THIS?"

"Why else would Jeremy have suggested it?" Miranda asked Drake.

And like he so often did, he had no answer to her own question so she didn't see any point in answering his.

She absolutely was *not* sure about this. But Jeremy had proved himself time and time again. It was hard for her, but she decided to trust him.

Clarissa Reese had gone back to see how her people were doing. She'd also promised to look into the lost CIA drones. Her phone had pinged as they were leaving the White House and Miranda managed to see the message. The CIA had just lost a small drone somewhere in DC.

Miranda knew what had happened to the MQ-9 Reapers, but the RQ-170 Sentinel's fate was still in question. She'd be surprised if they ever heard anything about it.

This loss didn't appear to be tied to any attacks, so

perhaps it was another problem, in which case it didn't concern her.

Or the hacker disposing of the evidence?

Yes, that must be it.

Miranda felt much better now. She always felt out of balance around unresolved issues.

Sergeant Lamont was driving the three of them—Drake, Lizzy, and herself—to the original SIMNET site in the Pentagon.

Which had been Jeremy's idea.

Perhaps between them at Eglin and herself in Washington, they'd be able to enter the simulation if necessary and quickly determine what was simulated and what was real world. If the hacker attacked on schedule, they'd be ready to help.

If the CIA had stopped them, all the better.

To prepare herself, Miranda built up the simulator's history in her mind, layer by layer. Just like nested spheres so that she could think about it in the present without having to think about all its past each time she tried.

DARPA had developed the first battle simulator in 1987.

By 1990, they were networking hundreds of simulators together. "Battle Labs" were soon formed at several major forts.

For the Army, the Close Combat Tactical Trainer and Combined Aircrew Mission Task Trainer had replaced SIMNET before 9/11. It had drastically improved their individual and battlefield tactics for their tanks, armored vehicles, and helicopters.

Soon the Air Force had joined in with massive thousand-station installations and America began to learn through simulated battles just what was possible.

With the integration of information from the Iraq and Afghanistan conflicts into the various branches' Directorates of Simulation, the learning had accelerated.

And apparently, so had the risks.

None of the major installations had ended up near Washington, DC, but there was a small training center in the basement of the Pentagon. Left over from the SIMNET days, it was kept upgraded so that commanders could interactively participate in the sim warfare. There were also a few stations set up for pilots on assignment to the Pentagon so that they could keep their skills at least moderately current.

Miranda checked her watch as they pulled into the Pentagon's garage.

Twenty-seven minutes.

80

MIRANDA PULLED ON THE HEADSET AS SHE SAT IN THE simulator.

The chair was too high but she didn't want to look like she didn't know what she was doing by searching for an adjuster.

Drake and Lizzy had pulled up office chairs close by, though thankfully out of her line of sight.

The head of the Pentagon's simulation department had done a poor job of hiding his displeasure at having a civilian in his facility—no matter that a four-star general had escorted her in here.

But when she tried to rest her hands on the controls, everything was wrong.

Finally there was a huff of exasperation from the department head. He stepped up and adjusted about six things faster than she could follow. It still wasn't right, but at least her feet were on the floor and her hands rested easily on the controls.

The big screen in front of her showed nothing but the night sky.

She slipped on the headset.

"Are you there, Jeremy?" Miranda barely whispered because of everyone watching. She didn't like being watched.

"Right here, Miranda."

"What am I doing here?"

"You're the pilot."

"Of what? I'm not military. The only jet I know how to fly is my Sabrejet." If only she could be aloft and gone.

Away from all these people.

But her jet had been sabotaged. Though Drake had promised that it was being well taken care of.

She'd wanted to go see it. Sit in its familiar old seat for a while. But sadly that wasn't going to happen. There just wasn't time.

"Okay," Jeremy spoke and she could hear keys rattling over the headset. "What's your station number?"

She found it and read it back to him.

More key rattles, then her Sabrejet's cockpit flashed up on her screens.

"The only real difference is that you tap the screen to change the status of a button. If you're fighting in sim, your actions will appear to be an F-35 Lightning II. If real world, well, we'll see what happens."

She took off down a late-night runway marked in a long line of lights. In moments she was aloft. The simulation did indeed handle like her Sabrejet. The main revelation was the canopy of the simulator was almost daylight bright. The night vision capability of the F-35 was truly a revelation. No wonder the pilot's helmets cost half a million each. They were amazing.

"How were you able to do this?"

"It's not just me. I've got a couple of Air Force programmers here with me. But Dad works at Microsoft. He's been the head programmer for *Flight Simulator* since forever. And that's the core of the Air Force's simulators. I learned how to program watching Dad write this code. Mom is on *Halo*. So gaming, flying, computers, battle scenarios— they all kind of came together when I started studying systems. And about the hundredth time I crashed an SR-71 Blackbird, I started reading NTSB reports. That's when I found yours and just got totally hooked. I— Ow! Cut that out, Holly."

Miranda finally understood why Jeremy was always so jittery around Holly. She perpetrated physical mayhem to get Jeremy to even pause for a breath.

"It's okay, Jeremy. Tell Holly, I give you full permission to talk to me as much as you need to."

"Are you sure, boss?" Holly came online for the first time.

"I'm sure."

"Good luck with that, Miranda. Jeremy, at least *try* to behave."

"Yes ma'am."

Miranda continued to familiarize herself with the simulated F-35 masquerading as a Sabrejet.

"Jeremy, let me see the real thing."

Suddenly everything changed. The steam gauge cockpit with all of its familiar dials and manual controls disappeared. In its place were LED readouts surrounded by control buttons all around the edges. Small diagrams showed her the changes to the controls. They were different, but not incomprehensibly so.

And the jet was fantastically responsive. She also knew enough to suspect that a professional F-35 pilot was riding the controls with her down in Eglin, smoothing out her rough edges, taking care of the engines, and other such issues.

"Who is flying with me?"

"Lt. Colonel Kiley is linked to your flight. There are also a few others along. Do you want to speak to them?"

81

"This is Kiley. I know it's late and some of you have already done multiple flights today."

Billy "Poet" Blake didn't know why Lt. Colonel Kiley was wasting his breath. He was so jazzed to be here at Eglin he might never sleep again.

Three major simulated flights in a single day? This was his kind of kickass.

"Tonight's flight lead is not, I repeat *not* an Air Force officer."

Billy leaned back out of the simulator enough to look at Toucan.

They traded shrugs. Something weird going on. Of course it had been a pretty damn weird day, so that wasn't news.

Another, deeper voice came on the air. "However, you should treat everything she says as gospel. I'm not in your direct chain of command, but consider this to be a direct order from the Chairman of the Joint Chiefs of Staff, General Drake Nason."

Billy swallowed hard and looked back at his own screen.

Then a woman's high voice spoke. "Uh, hi."

There was a weird pause, so Billy said "Hi" back.

A couple of the guys chuckled.

What kind of a clusterfuck was this going to be?

When she spoke again, it was pure business. "There have been five primary intrusions into the Air Force's simulation system over the last thirty-six hours. We are working on the root cause, but have not yet secured the source. There have been nine airframe losses and eight deaths not counting the F-35 Lightning destroyed over Syria."

"Wait, what?" Billy couldn't stop himself. "The debris I saw wasn't simulated?"

"Neither was the flight over the Gulf of Mexico. You were flying actual US drones against A-10 instructor pilots who lost their lives in—"

"That's classified, lady," Kiley's voice cut across hers.

"The pilots need to understand the stakes, Colonel Kiley."

"But—"

"Shut up, Kiley. Or get off the circuit." Again that deep voice of General Nason.

Billy didn't know what to do. He couldn't breathe. "I— We— I shot down...real people? *Our* people?"

"Yes," the woman said it like it was simple fact—dead flat.

"Son," General Nason's voice was soft. "There's a time for straightening all this out. There's a time for thinking and feeling. That time is *not* now. Right now your duty is to fly to the best of your abilities. This is the real test of any pilot."

"Yes sir." Oh great, no pressure to get his shit together. Just the CJCS watching over his shoulder. He closed his eyes for a moment and all he could see was the rounds he'd sent pounding through the back of the A-10's canopy to kill the pilot.

A guy who was expecting to be his trainer someday. Maybe next week, maybe tomorrow...now never.

He opened his eyes and shoved the image aside. How long would it be before he dared to close them again? How many years until he stopped seeing that image every time he did?

"In three minutes," the woman resumed in that *Iceman* chill voice of hers, "either nothing will happen, or we'll be in a major air battle. We don't know where in the world it will be happening. We won't know if it is real, simulated, or more likely both."

This time Billy leaned back and looked around of the simulator's screen in the other direction. Major "Ass-Face" Ashton's face was as white, well, an untanned ass.

82

"There it is," Jeremy announced. "The code just hit."

Miranda checked her watch as she sat in the Pentagon simulator feeling more out of place than anywhere in the last decade. Or two.

Midnight.

Exactly six hours from the start of the Gulf of Mexico operation. Usually she liked being right. There was a comforting symmetry when she understood how at least some part of her world worked.

This time she *hated* being right.

"Holy wow," Jeremy breathed out. "I've never seen anything like that. It just hit the firewall and splintered like a fireworks. We stopped some of it, a little anyway. There's code spreading throughout the system faster than we can do anything about."

Jeremy must have done something. The screen of her simulator went from a night view from a simulated F-35 to a tactical map of the world. It looked strange above the banks of her simulated F-35's flight instruments.

"Can't you just shut off the computer?"

"This isn't a PC, Miranda. It's one of the world's largest supercomputers. Even if there was a single master switch, which there isn't, it would shut down whole sections of Eglin Air Force Base. It could well kill more people that we could possibly save."

"We should have grounded all the A-10s. They're the targets."

"I don't think so anymore. Here," Jeremy's keys rattled in the background. "We have a flight of F-35's taking off out of Australia, except there aren't any F-35s in Australia yet—they're still on order. Maybe it's just to distract us. There are a hundred or more new events coming in and we don't know what's real."

"Are all of Colonel Campos' A-10s at Davis-Monthan still grounded?"

A brief pause while Jeremy asked.

"He says yes. Including everything at Nellis in Nevada. And Eglin's 96th Test Wing is still grounded pending the investigation of the three lost pilots."

"Good," Miranda wondered whether she should knock on her head or cross her fingers before she gave the next order. Unsure, she did both before speaking to Jeremy. "Delete all events involving A-10s over US soil and territorial waters."

"Okay, that's a lot of them cleared off."

"What's left?"

A map appeared across her simulation.

Israel, Britain, Vietnam…

"Jeremy?"

"Uh-huh."

"You said you were a gamer as well as a programmer."

"Uh-huh," his voice was so soft she could barely hear it.

"As a gamer, would you repeat a good play or go for a new one?"

"What are you saying?"

"What if out of all of this, only one piece is real. Which one would it be?"

83

JEREMY STARED AT THE SCREEN WITH NO IDEA. THIS WAS REAL
world. Real conflict. Not...

"What happens if I guess wrong?"

Miranda's silence told him what he really, really didn't
want to know.

He was supposed to save people. That was his talisman
as he sought the light side of the Force. That's how he'd
gotten himself out of hacking.

And ultimately, that's why he'd gotten out of gaming, too.
For the most part it removed him from society. Every hour of
gaming was like a drug—going to an easy escape.

Online, he was faceless and he belonged.

In school, he was the outsider frequently pissing people
off as he skipped grades and aced tests. *You're blowin' the
curve, man. Guess we're gonna beat the shit out of you 'til you
learn.*

He'd liked that social aspect of being online. Flying
together, fighting together, or even just sharing an adventure.

He really missed that kind of hypersharing. Everyone wired in for hours at a stretch.

Every communication immediate.

Focused.

No side conversation—except maybe about sex—which hadn't meant a thing at eight, nine, ten... He'd been out of gaming about the same time he noticed girls. They were much more interesting in the flesh than online. Even if he'd never been a real winner in that department.

It had taken a lot of effort to extract himself from gaming in Mom's *Halo*. But he'd been much slower about getting out of Dad's programming work on *Flight Simulator*.

That still didn't answer Miranda's question.

Then he remembered.

"The SR-71 Blackbird that I mentioned before."

"What about it?"

"I really only played with *Microsoft Flight Simulator* once. Dad loaded a pre-release of the next version onto my computer. He tried to show me, but I wanted to figure it out myself. I took the fastest plane—"

"The SR-71 Blackbird," Holly acknowledged from close beside him.

"Right. For twenty-six hours I didn't move. I didn't eat. I didn't pee."

"Too much information," Holly covered her ears and made a loud humming noise.

"All I did was keep working that SR-71 Blackbird. I'd zoom-climb up to a hundred thousand feet. Then, just before hard stall, I'd nose over and race down to the ground at better than Mach 3. I kept doing it until I could fly through an open hangar at Mach 3 without ripping off the wings."

"Jeremy..." He knew Holly's warning tone.

"No, this has a point. Really."

She raised an eyebrow as if saying, "Prove it to me." Then she tapped her watch to reinforce the message.

Right, he had to hurry.

"I didn't stop once I got it. I kept doing it over and over until I could do it ten times in a row without a failure. I didn't care how tired I was, how hungry, or how much my bladder was hurting. I was afraid it might burst it was hurting so bad, but I didn't stop. Not until I got it right ten times in a row. I *loved* reliving that success."

"Which means?" Miranda asked.

"Which means that the hacker is going to go back to their greatest success and try to repeat it."

"North Korea."

"North Korea," Jeremy agreed. Then he glanced at Holly and finally knew how to get her. "I never flew in *Flight Simulator* again. Too addictive for me. Besides, my bladder was in so much pain that I couldn't stand and I had to crawl to the bathroom."

Holly punched his arm hard enough to hurt.

But he didn't care and just smiled back at her.

Then she laughed that wonderful big laugh of hers that said he really did belong.

84

"WIPE EVERYTHING ELSE OFF THE SCREEN," MIRANDA SPOKE into her headset.

Jeremy did, then recentered her screen on just North Korea. Except there was nothing going on in North Korea.

Miranda squinted at it. She tried tapping her knuckles on the side of her head but it didn't seem to be bringing her any more luck.

"Expand it back out," Drake whispered to her. "South Korea *and* Japan. Especially Japan."

She passed the instruction on.

Suddenly everything was in motion. Planes, ships, active missile batteries.

"This is the simulation. How much of it is real?"

Lizzie had taken over one of the simulator's control computers. "Here. I'll overlay what our satellites are reporting."

Miranda's screen flashed and blurred.

"Sorry. I forgot about the angular distortion of the

satellite's view. It isn't directly overhead at the moment."

Everything distorted drastically, swirled left and right, then snapped into alignment.

Drake grunted. "Damn it. That happened really fast. The Japanese have actually relaunched their entire fleet. They probably never even tied up to the docks, just sat there at the ready. Look, they're flushing the F-35s back into the air."

"We have massive movement along the North Korean border," Lizzy announced.

"Our side or theirs?"

"Both."

Drake grabbed a phone, dialed, and then used that command voice of his. "Get the President back in the PEOC, with my apologies. Then get him on the goddamn line. Take us straight to DEFCON 3 for the entire Pacific Rim. No, there's not time to get him in the air. Besides, that's probably not a very safe place to be at the moment."

Miranda knew there hadn't been a DEFCON 3 incident since the 9/11 attacks.

"We have missile launches out of North Korea," someone in the background reported with perfect calm.

Miranda glanced aside. There were many more people in the room than there had been mere minutes ago. Some were on phones, some were on computers.

She turned and watched the simulations.

"Lizzy, why don't I see them in your satellite images? I should be able to because it's daylight there."

"Because..." Lizzy drew it out. "Because they aren't real."

"But the XC50 is reporting them as real to all of the Japanese systems."

"My god," Drake moved up to stand close beside

Miranda's left shoulder. "That crazy hacker is trying to start World War III."

"So tell the Japanese that it's fake."

"They won't believe me, but I'll try."

Miranda stared at the screen. Japan's defensive helicopter carriers turned into aggressive aircraft carriers by simply changing out the aircraft. And all three were powering west into the Sea of Japan. With each passing moment, more and more aircraft were taking off from the Japanese air bases.

Drake got off the phone, then swore vividly. "The Chief of Staff, Joint Staff of the Japanese Self-Defense Forces, just hung up on me. They're convinced it's real and they're going to launch everything they've got. Thank God we didn't sell them any bombers, but they've got over three hundred F-4s, F-15s, and F-16s, in addition to their first twenty F-35s."

"How do we stop it?" Lizzy asked.

"Well, they sure aren't going to stand down for the price of a few seared steaks," Drake told her.

Miranda looked up at him.

"Never mind. They won't be turning back just because we asked them to. I'm going to get the 7th Fleet out to sea, but if I start shooting down the Japanese planes, we'll have a whole different war on our hands." He turned away to say something to the President, who was on a screen she couldn't see.

Miranda stared at her own screen.

The answer had to be there somewhere.

What if it wasn't?

What if it was in the earlier crashes caused by the hacker?

"Jeremy, let's review the crashes."

85

"LET'S DO *WHAT?*" JEREMY COULD USUALLY FOLLOW WHAT Miranda wanted.

In fact, he'd been pretty proud about guessing her needs ahead of time. Like delaying to grab his pack when they'd gone to the CH-47F Chinook so that he could read the black box—before it blew up.

He hadn't seen *that* coming.

And he didn't see what she wanted now.

The general was right. World War III was shaping up fast on the screen. North Korea's perceived attack on South Korea and Japan would launch the Americans. Neither China nor Russia could ignore a war on their very borders.

Yet Miranda wanted to go back to—

"Let's review the crashes." She didn't often repeat herself. Miranda *was* a genius...

"Is this one of your sphere things?"

"That's an interesting question. A sphere greater than

one individual occurrence. One of interaction between lesser spheres."

"Stop her," Holly whispered urgently in his ear. "She can't stop herself from things like that. I thought you knew that."

Jeremy stared at Holly, her face just inches away as Miranda pursued the idea of an interactive sphere in superposition, inclusive of more directly discernible manifestations represented by individual crash events.

He *did* know that about Miranda. He'd just never thought of it as a problem.

But Holly was right.

He could see that he'd completely sidetracked Miranda from the fearsome issue at hand.

She didn't have a measure of magnitude, but rather focused on what was right in front of her to the exclusion of all else.

He turned from Holly and looked back at his list.

"Okay," he cut Miranda off in midsentence and tried to not feel awful about doing so. "I think we can dismiss the first crash in Achin, Afghanistan. Like an opening salvo, it was mostly a testing of abilities."

Holly hugged him hard from the side, kissed him on the cheek, and then ruffled his hair—partly dislodging his headset.

He straightened it and continued. "If the hacker's intent was to destroy an A-10, it was successful. But if it was to discredit A-10s in general, then it was a failure."

"Okay..." Miranda's voice dragged, then, "Next!" She'd made the switch back.

"The downing of Colonel Campos was even sloppier. An

attached mechanical device and the probable murder of the mechanic responsible."

"I was lucky to survive that," the colonel protested from somewhere on the system.

"Yes, but as it didn't show an aircraft failure, but rather direct sabotage, it's inconsequential."

The colonel started to speak again, but Jeremy just cut him off. The same way he'd cut off Miranda. The same way that Holly cut him off when he was rambling too much.

He'd never thought of the rambling as a problem in himself, but he could see it now.

And he'd always hated interrupting people. But it *was* a tool that seemed to work just as well as his wrenches worked on loosening a bolt. As long as he didn't have to use it very often.

"Syria was the first real success. The integration of real and simulated worlds."

"And I barely got out with my skin intact," one of the pilots called out. "I'm guessing that I was piloting an A-10PCAS. It's a remote-piloted version of the Warthog. The program was supposedly discontinued, but it's the only thing that fits."

"That's affirmative, Lt. Blake," Lt. Colonel Kiley backed him up. "It's classified, but it's out there."

Jeremy didn't want Miranda to get distracted so he moved on.

"Taking over the drones over the Gulf of Mexico was another mistake."

"A mistake? Hell, yeah," Lt. Blake again, sounding infinitely sad this time...and kinda pissed.

"Three A-10s were lost. No initial evidence that they were

shot down, but also no proof that they were failures either. Not a good demonstration."

"Then there was Korea," Miranda stated simply.

"Right. Because it was off your six-hour schedule, for whatever reason, we must assume that it was programmed quickly. Apparently only three of the four aircraft were sabotaged. If all four had been, we might assume navigation failures rather than reprogramming. That idea is supported by the fact that the aircraft were reprogrammed directly and never hooked into the Cray XC50 except for the report of their downing."

Miranda didn't say anything.

Jeremy looked at Holly and Mike as the silence stretched.

Mike stood close behind Holly with a hand resting on her shoulder. They both shrugged uncertainly. As Holly did so, she noticed Mike's hand. She nipped it hard with a sharp clack of her teeth. Mike yelped as he pulled it away.

"Then there's Korea," Jeremy finally prompted her again.

86

"No. Syria," the woman said flatly over the headset.

Billy wondered if she wasn't a bit daft. Though as he'd listened to the detailed horrors of what had occurred in the last twenty-four hours, perhaps she was the only sensible one.

"Mr. Pilot," she called out.

"You have a lot of pilots online at the moment," Kiley remarked.

"The one who flew into Syria."

Billy swallowed hard. "That would be me. Lieutenant William 'Poet' Blake, ma'am. I'm an A-10 pilot."

"Yes, I knew that. You also flew the RQ-170 Sentinel over the Gulf of Mexico."

"Yes ma'am. Even if I can never take it back."

"You didn't know. Why would you take it back? Everyone who saw it said you were very good."

He opened his mouth, closed it. How was he supposed to answer that?

Command never wanted a real answer, they just wanted... Damned if he knew.

"How can I be of service, ma'am?" Hopefully no more talk about interacting spherical concept spaces or whatever the hell mysticism she was into. This was really the woman that the Chairman of the Joint Chiefs said to trust?

"Lieutenant Poet, you took over an aircraft and flew it yourself from the simulator."

"Yes ma'am. I did." *Lieutenant Poet?* Well, he'd certainly never live down the Poet call sign after that. He'd be lucky if anyone used his last name ever again.

"Jeremy?"

"Oh, I get it. Hang on." He continued, sounding as if he was talking to himself. "How did they do that? Oh, I see. If they hacked the code like that, then I should be able to clip this section and— Oh, that's bad. That really, really shouldn't have worked. Seriously, someone needs to talk to the engineers of the GPS systems. I just walked right into the Nav system backwards from the satellites. Oh, that's a pretty code stack. Whoever did this is really awesomely good. Now, if I—"

Billy the Poet didn't get what was happening until his screen cleared and suddenly he was looking at the cockpit of an F-35 Lightning II. He'd fooled around with them in the simulator so it wasn't completely alien.

"All sim pilots," Jeremy spoke up. "You now have direct control of the Japanese F-35s as well as the flight leads on ten F-15 and F-16 squadrons. The latter are technically Mitsubishi F-2s, but they're basically F-16 Falcons."

"Get them turned around and back to base," the Australian woman ordered.

"If the pilot starts yelling at you in Japanese, just ignore him," General Drake announced.

Billy didn't just turn the plane around. He slammed the throttles to the wall and pulled up into an Immelmann. The F-35 Lightning climbed abruptly and kept going until it was flat on its back and headed once more toward Japan.

Then, instead of the simple half roll that would bring the plane right-side up, he did a three-and-a-half times-around snap roll. What did the pilot think as his plane spun in a straight-line wing-over-wing—completely out of his control?

Yeah. That's about how I feel, buddy.

Totally out of control.

He did a double snap roll the other way.

He had to admit that the F-35 was a fun plane.

Almost as fun as an A-10 Thunderbolt.

87

"Navy next, Jeremy."

"What was that?" Drake spun to face Miranda.

She didn't even look up from her screen.

"Do you have any Navy captains here?"

Drake was glad he'd called in the other Joint Chiefs of Staff as he'd rushed over from the White House. Being in the Pentagon, there were a number of their aides there as well. He directed anyone from the Navy or Coast Guard into ship simulators.

"Okay," Drake could hear Jeremy over the intercom. "Thankfully the Naval Support Activity Orlando shares this computer and the Japanese Maritime Self-Defense Force uses it for simulations as well. Okay, here are the helms of the lead ships linked into the Pentagon simulators."

"Turn 'em around boys," Drake could get to like this. "Or at least shut down their engines." Then he pictured someone doing this to his armed forces and felt sick. *Think about it later.*

The Japanese Chief of Staff, Joint Staff was much more cooperative when Drake called him back this time.

"No, General Yagi, I will not be telling you how we did that. In the future, please remember that when we say it's a false alarm and to not attack, we mean it."

He ignored the man's screeching for a while and finally, reluctantly, agreed to return control of the ships and aircraft to the Japanese.

He signaled Miranda, who whispered over the headset to Jeremy, then listened for a moment.

When she nodded, he informed General Yagi that he once more had control of his forces, then he hung up on him. It was indecently satisfying.

The pilots and ship captains in the room were cheering and applauding their success.

The few who really understood what was happening were collapsed in their seats.

Miranda Chase appeared unaffected by it all.

Once he assured himself that everything had returned to normal, or was at least starting to, he returned the nation's defense status to DEFCON 5.

Then he slapped his forehead and turned to the screen where he'd had an open line to the President.

He switched his headset so that they had a private circuit. "You're safe to leave the PEOC now, sir."

"I was wondering when you'd remember me."

"Sorry, sir."

"What are we going to do about Chase?"

"What do you mean, sir?" Drake glanced over to where she was still talking to Jeremy over her headset.

"I know she's got Top Secret clearance, but she was doing things even I didn't know about."

"Me either, sir. I don't think anyone did, maybe not even her. Should we give her a medal?"

"Very quietly. For that whole damn team. Then maybe lock her up so that nothing leaks out."

"I'm pretty sure that nothing could leak with that strange way she thinks."

Cole sighed. "Perhaps someday she'll give us clearance to know what she *is* thinking."

Drake laughed, "You don't really want to know, do you?"

The President sighed. "No, probably not. But at least buy her that damned new ejection seat she wanted as a thanks for saving the nation."

"You know that's like a quarter of a million dollars, right?"

The President didn't even blink. "Do it. Then get this cleaned up, Drake. I want full honors for every pilot who went down in this fiasco. Find a good cover story because that many 'training accidents' wouldn't sound good at all. I want to speak to any widows or parents personally."

"I'll get you a call sheet before sunrise, Mr. President."

"Thanks, Drake. Now shut this down. Lock it up as tight as you did the MQ-45 Casper fiasco and I'll give you a raise."

"You mean that you'll finally let me retire?" Drake had been on the verge of retirement when the newly elected President Cole had asked him to continue to serve.

"Only if I get to go first."

"Yes sir. And sir?"

"What?"

"At least your Wagyu beef is cheaper than her seat, Mr. President."

"Not by enough, Nason. Not by near enough," the President cut the connection.

88

Senator Hunter Ramson sat back in the luxurious armchair across the desk from Vice President Ricky Mulroney. It was one of the advantages to flying with the VP, traveling in Air Force Two on a beautifully sunny day.

He'd never been aboard any of the presidential aircraft. While it wasn't the grand 747, he had no complaints about the amenities aboard the modified 757.

Mulroney's onboard office was smaller than the pictures he'd seen of the President's office on the 747. A couch / daybed, two armchairs, and a desk. It had to be small enough to leave an aisle around the outside of the soundproof walls for people to travel the length of the aircraft.

Still...he idly wondered what it would be like to make love to Rose on that couch, with all of the business going on around them—aides, protection details, and the like. But she still insisted he'd never be running for the White House.

Too bad. He liked this plane and he would bet that he'd like the 747 even better.

The Secret Service hadn't appreciated the short notice on the trip, but they'd done Rio last year with the President, so, much of the groundwork had already been done.

Mulroney was good company at least. They'd just finished a delicious, if not fancy, lunch. He'd never been a French restaurant kind of guy anyway.

"Feels good to get out of DC," Mulroney toasted him beer to beer, a Pacific Northwest microbrew that he'd have to get more of—Walking Man Black Cherry Stout. "What's on the agenda?"

"Nothing tonight. I planned on taking it easy and then we'll start meetings tomorrow. Brazil is looking to expand their naval and air force purchase contracts. We'll tour some bases in the morning, then get down to real meetings tomorrow afternoon, see what they have in mind for force projections over the next decade or so. They've been buying Eurocopters, now Airbus, over Sikorskys, Swedish Gripens for their fighters instead of ours. Maybe we can tempt them with the Raptor or Lightning II."

"If they can afford it."

"If they can afford it," Hunter conceded the point. "Maybe we'll unload some F-18s on them. We do well with the Army. For the Navy, they buy from the Brits or build it themselves. We want them under our care but I doubt we'll get in there."

Mulroney shook his head. It was unlikely.

"But for tonight, I just want to relax and have a good

time." Rose had been very clear on what he could and couldn't say on this trip.

And even if I don't get to touch, I want to see just how pretty a sex trap Clarissa Reese has found for you, Mulroney. Knowing her, the bait would be a ten in any beauty contest, and would be—or at least have proof—that she was far younger than she looked.

If it was as neat a trap as the one that had taken out Senator Clint Howards, it was going to be a doozy.

Clint hadn't failed in his campaign launch—Clint had been driven out of the Senate entirely in under forty-eight hours.

The Chairmanship of the Senate Armed Services Committee was already his.

Reese might be as dangerous as a shark but—despite the failure of the A-10 ploy—it was the kind of shark Rose said he needed on his side.

And Rose was always right.

89

DAEMON SPENT FIVE HOURS MAKING SURE THAT HER equipment was fully scrubbed of any data and then buried five feet under the Oklahoma sod. Then she bleached the apartment.

At sunrise, she drove south from her place close by Tinker Air Force Base in a nondescript Ford F-150 pickup. It was old enough that it couldn't be hacked.

She left the Tesla Model S in the garage just in case she came back this way someday. The truck she could dump and would never care.

It was registered to a bloodsucking televangelist named Steph Right—properly named herself that because she'd stepped right into the money. SR's credit cards had also paid for Daemon's Tesla, which was *not* registered in Steph's name, as well as several other toys. If Steph stole from her followers in the name of God, Daemon had no problem stealing from her in the name of fun.

Fifteen miles south, at Max Westheimer Airport,

Daemon parked the F-150 illegally in a handicap spot. As she walked around to the private aviation hangars, she tossed the keys in the garbage.

A ticket and a tow for you, Steph dear. She wished she'd thought to buy a couple kilos of cocaine to stash under the seat, but too late now.

Daemon forgot about SR and the pickup.

She decided that it probably would have been better if she hadn't promised to ruin the entire A-10 fleet's reputation in just twenty-four hours. Turned out to be more of a stretch than she'd expected. She'd know better on the next job.

Those five events in twenty-four hours would have done it, if not for that woman in the Sabrejet. Daemon hadn't accounted for the unexpected variable.

Definitely time to move on.

And she wasn't going to get tripped up by some lousy airline delay like Mum.

She'd fly her own, thank you very much.

Daemon had done a little project for the Bolivian President and taken her pay in flying lessons. She'd worked her way through their tiny air force from the Piper trainer to Beech King Air. She'd finished her lessons in the President's own Falcon 50 ten-seater trijet. The autopilot and the luxurious bed in the back had made for a splendid final flight twenty thousand feet above the Andes' *Cordillera Central*. The President had demonstrated exceptional prowess between the sheets.

Waiting for her at the University of Oklahoma's Max Westheimer Airport was a pretty little—and delightfully rare as there were only eight of them so far—SyberJet SJ30.

Sabrejet to SyberJet, she hadn't even made the

connection. That primitive piece of Korean War crap to the very cutting edge of light business jet development. Choice was easy.

The SJ30 was a gift from Client F that he'd probably take back if he could.

Or maybe not, as it was also the price of her silence. She'd count herself well paid for her trouble, even if it hadn't worked as planned. As always, she'd arranged a little extra insurance for herself—set to deliver if she ever failed to log in for twenty-four hours.

As if.

She'd been practically hard-wired since birth. Actually, with Mum's going "freelance" after she left Compaq about when Daemon was born, she'd been born hacking.

The eight-million-dollar SyberJet had come with five passenger seats in the cozy cabin. Taking a hint from the lovely flights with the Bolivian President, she'd had it redone with a comfortable bed and a micro kitchen. It couldn't reach across the ocean in one hop, but it would serve very nicely.

The flight from Oklahoma City to Los Angeles was uneventful.

Due to flying west, it was still sunrise when she landed at Santa Monica Airport.

While she waited for the fuel to be topped up, she debated Haggador II's invitation. That was what had tipped her decision from flying east to Oslo over to west for Macau.

She'd pinged him before she'd shut down her station at Tinker.

He'd offered to meet her at the Spitfire Grill close by the

airport—to check out each other's vibe in the neutral territory of breakfastland.

Daemon had sent back a "What the hell, why not."

As they fueled her plane, she could just make out the restaurant between the terminal building and general aviation hangars.

He was probably there right now.

Maybe even watching her and wondering.

She turned her back on the place.

Sadly, it would be better to keep moving—Wizard Boy would still be pissed about her remote-hijacking his car. A pity as she had the bed right here in the plane for a proper post-breakfast feast.

Nope, wouldn't make Mum's mistake of waiting too long.

Daemon could get plenty of attention later, somewhere safe. Maybe she'd dye her hair from her born blah-brown or normal midnight-blue to red like Mum and Nicole Kidman. They'd go nuts for that in Macau.

She was also exhausted. But if stopping for sex was dangerous, stopping for sleep was worse.

Daemon filed her last flight plan under her current name—out to Honolulu, then Hilo.

Except once clear of Honolulu, a pre-scheduled block of computer code would finish wiping her current name from all records. Then Jenny Curtiss—for the old Curtiss JN-4 "Jenny" biplane—would turn south and arrive in Samoa rather than her filed plan for Hilo.

Maybe she'd hang with the Samoans awhile, or check out Fiji, before working her way up to Macau.

Once aloft and up to cruising altitude, she set the

autopilot for Honolulu and the alarm clock for an hour. The last thirty-six hours were really catching up with her.

She tried for a few Haggador II fantasies as she lay alone in the cabin's bed, but could feel his now-distant disappointment. The Bolivian President wandered through the cabin of her memory briefly but she fell asleep before the action got at all memorable.

90

Daemon woke with a jolt.

Not to any alarm. Somehow she'd slept through that.

The low thrum of smooth-running turbine engines lulled her for a moment, but she dragged herself up to check on the plane.

The clock said she'd been out for four hours. No big crisis, Honolulu was five hours from California.

She tried shaking her head. Just made her dizzy.

She knocked back half a Red Bull and a bag of gummy worms. Sugar and caffeine, that was the ticket.

Not much better, she was still weaving by the time she returned to the pilot's seat.

The first thing she noticed was the cabin's internal altimeter was falling. Falling?

The SyberJet had a sea-level cabin, the pressure wasn't supposed to ease as it did in most planes. It was falling, down through fifteen thousand feet, headed *back* to sea level?

How high had it been?

That would explain her not hearing the alarm and her fuzzy thinking.

But her head was clearing now.

More oxygen, more caffeine, and...

And the compass. There was something about the compass. The compass heading from Santa Monica to Honolulu should be two-six-zero, right where she'd left it.

It was now reading one-eight-two. Nothing out there except the Pacific Ocean and maybe bloody Pitcairn Island where the mutineers of the HMS *Bounty* had landed.

Squinting out at the ocean, all she saw was lots and lots of water. The sun was high—far higher than it should be if she was still racing west with the sunrise.

Her fingers felt leaden as she fooled with the GPS map.

One-eight-two.

Dead on Pitcairn Island.

Woo-hoo! Girl was good. She'd totally nailed it.

But wait...

Pitcairn was bad.

In addition to being a total nowhere place, it didn't even have a runway. Worse, it was showing over two thousand nautical miles away. Her plane was going to run out of fuel about a thousand miles too soon.

Nope.

She'd stick with Honolulu.

But then she looked at the GPS map.

Her pretty new SyberJet had flown five hundred miles out to sea and then turned south away from all land.

Not enough fuel to reach the islands—she checked the GPS—or *any* land.

Not Honolulu, Pitcairn, or Ecuador.

And those were only a few of the places she couldn't fly to. Samoa, Macau, Oslo... None of them.

Point Nemo—where they sent old satellites to die because there was no one there.

She was in the middle of the biggest land-free zone of any ocean.

Her closest companions would be the astronauts if the space station was passing by overhead.

She was going to plunge into the ocean a thousand miles from anywhere and she couldn't do a thing about it.

The GPS map blinked off.

Then all four of the LCD display screens lit brightly— her two and the duplicate two in front of the empty copilot's seat.

Cartoon versions of Harry Potter and Hermione Granger flew onto the leftmost screen on brooms. They did a loop- the-loop out the top of screen three back to two and then waved as they flew off the edge of screen four.

Wizard Boy and Witchy Lady.

She flicked the bird at them.

A little fleet of animated A-10 Lightning IIs followed them across, flying inverted, each with their wings raised— wingtips like hands to hold a white lily over their bellies. The little Warthog paintings on their noses all had cute Xs for eyes.

As the last A-10 Warthog slid off to the right, Harry and Hermione flew in again. Different screen antics this time, but the same trail of dead A-10s.

The third time Hermione was Smurfette, though it wasn't clear why.

Then Hermione was back while Harry yanked up his robe to moon her.

And again.

None of the controls worked to shut them off.

She tried the radio for a distress call. Maybe there was a ship nearby, if she could survive the landing.

They wouldn't transmit. And every one was pumping out KXXY—classic country from OK City. The only thing she hated worse than jazz.

She must have watched the Wizard geeks, and occasional Smurfette, fly through a dozen iterations, or maybe a hundred—all different—before she thought to pull off her shoe and use the heel to smash all four screens.

Daemon unbuckled and went back to lie on the bed.

As she lay down, she saw that they were flying across her flat-screen television as well. Beyond caring, she just lay there and watched them and their entourage of cartoon A-10s.

She really should have had sex with Haggador II before she died.

Yep. Too late for that too.

91

As Stefon Gabriel started his Mercedes-AMG GT R roadster, a message pinged onto his console display.

A video. He tapped play as he rolled out of his townhouse's garage high on San Francisco's prestigious Russian Hill, but stopped before crossing the sidewalk onto the road.

A small black dot at the exact center slowly expanded. A low rumbling sounded from his sound system. It kept growing until it shook his car.

The dot resolved into an A-10 Thunderbolt II Warthog.

Shit! No one in that whole operation was supposed to know who he was. Even that asshole Hunter Ramson didn't know.

He could see the massive gun set in the mouth of the hog's toothy grin.

A load BRRRRT sound, characteristic of the GAU-8/A Avenger rotary cannon, roared into the car.

He caught himself cowering in his seat and forced himself to sit up straight.

His clients had been *beyond* furious at the failure of his plan to discredit the A-10s. Over twenty million down the drain and nothing to show for it. Now they wanted him to repay those costs.

This must be part of their intimidation plan.

Eight million of it should have been easy, except that Daemon bastard had taken the SyberJet thirty-six hours ago. And other than a brief stop at Santa Monica—his people had been less than an hour behind—the plane had evaporated along with its pilot. Like it had fallen off the edge of the map, it hadn't been reported landing anywhere.

It was that damn senator's fault. Maybe Stefon could choke the money out of him. Or that CIA bitch who had recommended this hacker in the first place. They both owed him.

And if they didn't pay? Well, they didn't know who he was, but he could certainly splash their identities far and wide.

Whoopsie!

Displayed in bright red letters on the screen.

"What the hell?" But no one answered. He sat alone in the car, staring at the screen.

I haven't logged in for over 24 hours.

I must be dead.

So sad.

A frowny round-and-very yellow emoticon wept a stream of tears so bountiful that he actually checked the leg of his pants to make sure they weren't getting wet.

It must be the hacker. Dead? Good. Worth the eight million.

*By the way...*the frowny face stopped crying and smiled brightly...*You're dead too—Client F.*

He froze, unable to move. No one should know that name belonged to him.

He held his breath, not by choice but because he'd forgotten how to breathe.

But the car didn't explode like in the movies.

Nothing fell on him.

VX gas didn't pour out of the car vents.

I told the CIA exactly how to find you.

And the cheery yellow emoticon winked.

He laughed at the screen. It had to be the hacker. "You screwed up, asshole. Who do you think told me to hire you in the first place? Got your contact info straight from that blonde bitch."

I told them hours and hours ago.

He ignored the hard clench in his gut and the winking face that he couldn't clear off his screen. Getting out of here seemed smart, so he pulled out to the brickwork on Lombard Street. Again he paused—because of all the asshole tourists who thought the street winding down the face of Russian Hill was somehow theirs.

Nope. All clear at the moment.

Except for directly across from his house, there was a car parked. It was pointed straight down the hill with the driver looking straight ahead across the city out to the ocean. Nobody was supposed to park on Lombard.

The tinted rear window rolled down.

A stunning woman, with her white-blonde hair back in a

severe ponytail, sat in the back. As casually as a runway model, she turned to look directly at him.

Then, in seeming slow motion, she raised a handgun with a long silencer on it.

That's when he recognized her. She was the CIA bitch who'd told him to hire that goddamn—

The first shot shattered his windshield and skittered aside to plunge into the Mercedes' headrest.

"No! Wait!"

The next two caught him in either shoulder as if pinning him to the seat.

The pain exploded into his brain like nothing he'd ever imagined.

When he opened his mouth to scream, the last shot entered through his open mouth and cut his spine.

With the last of his fading sight, he watched her turn just as slowly to face front and raise the tinted window. The driver pulled ahead into the quiet evening without once turning in his direction.

The video winked again through splatters of his own blood, then blanked.

His foot slipped off the brake. The Mercedes rolled slowly sideways across Lombard and stopped when it bumped against a brick wall.

92

It was three a.m. and bitterly cold for Washington, DC, even in November.

Miranda's plane had spent a day under a hastily erected Quonset-style tent on the JFK Hockey Fields. The perimeter secured by National Guard and the plane serviced by specialists from Andrews Air Force Base.

Miranda had spent the day asleep.

Drake was hoping to get to sleep soon himself. Now that the detailed interviews had been completed and the deep code unraveled to lay out exactly what had happened in that horrific twenty-four hours—especially what was in the simulator and what wasn't.

The detailed code that had infected the simulation computer and the aircraft had been delivered to the right people. Security patches to block any similar attack were promised quickly. *Very* quickly after he threatened to cancel all future military contracts with anyone who didn't deliver by the end of the week.

He'd spent nine of those hours down at Eglin and only returned to Washington an hour ago to put the last of the mess under lock and key.

Now he stood out on the southeast corner of the Ellipse in front of the White House to watch the final piece be put in place.

The wind was from the west, so they'd towed Miranda's Sabrejet to the bus parking area just east of the Washington Monument.

No press was in sight...yet.

The few passersby who'd asked had been told that the ancient plane was headed to the Smithsonian Air and Space Museum at the head of the Mall. A few had snapped photos, but no one had stayed to watch on the bitter November night.

At precisely three in the morning, Miranda was escorted to her Sabrejet.

Very quietly, in a smoothly coordinated plan, the police closed Constitution Avenue from the Washington Monument to the Lincoln Memorial.

A generator, trucked over from Reagan National, was started and plugged into her Sabrejet.

After a successful engine start, they unplugged, pulled the chocks from her wheels, and a pair of runway conductors waved her forward with red wands.

Out of the bus parking area, they signaled her for a right turn onto 15th Street Northwest. Four lanes wide, her wingtips reached from shoulder to shoulder. The two conductors walked backward for the half block, stationed in front of each wingtip to make sure she was clear.

Left onto Constitution.

Drake held hands with Lizzy at the southeast corner of the Ellipse. The White House shone brightly behind them and he'd wager that the President was at his window to watch the show even if his press people hadn't wanted him involved.

The press had taken the cover story hook, line, and sinker. The "unplanned mechanical failure" and the NTSB's lead investigator saving her own life on her way to consult with the Pentagon over the tragic recent losses.

No mention of the White House.

Nor the CIA.

His own presence at her landing had somehow slipped by mostly unremarked.

He and Lizzy waved with their free hands as Miranda lined up at the corner of 15th and Constitution, pointed west.

Miranda waved back by flapping the ailerons at the trailing edges of her wings as she sat in her brand-new seat.

Then the engine roared to life, a shot of blue fire poured out the rear exhaust port, aimed at the distant Capitol Building. *Couldn't happen to nicer people,* but Drake kept that thought to himself.

For the length of a breath, the plane strove forward against locked wheels while they covered their ears.

Then Miranda released the brakes and the plane raced ahead.

She accelerated past the Ellipse, the World War II memorial, and the Constitution Gardens.

The Sabrejet shot aloft somewhere between the National Academy of Sciences and the Lincoln Memorial.

Then it turned northwest over the Potomac and raced

away exactly on schedule—during a planned gap in the Reagan National Airport's pattern.

"You really know how to show a girl a good time, Drake."

He took Lizzy's hand again. "Just trying not to be some average boring guy."

"I think you have that covered."

Then, as the police reopened Constitution Avenue and melted back into the night, Lamont pulled his car around the corner and rolled up in front of them.

"Lizzy?"

"Mmm," she sounded sleepy. It made sense; it was three in the morning after all and neither of them had slept last night.

Maybe it wasn't his best idea. But maybe it was.

"We're both exhausted."

He could see the disappointment on her face.

"But I sure wouldn't mind waking up next to you in the morning."

Her radiant smile was all he needed.

He definitely didn't need Lamont's thumbs up as he held the door open for them.

93

"Wow! That's a huge turkey," Jeremy flapped his arms as if it was eight feet wide.

Miranda did her best not to laugh.

It wasn't that big, but it *was* Dillinger. She'd slept much better these last few nights without his shrieking two a.m. gobbles outside her island window.

She'd made the turkey and stuffing.

Jeremy had brought wine from Oregon and Washington vineyards, "That Cassidy Knowles blog rated these just super high." And she'd been right; they were very good and Miranda was feeling just a little bit loose already.

Holly had claimed "no skills with that stuff" and found an unlikely place called the Australian Pie Company close by the SeaTac airport.

"They specialize in meat pies—no real wonder—they're from Oz after all. But I got us a whole box of their dessert treats for later." Peach puffs, cheesecake turtles, some kind of apricot cake. And she'd brought enough for many times the four of them.

Mike had shown a surprising facility in her kitchen and had created appetizers of spinach and artichoke dip on fresh-baked rye crackers, corn pudding, and real cranberry sauce. He'd also manhandled her attempt at gravy into a thick luscious wonder over rough-mashed potatoes with the skin on.

Now they sat at the big table in the main house. Even with all the leaves taken out, the four of them sat at one end and enough food for three more teams sat at the other. They'd each made their first foray down the table and now sat staring at their full plates.

She and Jeremy sat to one side and Mike and Holly to the other.

The two of them had sparred over having to sit side-by-side—"Even on the same continent is too close," Holly had declared. But Miranda noticed that they also sat far closer together than she and Jeremy did.

The team had tried to place her at the head of the table, but that had been Dad's spot and she never sat there. She also wondered if it hadn't been John Wayne's spot as well when "The Duke" had hunted here.

For a moment she wondered what it would be like to have Colonel Campos sitting here with them all.

She'd liked him.

It might even be nice.

But unless he crashed another A-10, it wasn't likely that she'd ever see him again.

Even if she did, she wouldn't seat him in the head chair.

That belonged to Sam Chase. She imagined her father

sitting there, posing some challenging thought experiment over a slice of pie made from island apples.

The walls were paneled in dark Douglas fir, and big beams of the same created a lofty cathedral ceiling. The fire was crackling and the house was warm against the fast-descending night. A dusting of an early snow lay over the fields, but would probably melt by tomorrow. It wouldn't matter, the planes—both the Sabrejet and the Mooney—were tucked away snugly in the hangar.

Miranda sighed.

She'd forgotten these times.

Mom and Dad. Her and Tante Daniels. It seemed there were always more. Tante Daniels was beautiful and often had male guests. Visitors, friends—who she now understood had probably been fellow CIA agents or aviation specialists.

She'd been exposed to flying a wide variety of planes long before she was legal to fly them. Almost everyone had been willing to take "Sam Chase's kid" aloft for a ride. A ride that she'd always done her best to turn into a flying lesson since long before she could reach the rudder pedals.

Mike raised a glass.

Holly and Jeremy did the same and Miranda almost knocked hers over in her hurry to join them.

"You cracked another one, Miranda. Well done, you."

Holly and Jeremy were nodding in agreement.

"I, uh..." she looked down at her plate and tried to figure out what to say.

Saying she couldn't have done it without them seemed too mundane, even if it was true.

Saying that she was glad they were here was also true, but it wasn't enough.

It shouldn't be even about the NTSB.

It should be about…how she felt.

How did she feel?

Like…

She looked up and raised her glass a little higher.

"I can't think of any other people I'd rather do it with."

Jeremy offered her one of his goofy-happy grins.

Mike placed a hand on his heart and made a humorous "Awww" sound.

But Holly tipped her glass ever so slightly toward her and whispered in a way that Miranda knew only she could hear.

"No one I'd rather *be* with either."

Right. That's exactly what Miranda had meant to say.

———

If you enjoyed this, keep reading for an excerpt from a book you're going to love.
..and a review is always welcome (it really helps)…

MIRANDA CHASE RETURNS

COMING IN 2020

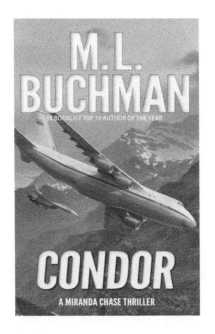

CONDOR (EXCERPT)

MIRANDA CHASE #3

"Favorite airplane?"

"Oh, c'mon, Jeremy, ask her a real question. We all know Miranda's favorite plane," Holly teased him.

"My F-86 Sabrejet," Miranda answered calmly. For twenty years she'd flown the old jet and knew it as well as the back of her hand. She liked its familiarity. Just as she liked the familiarity of this house. She'd grown up here.

Though it was still slightly uncomfortable having visitors to her island.

No, not uncomfortable. Merely...unfamiliar. Yes, that was a better way to think of it.

"Ehhhh!" Holly made a rude sound like a plane's stall-warning buzzer. "So not on, Miranda." Holly's Australian accent was even thicker than usual as she sipped her second beer of the evening.

Before Miranda could respond that she knew her own mind—which she wasn't always sure of, though she was this time—Jeremy raised his hand.

"Wait! I know. I know!"

"Don't have to raise your hand, buddy." Mike winked at Miranda from his armchair near the fire. He sat as neatly as ever—a slim, elegant man with short dark hair, a dress shirt, and custom-tailored slacks.

She sat on the sofa with Holly. Actually, Miranda sat on the sofa whereas Holly slouched so low she was almost horizontal—her feet on the coffee table, sticking her toes out toward the fire in the big beach-cobble stone hearth. Her socks didn't match.

"It's any plane that hasn't crashed," Jeremy proudly announced his answer.

While the others laughed and nodded, Miranda considered. The four of them were the lead crash investigation team for the National Transportation Safety Board. Yes, any plane that was fully functional *was* a very good thing.

But still, she liked her old Sabrejet very much.

"Jeremy's favorite site investigation tool?" Mike called out.

Holly giggled.

Miranda had no idea why.

Holly whispered to her, "Can you imagine him picking out a single favorite tool?"

"Oh," Miranda understood the joke now.

Jeremy had a bigger field pack than the other three of them combined.

"His hammer," Holly suggested. "The one he actually offered to that colonel who wanted to bust up his phone for constantly giving him bad news."

Though the event occurred several months in the past,

Jeremy blushed brightly enough to be seen by the firelight despite his Vietnamese tan complexion.

"No, his program for reading Cockpit Voice and Data Recorders, even if he isn't supposed to have one. He secretly wishes he was James Bond," Mike teased him.

"No," Holly shook her head hard enough to flutter her rough-cut blonde hair over her shoulders. "He wishes he was Q, Bond's equipment geek."

"No," Jeremy spoke up a little hotly, "but *he* wishes you both had fallen into the ocean and been eaten by orcas on the way here."

"You'd have been whale food right along with us." Mike accurately pointed out. He had flown the three of them out to her island in Washington State's northern Puget Sound for the weekend. Holly was the one who'd suggested the Spring solstice was a good excuse for a party.

"Would have been worth it," Jeremy mumbled.

There was a brief silence in which the only sound was logs shifting in the fireplace.

"What *is* your favorite tool, Jeremy?" Because now Miranda was curious.

He looked down, and she was afraid that she'd somehow embarrassed him even further than Mike and Holly had.

Then he reached for his shirt pocket and pulled out a pen.

"A pen, mate? Really?" Holly turned to Mike. "Have you ever seen him even use a pen? Everything in the world is on his tablet."

Mike just shook his head.

Miranda could remember three instances. They'd been

together as a team for almost six months, yet three was all she could recall.

"You gave it to me on the first day I joined your team. It's everything I ever dreamed of."

"Miranda's *pen?*" Mike scoffed.

"Being on Miranda's team," Jeremy said softly.

Holly, who never looked touched, looked touched. She turned to Miranda.

"He's so damn sweet," she whispered, but loudly enough for everyone to hear. "Can we keep him?"

Miranda didn't know why she wouldn't. He was an exceptional airplane systems specialist.

"Holly's favorite soccer team?" Mike asked.

"The Australian Matildas," they all called out in unison. Their four Matildas hats were all lined up on the mantle.

This time Miranda was fairly sure it was right that she joined in on the laughter.

———

Captain Dimitri Voskov hunched against the March chill while he watched the loading process, and wished he was anywhere else.

His plane was *the* heavyweight champ for cargo hauling. Known as "Condor" in the west, his Ukrainian Antonov AN-124-150 Ruslan could carry up to a hundred and sixty tons in a single load. Its lone big brother, the An-224 Mriya "Cossack" didn't really count as there had only ever been one in existence.

He'd gone to the restaurant along the Helsinki airport cargo road for a change of pace from their own on-board cooking. The meat soup could have been century-old reindeer hide—it had certainly tasted like it—and the waitress had been a dour battleax. Not even any fun flirting to break up the monotony.

At least there was no deadhead this time. As a specialized cargo hauler, too often they flew empty from a delivery to the next pickup.

Here in Finland, they'd dropped off a geothermal power generator built by the Brits and were picking up a load of Russian helicopters—helicopters that defecting Russian pilots had delivered into Finnish hands. No surprise, they were now getting handed over to the Americans—so greedy for examples of Russian technology.

His real mistake was delaying at the restaurant too long over scorched coffee and the last slice of Kakku pie which was even worse than it sounded. The loadmasters had started the loading while he'd been at dinner. Now, it was three in the morning, the terminal was closed, his gut was roiling with the heavy meal, and he couldn't get to the cockpit.

Much of the Condor's design had been taken from the American's C-5 Galaxy, and just made bigger. Voskov rubbed his hands together to no effect then tucked them back into his pockets—he just wished they'd provided flight deck access during loading.

The four-engine cargo jet was a massive open tube with a rear ramp behind clamshell doors. The front nose swung up like a king-sized garage door to expose the front ramp. The Condor could even kneel—lowering its front landing gear to facilitate drive-on loading.

However, during loading, the stair up to his cockpit

home was cut off. That left him to stand in the biting cold and watch his loadmasters do all the work.

All he could do was look longingly up at the nice warm living area four stories above him. He should be kicked back on his bunk, sleeping or watching a Scarlett Johansson movie (he had every one of them, at least all the ones she was blonde in, and most of Jennifer Lawrence's, even *The Hunger Games* when she wasn't blonde).

"How much longer, Portnov?"

"You whine too much, Captain."

"Fine. I'll just leave you here to freeze your ass off."

"Then who would unload your helicopters in America?" Portnov slapped him on the back and returned to loading the next helo into the Condor. A painfully slow process.

Of course, the least gouge in his hull could ground them for a week. And if everything wasn't perfectly balanced fore and aft, he'd crash on takeoff.

Voskov paced back and forth, because it was that or die cold in Helsinki which sounded like a bad movie that he wanted no role in. He was always amazed at the volume Portnov managed to move in and out of their plane. Somehow it looked so effortless when Portnov was the loadmaster.

Damn but this took longer than a Ukrainian spring.

It looked like a whale's maw gobbling up anything they fed it.

He glared across the field at the now darkened restaurant in the terminal. She was long gone, but right now even that dour battleax looked like a good option.

ELAYNE KASPRAK HAD WATCHED THE WHOLE OPERATION SINCE the Antonov AN-124 had landed before she'd decided on her approach. It was the arrival of the captain—conveniently unable to retreat to his flight deck—that gave her the solution to boarding the aircraft.

It had taken less than five minutes to liberate an airport security car from the Helsinki motor pool. Acquiring a uniform had been harder. Finding a real guard who was small enough that she wouldn't look ridiculous in his uniform had taken almost twenty minutes. She hoped that the guard woke up before he froze to death in just his long underwear. The one bit of attire she hadn't needed—it would only get in the way.

On her return, the captain was still there, trying to huddle out of the wind and not even pretending he was in charge. Time to prove that he truly wasn't.

She parked her clearly marked vehicle close, but not too close. Visible, but in the shadows. Elayne planned her walk carefully. Casual, friendly. Not some sexy slink.

Just a cop on patrol...and just as bored as you.

"*Hyvää iltaa,*" she wished him a good evening in Finnish.

"*Tak?*" Ukrainian.

She was fluent in Ukrainian, and six other languages, but he'd know that her accent was too Russian. "Good evening?" she asked in intentionally awkward English.

"Ah! Good evening." He finally focused on her face and most of his shivering went away.

Elayne knew why she'd originally been recruited by the SVR. The Russian Foreign Intelligence Service needed beautiful spies. But she was also the daughter of a Spetznaz colonel and could outfight nine out of ten men, despite her stature. It hadn't taken her long to ascend to the operations department of Directorate S. Then from S to Zaslon—the most secret and elite black ops team in the entire Russian Federation—in just two more years.

"Good evening," he said in a much warmer tone as he stood straight and squared his shoulders.

"Slow loadings?" She nodded toward his plane.

"Damned slow. Made the mistake of going to the café rather than hiding in my bunk."

"Tell that you did not the eating of Madame's meat soup?" She had watched him do precisely that.

At his expected groan, she laughed sympathetically.

"If you walk three more blocks, there very good steak."

He groaned more dramatically, "I didn't need to know that." His English was almost as good as hers actually was. Better to let him think she was struggling to keep up with him.

She removed her hat. After all, Helsinki was tropical compared to where she'd grown up in Polyarny submarine base near the Arctic Circle. That let her long white-blonde hair fall loose over her stolen parka's shoulders. Truth be told, she was missing the guard's long underwear at the moment as the wind was quite bitter.

Elayne paid attention to the six helicopters being loaded. It gave the captain time to look his fill.

She was glad that it wasn't her job to hunt down the pilots who had betrayed the motherland by delivering these to the West. She'd castrate them slowly then make them cook and eat their own balls before she cauterized the excision point with a blowtorch.

There was a hard metal-on-metal bang from inside the

Condor. By the lights inside the cargo bay she could see that it was just one of the loaders cursing at a freezing cold pry bar he'd dropped on the deck. The sound had been echoed and reinforced as it blasted out into the darkness. Her own breath was clouding so thickly that it was blurring her vision.

But not enough to hide what was in the cargo bay.

A Kamov Helix that looked to have all of its Airborne Early Warning system's electronics still intact. Two Kamov Alligator attack helos and a fully-armed Mil Havoc as well. One of the brand-new Kazan Ansat multi-role birds. The last one was a monstrous Mi-17 gunship that shouldn't fit inside any aircraft—at least nothing less than the Antonov.

It was an incredible intelligence haul.

"Sorry, Captain."

"What?"

Elayne remembered herself. "Sorry that you must stand out in such colds."

And sorry for you that you were assigned to carry the wrong cargo. Not your fault, but that doesn't change anything.

"Would you like to warm up in my car?"

"That would be very good. Thank you."

Very nice, she corrected him in her thoughts.

She'd left the heater on high, they both soon shed their jackets. He wasn't the handsomest man, but he clearly worked hard to stay in shape. Seducing him there in the shadows of her stolen but warm car was laughably easy.

And surprisingly good, once his hands warmed up.

He was a skilled lover, better than any she'd had in a long time. Best of all, there would be no loose ends to worry about—ever.

———

Dimtri Voskov set up on final approach into Fort Campbell and daydreamed of what wonders awaited him in Kentucky.

The load of Russian helicopters would go to the 160th Special Operations Aviation Regiment—SOAR was the US Army's secret helicopter regiment and no concern of his.

Kentucky though...

It wasn't the land of petite Scandinavian white-blondes, but he'd been in the American South enough to appreciate the seriously built gold-blondes as well—even when it was dyed.

No one would match the Helsinki Airport security officer who wore nothing under her uniform. That would be asking too much. But she left him to dream. She'd also left him a phone number and first name—Valery. Valery, a female name in the West and a male name in Russia; it fit her strength well. She had the finest body he'd been invited to plunder since a fiery Irish redhead on a layover in Shannon three years before.

While finishing the tie-downs and doublechecks, Portnov had lowered the cockpit stairway and he'd given Valery a tour upstairs.

Bunks near the back of the compartment—just ahead of the wings. Enough for the three loadmasters and the four-man flight crew. A small lounge, bathroom, and a decent kitchen.

She hadn't looked very impressed until they reached the cockpit. He gave her the full tour and grabbed a couple of nice feels.

"May I use bathing room?"

"You know the way."

On her return, Valery had asked in that charming mangled-English of hers as she closed the cockpit door, "Does these doors lock?"

He'd reached across her, latched it, and tried to take her right up against the door.

Instead, she'd guided him to the pilot's chair. Sliding it to the back of the stops, there was just room for her to straddle him.

Over Valery's bare shoulder and out the windshield, he'd caught Portnov looking up in surprise, then grinning.

Plenty to grin about here.

The only thing more amazing than her hair, face, and breasts had been what she could do with her hips.

She would start a motion somewhere deep inside that built in a slow gyration to—

The radio hauled him back to the present. "Antonov, this is Campbell Army Airfield. You're cleared to land Runway 23. Winds light and variable."

"Roger, Tower." Everything looked good.

Everything.

Including the updated schedule from the home office that said they'd be back in Helsinki in just three weeks.

He rode the big plane down the glideslope. He had plenty of runway, but still got the main gear on the pavement in the first five hundred feet. Nose gear down at a thousand.

It would be good to get out of the cockpit and stretch. He might not even go barhopping. Maybe he'd just hit his bunk, think about Valery, and count the days until they were back in Finland.

WHEN CAPTAIN DIMITRI VOSKOV PULLED BACK TO ENGAGE THE thrust reversers on the four brand-new GE CF-6 engines, a small switch was engaged. It had been placed by SVR Zaslon Major Elayne Kasprak as Voskov had buried his face in her breasts—so skilled with his tongue that she'd almost missed the proper placement.

The small switch sent a signal to a receiver she'd placed fifty feet behind the cockpit. She'd hidden it beneath the rearmost bunk while ducking out of the cockpit to use the bathroom.

The receiver was attached to a detonator.

The detonator had been rammed into the heart of a shaped charge.

The C4 plastique explosive detonated, punching through the crew cabin's rear pressure wall and the central wing tank close behind it.

It also incinerated Loadmaster Portnov and the Swedish *Aktuell Rapport* skin magazine he'd been using as a visual aid while he imagined Voskov's blonde going down on him in the last bunk.

In the cockpit, the sound was no louder than a blown tire on the main gear.

"Shit!" Voskov checked the indicators, but no red warning lights. Hopefully not a brake fire, or a broken wheel axle. *Please let it just be the rubber.*

The central wing tank had been run mostly dry during flight. Now it was filled with fuel vapors and nitrogen that had been pumped in as the tank emptied to decrease the chance of fire.

The hole punched by the shaped charged not only heated the remaining fuel above the ignition point, but allowed oxygen to rush into the breached tank.

Four seconds after the thump sound in the cockpit, their speed was down to a hundred knots. The plane wasn't pulling to either side, so Voskov decided the problem might not be too terrible.

Two thousand feet of runway gone, eight thousand still clear ahead. Under normal operations, the Antonov would need only a thousand more feet before turning off onto a taxiway—for all their size, helicopters didn't weigh much, less than a third of the Condor's load limit.

At that same moment, a fireball followed the stream of oxygen and flashed back through the original penetration in the tank and the cabin's rear bulkhead.

It ignited the entire crew cabin and killed the other two loadmasters.

Other than a sudden inward bulging of the closed cockpit door, the active flight crew, including Captain Dimitri Voskov, remained unaware of what was happening behind them. The copilot had opened his small side window to smell the fresh Kentucky air—splendidly warm and lush in mid-March—so their ears didn't even pop at the sudden overpressure.

Five seconds after the initial blast, the building explosion inside the fuel tank exceeded critical rupture.

Both of the central tanks' side seams failed at a hundred and thirty-seven percent of design maximum.

The shrapnel blew through the wing tanks to either side, spilling the three thousand remaining gallons of reserve Jet-A fuel into the wing structure. From there, it cascaded down onto the runway through mechanical openings for flaps and landing gear.

At seven seconds past ignition, both wings exploded internally. Bits of fuel tank and wing covering were blown so high that they didn't return to the ground for forty-two seconds.

If the wings had broken free, the fuselage might have survived.

Instead, they kept spilling fuel and feeding the fire now building along either side of the fuselage.

Captain Dimitri Voskov's last act fully damned the plane.

He stood hard on the brakes for an emergency stop.

It worked.

The Antonov AN-124-150 Condor squatted in the middle of its own fire and burned.

Directly below the cockpit and crew area, the armament on the Mil "Havoc" heated past critical.

An Ataka-V anti-tank missile was the first to go. The blast ignited the three other missiles in the rack as well as the five smaller weapons in the S-13 rocket pod. This in turn triggered the Product 305 air-to-air missile that the West had yet to inspect.

The combined blast was sufficient to separate the already weakened connection between the cockpit and wing assemblies. As the sides of the hull blew outward, the cockpit section was blown upward.

Because its attachment at the nose held longer than at the wing, the sixty-foot-long section swung upward like a giant second hand, trying to fly one last time before breaking free and landing on its back ahead of the fire.

It didn't matter. There wasn't anyone left alive in the

inverted cockpit assembly that now lay on Runway 23 at Fort Campbell, Kentucky. The acceleration of the explosion had snapped Dimitri Voskov's neck, the last survivor aboard. His final thought hadn't been about his beloved Antonov Condor or Valery's amazing body. All he knew was how much his neck hurt.

Of the helicopters, not so much as a single instrument of Russian technology survived intact.

As always, Major Eleyna Kasprak had gotten her man.

———

MIRANDA'S PHONE INTERRUPTED HER ATTEMPT TO MAKE THE others say, "Ewan McGregor."

It was Charades, but she didn't know who Ewan McGregor was.

When she'd asked Holly for help—it was guys versus girls—she'd whispered "Star Wars" as if that explained anything.

"Timer's still running," Mike called out as she stopped to answer the call.

Good. Maybe it would run out before she was done with the call. No, Mike was tipping the tiny hour glass onto its side to stop the running sand.

"Hello?"

"Where's your team?" Miranda had always appreciated that General Drake Nason didn't waste his time on unnecessary niceties.

"Holly's on the coach, Mike is in my mother's armchair,"—Mike looked down as his seat as if that was somehow shocking—"and Jeremy's sitting on the floor by the coffee table."

Drake's soft laugh made no sense. "Okay. Where are *all* of you?"

"At my house."

"Where is *that,* Miranda?"

Oh. "I live on Spieden Island in the San Juans of Washington State, United Sta—"

"Yes, I know that Washington State is in the US."

"—States. Okay, well that's where we are."

"How fast can you get to Kentucky?"

ABOUT THE AUTHOR

M.L. Buchman started the first of over 60 novels, 100 short stories, and a fast-growing pile of audiobooks while flying from South Korea to ride his bicycle across the Australian Outback. Part of a solo around the world trip that ultimately launched his writing career in: thrillers, military romantic suspense, contemporary romance, and SF/F.

Recently named in *The 20 Best Romantic Suspense Novels: Modern Masterpieces* by ALA's Booklist, they have also selected his works three times as "Top-10 Romance Novel of the Year." NPR and B&N listed other works as "Best 5 of the Year."

As a 30-year project manager with a geophysics degree who has: designed and built houses, flown and jumped out of planes, and solo-sailed a 50' ketch, he is awed by what's possible. More at: www.mlbuchman.com.

Other works by M. L. Buchman: *(* - also in audio)*

Thrillers

Dead Chef
Swap Out!
One Chef!
Two Chef!

Miranda Chase
Drone*
Thunderbolt*
Condor*

Romantic Suspense

Delta Force
Target Engaged*
Heart Strike*
Wild Justice*
Midnight Trust*

Firehawks
MAIN FLIGHT
Pure Heat
Full Blaze
Hot Point*
Flash of Fire*
Wild Fire
SMOKEJUMPERS
Wildfire at Dawn*
Wildfire at Larch Creek*
Wildfire on the Skagit*

The Night Stalkers
MAIN FLIGHT
The Night Is Mine
I Own the Dawn
Wait Until Dark
Take Over at Midnight
Light Up the Night
Bring On the Dusk
By Break of Day

AND THE NAVY
Christmas at Steel Beach
Christmas at Peleliu Cove
WHITE HOUSE HOLIDAY
Daniel's Christmas*
Frank's Independence Day*
Peter's Christmas*
Zachary's Christmas*
Roy's Independence Day*
Damien's Christmas*
5E
Target of the Heart
Target Lock on Love
Target of Mine
Target of One's Own

Shadow Force: Psi
At the Slightest Sound*
At the Quietest Word*

White House Protection Force
Off the Leash*
On Your Mark*
In the Weeds*

Contemporary Romance

Eagle Cove
Return to Eagle Cove
Recipe for Eagle Cove
Longing for Eagle Cove
Keepsake for Eagle Cove

Henderson's Ranch
Nathan's Big Sky*
Big Sky, Loyal Heart*
Big Sky Dog Whisperer*

Love Abroad
Heart of the Cotswolds: England
Path of Love: Cinque Terre, Italy

Other works by M. L. Buchman:

Contemporary Romance (cont)

Where Dreams
Where Dreams are Born
Where Dreams Reside
Where Dreams Are of Christmas
Where Dreams Unfold
Where Dreams Are Written

Science Fiction / Fantasy

Deities Anonymous
Cookbook from Hell: Reheated
Saviors 101

Single Titles
The Nara Reaction
Monk's Maze
the Me and Elsie Chronicles

Non-Fiction

Strategies for Success
Managing Your Inner Artist/Writer
Estate Planning for Authors*
Character Voice
Narrate and Record Your Own
Audiobook*

Short Story Series by M. L. Buchman:

Romantic Suspense

Delta Force
Delta Force

Firehawks
The Firehawks Lookouts
The Firehawks Hotshots
The Firebirds

The Night Stalkers
The Night Stalkers
The Night Stalkers 5E
The Night Stalkers CSAR
The Night Stalkers Wedding Stories

US Coast Guard
US Coast Guard

White House Protection Force
White House Protection Force

Contemporary Romance

Eagle Cove
Eagle Cove

Henderson's Ranch
Henderson's Ranch*

Where Dreams
Where Dreams

Thrillers

Dead Chef
Dead Chef

Science Fiction / Fantasy

Deities Anonymous
Deities Anonymous

Other
The Future Night Stalkers
Single Titles

SIGN UP FOR M. L. BUCHMAN'S NEWSLETTER TODAY

and receive:
Release News
Free Short Stories
a Free Book

Get your free book today. Do it now.
free-book.mlbuchman.com